GONE

M K TURNER

127 Publishing

This edition published 2024 by 127 Publishing

Paperback ISBN 978-1-0686749-4-5

Hardback ISBN 978-1-0686749-5-2

Also by M K Turner

Meredith & Hodge Series

The Making of Meredith
Misplaced Loyalty
Ill Conceived
The Wrong Shoes
Tin Soldiers
One Secret Too Many
Mistaken Beliefs
Quite by Chance
Family Matters
Not If You Paid Me
A Measure of Guilt
Meredith & Hodge Bear Witness
Web of Deceit
Error of Judgement
Chance Encounters
Enough
Gone

Bearing Witness Series

Witness for Wendy
An Unexpected Gift
Terms of Affection
Meredith & Hodge Bear Witness

Little Compton Mysteries

The Murder
The Abduction
The Burglar

JJ Jenson Series

An Ill Wind

To Kill Two Birds

Too Many Times

Others

Who Killed Charlie Birch?

The Cuban Conundrum

Murderous Mishaps

The Recruitment of Lucy James

This book is dedicated to Archie, our beloved White German Shepherd possibly the soppiest dog you could ever meet, who we lost during the writing of Gone.
And, to YOU, the reader, for giving me a reason to keep making stuff up.

Acknowledgements

Edited by Sharon Kelly & Jill Buss
Cover by: https://www.behance.net/lwpmarshala1e9
And of course, my wonderful beta readers

Chapter One

2016 – Brandon Farm

Louise could taste blood, and lifting her fingers to her lips, pressed them softly against the pain. When she pressed her tongue forward, it found its way through her lip to her fingertip, and she cursed. That would scar. Yes, this was a cushy number for the best part, but not cushy enough to put up with this shit. Been there and done that.

As the familiar thumping on the floor above began, Louise lifted her eyes, but instead of releasing a string of abuse as intended, she covered her head with her hands and opened her mouth to scream.

Anyone listening wouldn't have heard a scream, only the grunt as the hammer smashed into the side of her skull before it was raised again and again.

"What have you done? Stop hitting her. You can see she's dead." An odd choice of words, as they couldn't see, as their eyes were screwed shut against the horror of it.

The thumping stopped and their eyes opened.

"Why? Look at what you did. I suppose you want me to help you clean this up now, don't you? It's the last time. I'm warning you. This is the last time. Nothing is worth this. Poor Jasmine. Poor Thomas."

Chapter Two

2024

DCI John Meredith nodded at Daisy and tapped his spoon against his mug before walking to stand next to the screen in the Cold Case Review Team's new office. His team fell silent and Meredith pointed at an attractive young woman with curly red hair and perfect teeth who smiled at the camera.

"Louise Marshall. Went missing in 2010. She was thirty years old. A farmer on the outskirts of Reading found her body buried in one of his fields in 2018. She'd been dead for some time, but according to the forensic pathologist, not as long as the eight years she'd been missing. We have their report. You'll get it later. Their best guess is that she'd been dead for around two years. The soil on that side of the farm is boggy as it's close to the Thames, and it floods frequently. The boggy condition at the location of the burial site caused partial mummification of the remains. Her skull had been smashed repeatedly with a hard, blunt instrument, probably a hammer. She had a broken arm which had healed in the last year or two of her life, and she'd given birth to a child, probably in the six to nine months prior to her death. That would make her child, assuming it survived, about eight years old."

DS Tom Seaton raised his hand. "Are we all working on this one, and why have we got it? I'm not complaining, because I think we could do with getting our teeth into something. But surely the Thames Valley team in Reading should have this, shouldn't they?"

"I'm getting to why, and yes, this will be a team effort because if you hadn't noticed, we're a little short of staff." Meredith pursed his lips and looked at his feet.

CCRT members Patsy Hodge, who was also Meredith's wife, and Linda Trump, the team's Girl Friday, were on extended sick leave. A serial killer the team had been hunting had attacked and almost killed Patsy, leaving her with a fractured skull, a compound fracture of her arm, and issues she wouldn't talk about.

Linda had come to the rescue in the nick of time, and had taken a knife, repeatedly stabbing the man, resulting in his death. Physically, Linda was unharmed, mentally she was learning to accept her actions. Linda was having counselling, Patsy was insisting she was okay. It had been over three months and Meredith knew Patsy was anything but okay. At first, it seemed as if she was coping well and it was just the physical injuries that needed to heal, but now, mentally, she was becoming more and more troubled.

Meredith tutted at his thoughts and looked up. "And, Seaton, if you let me finish, all will become obvious. A few miles up the road, on a different farm, another body was dug up late last year. No mummification, but a hole in the skull. And it was this young woman. Daisy, do the honours."

The image changed to another young woman of a similar age and appearance. On Meredith's nod, Daisy pulled the first photograph back, and the two women smiled out at the team.

"Jasmine Jones. Jasmine was twenty-five when reported missing in 2002, and the pathologist's best guess is she died approximately ten to fifteen years before being found last year. There wasn't much left to go on. For the purposes of the investigation, we'll assume she died between 2008 and 2013 but keep an open mind. So, in answer to your question about why us? Louise lived in Bristol and Jasmine in Worle. On the day they went missing, they had both purchased a ticket from Bristol Temple Meads to London Paddington. Neither of them made it to London because they both got off at—"

"Reading," George Davis announced. "Who dealt with the misper files?"

"Swindon," Meredith finished his sentence. "So, the theory is they were either buying a ticket to Paddington to confuse any search, both having the same mission in mind and intending to get off at Swindon, or someone on the train convinced them to get off there. I've asked for the footage of them leaving the Swindon station, but while we wait, I'm told both left alone, both got into a taxi. No taxi driver working on those days could remember them. We've not started yet, I know, but I can't see that a taxi driver in Swindon got lucky twice, unless he liked red curly hair. It's a theory but it doesn't explain the purchase of a ticket to Paddington."

"Sounds like a hard slog, but good we're working again after weeks of sorting out this place. Don't you think, Guv?" DC Will Kent asked.

"Chief Constable Carrington thinks it's a good fit for us. I don't. Too much geography involved, but no one ever listens to me. Now, much as I know you love the sound of my voice, Daisy will now hit the send button, and you'll all have your own copies of everything I have. Spend the rest of the day going through it, and tomorrow we'll cover what happened the day they went missing, and you can put forward any theories you might have, and we'll get a strategy together. Seaton and Kent concentrate on Louise, George and Trump, Jasmine. Carry on." Meredith closed his notebook. "I know there can't be any questions yet. Not even stupid ones."

Meredith went back to his desk and knocked his phone with the notebook to activate the screen and see if he had any messages. Nothing. With a sigh, he dropped onto his chair and clicked open the file on Louise Marshall. Meredith had read it cover to cover twice, but now he'd start noting the actions required. He'd been angry when Chief Superintendent David Ashworth had called about it. But not now. It still wasn't a good fit, but now he needed the distraction.

At five thirty, satisfied with his notes for the next morning's briefing, he called across the office.

"That's it. Get your coats. Eight thirty in the morning because who knows when we'll have a normal working day again."

As the others got ready to leave, George Davis walked to stand in front of Meredith's desk, and keeping his voice low, asked, "How's Patsy? You haven't mentioned her, other than to say getting there."

"Because I don't know. Her injuries are finally repairing themselves. Plaster comes off her arm in a couple of weeks. Blood clot has been sorted, painkillers have stopped, but...I don't know, George, she's not herself.

She's not...Patsy. She says all the right things, she's up and about and doing what she can with her arm still in plaster, but she's...I don't know, she's lost her spark."

"Still refusing to see the counsellor? Louie was telling me Linda loves meeting with hers. Perhaps ask Linda to convince her."

"Yes, I might do that. Thanks, George, get off home or I'll be in your wife's bad books again. And, George, keep that to yourself."

"Goes without saying, just support her, Meredith. All you can do is love her at the moment. She'll get there. This is Patsy we're talking about."

Meredith nodded, unable to answer as he swallowed back the lump in his throat. It wasn't Patsy. It was the shell of Patsy. He called over to Louie Trump.

"Trump, are you in a rush, or do you have time for a pint? Just a quick one. I need to get home."

Trump also wanted to be at home with his wife, but DCI Meredith wasn't himself. Perhaps he might open up. He glanced at the clock and nodded.

"Give me two minutes to call Linda, and I'll be with you."

• • • • ● • ● • • • •

"So, how's Loopy doing?" Meredith asked, wiping the froth from his top lip.

Meredith frequently gave his colleagues nicknames. Linda ended up with Loopy because of her flamboyant and eccentric personality. She was colourful in all aspects.

"Okay, thank you. She's getting there. She suggested going to see my parents this weekend as she fancied some sea air. As you know, she's not wanted to do much of anything, so I agreed, despite the destination." Louie smiled and sipped his drink. "And Patsy? Linda said she called her the other day, but Patsy was in the middle of something, must have forgotten to call back. And what about you? How are you? Because if you don't mind me saying, you've not been yourself. I think it's too easy to forget the effect these things have on the partners of victims. I was a total mess at the beginning."

"I'm fine, and I don't need a bleeding heart, Trump. But thanks for the consideration. Loopy is getting on well with this counsellor, then? It's working?"

"Oh yes. We're not out of the woods but we're now allowed to have sharp knives in the kitchen, although out of sight, and Linda won't touch them. She's still clingy. No, that's not the word. She's overly affectionate and requires a lot of...affirmation of acceptance, I suppose, so I won't stop long. I have to text her every hour or she's asking me if I'm okay. I might keep the new case to myself. She was content when I was organising desks and unloading stationery. I don't want her to think I'm in danger. Because that's her biggest problem, seeing danger where there is none, that and wondering how I can love a woman who killed someone. Maxine has taught her some process for breaking things down. I didn't understand it myself, but then, you know what Linda's like. Why stick to the basics when explaining the full manual is possible?"

"That's good. Really great news," Meredith replied with a smile, the first he'd managed all day.

Trump looked at Meredith's full pint. Whatever the reason for the invitation, drinking wasn't top of the list.

"I hope I'm not overstepping the mark but why don't you just say it? It's clear you have something to say, and we've known each other long enough for you not to need to hesitate. However sensitive a subject it may be."

"She's not right, Trump. Body is healing, mind is anywhere but with me. She says all the right things, even manages a smile now and then, but she won't see anyone. I'm walking on eggshells, and I don't want to push her and get it wrong. Now we have the twins, I thought Christmas with the grandkids would be wonderful. I couldn't wait because I've always hated Christmas. I still do now. It was dire. Absolutely fucking dire. I'm not sure how much the others noticed, but she went on to autopilot. Smiled in the right places, said the right stuff but with no passion. None. The words that come out of her mouth bear no relation to the look in her eye or her body language. I want to help but she doesn't think she needs it, and I don't know what to do for the best."

Trump gave a solemn nod. "That's tough. My only advice is to keep doing what you're doing. For the first two weeks, all I seemed to do was hold Linda."

Meredith barked out a snort. "If only. I'm too frightened to go anywhere near her. I'm terrified I'll break her. If this carries on much longer, it will be me that needs help. All I want to do is...anyway, time's running away with us. Drink up." Meredith took a sip of his pint and set it back on the bar. "Tomorrow's another day." Sliding off the barstool, he left his unfinished drink and headed for the door.

Trump followed him, resisting the urge to put his arm around Meredith or pat him on the back as they left. "I'll have a word with Linda, or perhaps Maxine. That might be best at first, and see if getting them in the same room might help."

"I'm home."

Patsy looked up as Meredith put his head round the door, and tried for a smile. It failed.

"How was work?" she asked.

"Okay, opened a new case. For us, that is. It's obviously a cold case." Meredith smiled.

"Yes, I got that. Is it interesting?" Patsy closed the book she'd been staring at and placed it on the table.

"They're all interesting, but do I want it? No. Have you eaten?"

"No. I thought I'd wait for you." Patsy pushed herself up.

"Don't move. I'll jump in the shower first, and how about we treat ourselves to a takeaway? I'll go shopping tomorrow and buy us something nice. Unless you did the shopping, you were going to do it online. Did you get to it?" Meredith asked, knowing full well the only items in the kitchen would be the leftovers from the shop he'd done at the weekend.

Patsy banged her palm against her forehead. "I knew there was something I was supposed to do. I'm sorry, I'm pretty useless, aren't I?"

Meredith walked into the room and smiled at her. "No. You're pretty bloody wonderful. You've got enough to think about." He leaned forward to kiss her but caught the twitch of her shoulders as she froze and he stepped away. "Perhaps we can go together? Now, after I shower, or tomorrow?"

"Or perhaps you can learn to use the bloody computer for anything other than work, and log in and do it the easy way," Patsy snapped.

She seemed horrified at the thought of going shopping or doing something with Meredith. Perhaps both. Meredith aimed for comedic effect and clasped his hand to his chest. "I'm wounded. I can use a computer, not efficiently, as Loopy always points out, but we'd end up with a load of pasta and a couple of frozen pizzas, and I'd get bored and forget the stuff we needed. If huge juicy steaks or, I don't know, something tasty was put under my nose, without a million clicks, I'd buy it. But point me in the right direction. I'm willing to do it online."

Patsy opened her mouth to snap a response, but thought better of it. She composed herself and the false smile was back. "You said you were going to shower. You do that, I'll get the laptop."

Meredith nodded and headed upstairs. He'd do anything for Patsy, but knew it was only a matter of time before he snapped back. And then what? He took his time in the shower. When he got dressed, he pulled on some jogging bottoms and a T-shirt Patsy liked him in. As he dressed, he heard his phone ringing down in the hall, but knew he wouldn't get there in time, and when the landline rang, he paused in the bedroom doorway, and waited for Patsy to answer it. She didn't, and he heard his daughter's voice as she left a message.

"Hi, Dad, hi, Patsy. Hope you're feeling better and that arm isn't too itchy in the cast. Johnny and Katy say hi. Well, they don't. They either send a soppy soggy raspberry or a wet fart. But they mean well. How do you fancy coming to us for dinner on Friday? Peggy is moaning. She hasn't seen you since Christmas. Anyway, let me know as soon as. Love you."

Meredith walked down the stairs, fixing his own smile in place. He found Patsy sitting in silence in the living room, the laptop nowhere to be seen.

"That sounds nice. Do you fancy it?"

Patsy's chin trembled, and she shook her head.

"No problem. I'll call her later and let her know. Now what do you fancy to eat? I vote Chinese."

Patsy swallowed. "You go ahead. Not for me, I'm not hungry."

"Why's that? Did you have a big lunch?"

Patsy nodded. Meredith knew she was lying.

"By the way, Trump said that Linda was going to pop in and see you. That's something to look forward to."

"Yes. Nice. Order your food." Despite her agreement, Patsy's head was shaking.

As Meredith ordered his food, he considered his options and reached a decision. They were approaching shit or bust time. He sat in the chair opposite her rather than next to her as he used to.

"I've decided I'm going to retire. I'll probably tell them tomorrow."

Patsy's head shot up. "Why?"

"Because I'd rather be here with you learning how to shop online than wading through a bog in Reading."

"A what...There's no need. I'm fine. Tell me about the new case."

"You're not, but you will be, and no, there's no point, I won't be working it."

"Yes, you will. If nothing else, you'll have to give notice."

Patsy's voice had an edge. She was clearly upset at the thought of Meredith retiring, and he didn't know if that was because she didn't want to spend more time with him, or she was worried about her own job. Meredith opted for the former.

"I'm owed, Patsy. We're owed. There won't be an issue. We can book a holiday, fly away from this damp, miserable weather."

"We could do that anyway, only you won't fly. So what was the point of saying that? Don't treat me like a child, Meredith. Or do you realise that without the job you'll be so bored stuck here with me that even getting on a plane would be better?"

"What I realise is that you need me. I want to be here for you, and I can't be while I'm working. I know you're struggling at the moment, and it's getting worse, and I think it would help if you weren't stuck in this house alone every day."

"Oh no. No, you don't, Johnny. You're not pinning that on me. I'll be fine, I'm getting there. If you retire and I have to put...take the blame for that, I'll never get there. I'm going to bed."

Patsy flew from the room. Sitting in the silence of the living room below, Meredith heard a door slam and her sobs arrive. He took the stairs two at a time. Pulling her into his arms, he buried his face in her hair as he stroked her back.

"Please don't cry. I'm here. Tell me how I can help you." It was the closest he'd been to her for weeks, and he pulled her closer. "We can sort this. It will be okay, I promise."

She didn't respond, but her tears had almost subsided when the doorbell rang.

"That's only the food. We can ignore it."

Patsy pushed him away. "Go and eat. I'll have a bath."

Meredith opened his mouth to speak, and she shook her head. "Please."

He listened to the running water as he ate another solitary meal at the kitchen table. As he cleared the cartons away, he heard the gurgle as the bath water was released. By the time he'd got upstairs, Patsy was in the spare bedroom. He listened at the door. She was crying again. He went in to her and sat on the edge of the bed. She rolled away from him.

"Tell me why you're crying. Right now, what's making you so upset? Come back to our room."

"You're going to leave me, Meredith. I might as well get used to it." Patsy sniffed.

"I will never leave you. Ever." Meredith tried to roll her towards him, but she shrugged him away.

"You will. You might not want to yet, but you will."

Meredith slapped his hand hard on the bedroom wall. "Stop it! Stop it! You have enough to deal with without making stuff up. You need to see someone, Patsy. If you won't see the counsellor, I'm taking you to the doctor's. Tomorrow. Right before I tell them I'm retiring. Because you might want me to leave, but I'm going nowhere. I'm going to be right here."

Patsy turned to look at him. She could only see his outline as the light was behind him. "Let's discuss it in the morning. Close the door behind you. The light's hurting my eyes."

Meredith resisted the urge to slam the door in frustration. He went downstairs and picked up the phone. "Trump. Sorry to disturb you, but I'd like two favours. The first is the contact details for Linda's counsellor, the second is to see Linda. I need to make sure it's going to be right for Patsy, but I don't want to upset Linda, ask her if that's okay."

"Of course, I'll speak to her. She's just gone up to bed. Will tomorrow be soon enough?"

"Yes, of course. I'm sorry to bother you. You've got your own problems. I just don't know if I'm on my arse or my elbow."

"It's no bother, and I'm sure Linda would love to see you."

Meredith went to the kitchen and opened a bottle of wine. His preference would have been the whiskey, but he didn't want to go down that road again.

Chapter Three

2019 – Brandon Farm

Three-year-old Thomas sat at the table and looked at his grandmother.

"She can take me to school?" he said, looking at the woman sitting opposite.

"No, because she has things to do, and who's she, the cat's mother?" Cissy shook her head. "It's Mummy, or Mum if you like, but not she."

Thomas looked from one to the other. "Sorry, Mum."

"That's okay, Tommy. Perhaps I'll pick you up after football. I'll come with Granny, shall I?"

"Yes please."

There was a knocking on the ceiling, and everyone looked up.

Cissy got to her feet, feeling every one of her sixty-two years. "I'll go. Jasmine, we need to do your roots as soon as I get back from school. We also need to talk about you know what. Mark is becoming impatient. You know what you signed up for."

Susan Beddow, now known as Jasmine, watched Cissy open the door to the stairs, and listened to her slippers slap each one as Cissy made one of many trips up to the front bedroom. And she thought about Mark as she twisted the gold band on her finger. He was a handsome man, well built, and he clearly liked her, but could she do it? When Cissy found her, Susan had been prepared to do anything she was so desperate. Anything not to have to go back. And this was okay, wasn't it? She'd even considered prostitution, so this was the same, wasn't it? Just more comfortable.

When Susan had arrived at the farm, she'd been expecting someone resembling Shreck because otherwise it would be too good to be true. So had been pleasantly surprised when she met Mark. He wasn't the brightest bulb in the box but nor was she. He said nice things, but he didn't smile. Not really. Mark showed little emotion about anything. Susan judged his mood by the tone of his voice. Thomas certainly had his father sussed too, knew when to agree and when to settle with his toys.

Cissy must have known it wouldn't be easy for her because she agreed Susan could have a few months to settle in. So Susan had expected some sort of courtship. There had been none, nothing, not even a bunch of daffodils from the field. Not unless you counted the staring. Now it appeared it was time to make her mind up. She could just leave and put herself back to square one, or she could let him have what he wanted, and pretend to be his wife in all matters. How bad could it be? She might even enjoy it.

As though summoned by her thoughts, Mark came into the kitchen and stamped his boots on the mat.

Susan smiled at him. "Hello, Mark, it's not very nice out there. You must be freezing. Do you want a cup of tea?"

"That'll do for starters." He returned her smile with a wink. His lips made no attempt to smile. "Where's Mother?"

"Up with your dad. He banged."

Mark rolled his eyes. "How is he?"

"I don't know. I haven't seen him. Do you mind me asking what happened to him?"

Mark lifted his shoulders. "Ask Mother. she'll tell you if she thinks you need to know. Are you going to get me something to eat? You'll be off to preschool soon, won't you, son?"

"Yes, Dad. It's soft football day."

"Score a goal for me." Mark returned his attention to Susan. "Jasmine, move your arse. I've got a lot on. Just bacon and egg will do."

Susan walked to the cooker and wondered if she'd ever get used to her new name. Placing two rashers in the pan, she turned to Mark. "One egg or two?"

"Two. I like you in that dress. Doesn't your mum look pretty, Thomas?"

"Yes, but she's still a girl."

In a rare show of emotion, Mark barked out a laugh and thumped the table, startling Thomas.

"That she is, but they have their uses. You'll find that out when you get older. If you've finished that, put the bowl in the sink and get your shoes on, then find out where your grandmother has got to. You don't want to be late. Your mother and I have things to do. Don't we?"

Mark's eyes didn't leave Susan, and a shiver ran up her spine. He didn't need to say what.

Susan turned back to the pan, cracked the egg, and listened to the hiss as it landed in the hot oil, trying to calm her thoughts. She knew Mark was looking at her. He was always looking, and it was flattering for the best part. It was nice to be admired; it had been a while, and she doubted she'd have that conversation with Cissy before she'd had it with Mark. Her hand shook a little as she flipped the egg over. Why was she so nervous? It's not like she was some innocent virgin. She'd known this was coming.

When Cissy reappeared, she lifted her keys from the hook. "I'm popping into the shop on the way back. Father wants some mints. Is there anything we need?"

Susan told her she didn't think so, and Mark ignored her. Mark never joined in conversations about his father.

"Good. Come on, Thomas, have you got your boots? Good boy. Say goodbye to your mum and dad."

"'Bye." Thomas pulled the strap of his kitbag over his shoulder.

"'Bye, Thomas, good luck at football." Susan smiled and waved before she stacked the crockery on the table. She waited until they'd closed the door before carrying the dishes to the sink and lowering them into the suds, She began the washing up. "He's a lovely boy. You must be proud of him." She was becoming nervous. Mark had not stopped staring at her since he'd come in and she didn't want to look round to check. She jumped as his hands grabbed her hips. He moved quickly and quietly for a big bloke. "Oi. Cheeky, you scared me."

Susan forced her laugh as her heart thundered in her chest. Mark pressed himself against her, his intentions confirmed. His hands slid from her hips down to the hem of her skirt, and he hiked it up. Goosebumps jumped to attention on Susan's exposed skin. It seemed she could feel every one of them. Was that the cold air, or was she enjoying this? Deciding to go with the latter, she pressed back against him before turning round to face him. His eyes were glazed.

"I think you've got something on your mind." She stood on tiptoe and tried to kiss him.

"Take your knickers off," Mark replied against her lips, thrusting his hips into her.

"Shall we go somewhere more comfortable?" Susan tried for another kiss.

"Take them off. Now. I won't ask again." His eyes travelled from her face down her body and back again. "Take it all off." He grabbed the dress, still concertinaed around her waist, and forced her arms into the air as he hoisted it off, tossing it onto the floor.

With trembling fingers, Susan unhooked her bra and allowed it to fall to the floor at their feet. His eyes flicked to her breasts and back again. Embarrassed, she lowered her head. This was going to happen, and she couldn't lie to herself, his passion for her was turning her on. It had been a long time. She just wished they weren't in the kitchen. As he unzipped his trousers and lowered them, she smiled. Perhaps this wouldn't be so —
The blow came from nowhere. One minute his hand was sorting out his trousers, the next it was colliding with her face. Susan screamed, and he clamped a hand over her mouth.

"I said take them off." Mark's eyes left hers and searched the draining board. With his free hand, he lifted a knife and showed it to her before he slid it down along her hip, and with a flick of the wrist, sliced through the seam of her knickers. "Off." Susan wiggled her hips, and they slid down her legs. Mark's hand slid from her mouth to her neck and his fingers dug into her skin. "No more screaming. Turn around."

Susan did as instructed. She didn't make a sound as he took what he wanted, but watched as her tears splashed onto the bubbles in the sink. The man was a psycho.

Mark straightened his clothes and turned her to face him. "No answering back, do as you're told, and there will be no need of this." He flipped a tear away with his thumb. His touch was gentle. "Now get dressed before me mother gets back, and move your stuff into my room. You'll be sleeping in there from now on. I'll be working on the fence if anyone needs me. Bring my lunch down at one."

When Cissy returned, Susan was sitting at the table, and turning to face Cissy, she burst into tears.

Cissy looked at the marks left by her son and tutted. "I'm sorry. It's my fault I should have spoken to you yesterday. Come here. Let's sort you out."

Susan jumped to her feet. "It's not your bloody fault. He's bloody mad. He whacked me, then he raped me."

"Come on, now. No need for language like that. None at all. You're his wife. It's what you agreed to. There's four grand in that account now. You were being paid but not keeping to your end of the bargain."

"I agreed to pretend to be his wife, to be a mother to Thomas, to help you around the house. But you said the sex would be when I was ready, not when he fancied taking it. I can't do this. Look at the state of me."

"Did you argue with him, Jasmine?" Cissy had reached Susan and pulled her into a hug.

"No. I just didn't take my knickers off fast enough." Susan had stopped crying and enjoyed the comfort of being hugged, so she didn't pull away. It was a long time since anyone had shown her any affection. It was the reason she thought this might work. They needed her, and she needed...someone.

"Hmm. So you were considering it then? You hadn't said no."

"Yes, I was going to do it. I was nervous, but I was going to make the best of it, and I even thought I might enjoy it. Then he whacked me. And took me over the bloody sink, for God's sake. That's not what I signed up for."

"Then that's alright. Wouldn't have happened if you'd been quicker. This was a blip, that's all. First time nerves. Men have needs. You must know that. He's waited a long time for you. I'll have a word. Did you move your stuff into his room?"

Susan nodded. She'd been too frightened to do anything else.

"Good girl. Now let's get that hair sorted. You'll look pretty as a picture and we can begin afresh." Cissy led Susan to a chair and sat her down. Then pulled her phone from her pocket and clamped her tongue between her teeth as she concentrated, tapping away. When she'd finished, she showed Susan the screen. "There, another two hundred in your account. My apologies, I left it too long. Now let's get you sorted."

By one o'clock, Susan had a mop of red curls bouncing around her shoulders. At first she didn't think she'd like being a redhead, but it was better than her usual mousy colour, and it suited her natural curls. As she wrapped Mark's sandwiches in greaseproof paper, her hands shook, and Cissy placed her hand on her shoulder.

"Don't be nervous. It'll be fine, Jasmine. Just be nice. You're a nice girl. It won't be hard."

Susan zipped up her coat and nodded. She reached the door and turned back when Cissy called her.

"Jasmine, don't forget his tea." Cissy held up the flask.

Susan's stomach flipped at the thought of telling Mark she'd forgotten his tea. As she set off down the lane towards the broken fence in the bottom field, she thought about what Cissy had said, and looking around to make sure no one was watching, she balanced Mark's lunch on the hedge and removed her knickers, shoving them into her pocket. He wouldn't catch her out twice.

Mark watched her clamber over the bank and held out his hand to steady her as she reached him.

"You're late." Mark sat down and looked at her.

Susan froze. "Yes, only a few minutes though. It was your mum. She wanted to do my hair. What do you think?" She swished her curls around her shoulders.

"Looks like it should. Nice." He held out his hand for his sandwiches.

Susan passed them to him and placed the flask on the bank. "Thank you. There you go, I'd better get back. I promised Cissy I'd do the veg. We're having a hotpot tonight."

"She'll be fine. Sit down." Mark watched her sit on the plastic sheeting next to him.

Blowing out a breath, Susan looked him in the eye. "I moved my things. I'll sleep in your room tonight."

Mark bit into the sandwich and nodded. "Did you make these?"

"Yes. Extra pickle because you like it."

Mark nodded again, still looking at her as he took another bite. Susan was desperate for him to say something, preferably nice, like some sort of approval to make this pretend life easier.

"Shall I pour you some tea?" Susan asked. "I put sugar in it so you don't need to bother."

"Not yet."

Susan sat looking out at the field while he sat there eating his sandwich and looking at her. As he screwed up the wrapping, she placed her hand on his knee. "Can we talk? About...about, you know."

Mark looked from her face to her hand and back again. "What?"

"Us. This arrangement. Me being your wife." Susan threw her arms into the air. "All of it."

"You mean sex." Mark's eyes narrowed a little.

"As well, yes. I don't want you to hurt me, Mark, because I don't deserve that, and I'm doing my best."

Mark's eyebrows rose. "Are you? You made me wait too long."

"I know, and I'm sorry. I should have realised, but I was nervous. Mark, I'm on the wrong side of thirty, so I'm not innocent, but I don't really know you. You're so quiet. Perhaps you can tell me about yourself, or not. I mean we could talk about what you like, what you don't like, you know that sort of thing, then perhaps you won't need to hurt me because I won't get it wrong. I want to be a good wife, Mark. I know you don't love me, but I want to make this easy on both of us."

Mark looked surprised. "I do love you, Jasmine. Why would you say that?"

Susan watched his hands clench into fists. "I didn't know that. You didn't tell me." Her mind was racing. She'd known it, of course, but this confirmed it. The man wasn't right in the head. How could he love her? He'd only known her a couple of months and had barely said a word to her. He was shy, she decided. Shy and had a temper, and she was winding him up. Closing her eyes and crossing the fingers on the hand shoved in her pocket, she bumped her shoulder against his. "Shall I tell you a secret?"

Mark's fists clenched tighter and she could see the whites of his knuckles. "I don't like secrets."

Shit. That didn't work. Susan clambered to her feet. "You'll like this one. I haven't got my knickers on. I didn't want to make you cross again." She pulled them from her pocket and held them scrunched up in her hand. "My bum is freezing."

"Show me?"

Susan held the knickers out. They fluttered in the breeze as though pegged on the washing line. But knowing that's not what he meant, she decided not to push her luck. Shoving her knickers back in her pocket, she unzipped her coat and pulled up her skirt. Her cheeks were on fire, and she stumbled over her words. "I won't lie to you, Mark, and I'll never keep secrets from you. Not real ones, only fun ones like this." Mark didn't respond, but his hands had relaxed. Feeling more confident, Susan stepped forward. "We can make this fun, Mark. You'd like that, wouldn't you?"

"Fun? I like sex, not fun. Come here."

Hoping her knees wouldn't buckle, Susan stepped forward. "Yes, fun sex. Sex is better when it's fun. Give me your hand." Her hands were shaking as she held them out. To her relief, Mark raised his hand. He looked confused now, not angry. This might work. Taking his hand, she squeezed it. "If you make me want you, make me want to have sex like you want to, it will be even better. Would you like that?" She heard her own words. She was talking to him like she would a child, and she studied his face.

Mark didn't respond, confusion still clouded his eyes, and Susan had a moment of pure clarity. If she pleased him sexually, not just accepted it, and made him enjoy it more, not just scratched an itch, she'd have complete control. As she moved his hand closer, she thought back to her first time; it had been awful, but the young lad had followed her around like a puppy afterwards. She'd controlled him. They did what she wanted, when she wanted. Perhaps she could do the same again.

"Now do what I tell you. We're going to have some fun."

• • • • • • • • • • •

Collecting the flask, which had rolled down the bank, Susan handed Mark his hammer. "There you go. I'd better let you get on with some work. See you later."

Mark didn't stop watching her until she had disappeared over the hill. The confused look remained, but as he lifted the roll of fencing onto his shoulder, he smiled.

Chapter Four

"Trump, talk us through your thoughts on Jasmine Jones. What do we know about her? What might we assume?" Meredith leaned back in his chair as Trump got to his feet.

"Jasmine was placed into care at the age of twelve by her mother. A single mother, diagnosed with terminal cancer, who didn't want her daughter to watch her die. There's a copy of the letter she wrote Jasmine on file. It had Linda in floods. Jasmine became—"

"Linda has read the file?" Meredith sat up.

"Yes, sir. She wants to keep in touch with what's going on," Trump answered.

"Linda sent him in with a list of suggestions for me. Can't wait for her to come back, both of them." Daisy smiled. "Putting up with you lot on my own is hard work. How's Patsy, Guv?"

"Getting there. Carry on, Trump."

"Once in care, Jasmine became a troubled soul. Had several juvenile arrests, no charges, all minor stuff. At seventeen she went to live in a house with similar young people, four of them sharing. She got a job at a local supermarket and everything went quiet, at least on the police front. Two years later, she moved in with Carl Mason. He was twenty-five, six years her senior. They lived together for six years. The few friends who gave statements said it was..."

Trump looked at his notes. "A love job and the real thing. They couldn't believe she'd done a runner. But do a runner she did. According to Mason, he came in from work and she wasn't there. He tried calling her, called her friends, checked she wasn't doing a late shift. At eleven thirty, he called the police and reported her missing. He was told to attend the station to do the paperwork the next day if she hadn't turned up. Three years prior to moving in with Jasmine, Mason was arrested for GBH against the then girlfriend. Broke her arm when he caught her dancing with someone else. She dropped the charges, but they didn't get back together. There was no record of him being violent towards Jasmine."

"Do we know anything else about him?" Kent asked. "Anything else on his record?"

"No, to both questions. He was a good bloke who doted on Jasmine according to the 'love job' friends. But given his history, the local team did search for her. Her bank records revealed the purchased ticket to Paddington, but as she didn't get off the train there, they checked the other stations, and as we know, Jasmine was seen leaving the station at Swindon and getting into a taxi alone. They found nothing out of the ordinary in her actions in the months leading up to her departure, and the case was closed. Until her body turned up."

"That's it? That's all we have to go on?" Seaton asked. "Did she use her bank account again?"

"I'm afraid that's all we have, yes, and I don't know about the bank. It's on my to-do list. She certainly hadn't from buying the ticket to the team closing the investigation. The next time Jasmine's name came up was last year, when her body was discovered and DNA confirmed identity."

"So, if we take the earliest date on which she might have died, 2008, where had she been for six years? She was living somewhere in the intervening years. Even if it was on the streets, someone must have seen her." Meredith pointed his pen at Seaton. "Over to you. Tell us about Louise."

"Not much to tell. Miss Average until she disappeared. Louise had been married. It lasted three years, they split up a year before. She had a restraining order on her ex, Ricky Marshall, and was in the process of divorcing him. He was also given a nine months' suspended sentence for ABH, which hadn't expired at the time of Louise's disappearance, which was reported by the woman she rented a room from. Her landlady was convinced Marshall was responsible, and given the history a full investigation followed. Marshall had a cast-iron alibi. He was in Ibiza on a stag do, and then the purchase of the train ticket and the footage from Swindon emerged. Case closed. As with Jasmine, Louise was alive for six years or so between going missing and being murdered."

Meredith smiled as Seaton got to his feet and nodded at Daisy. They must have been discussing the case out of hours. An Ordnance Survey map appeared on the screen.

"I've had a look at the map. Here's Swindon, here's roughly where they found the bodies, and here in between is a lot of farmland and very little housing. Also, just up the road from the burial sites is Pangbourne Station. There's not a direct line to Swindon, but it takes less than an hour to get there by train, even with the change at either Reading or Didcot. Did they double back to the station or did they get to their destination by taxi? I couldn't find anything on a televised or media appeal. Was there one, because if there was I can't find any reference to it?" Seaton asked.

"An also ran mention on the local news. I'm not even sure if there was a photograph. Is that part of your plan?" Meredith asked in reply.

"I think it should be. They had to be living somewhere local. I mean, how far do you travel with a body you need to dispose of? And for what it's worth, I reckon they were living somewhere rural because, and I'm guessing here, neither was reported missing a second time. Not unless they had taken a new name. I've added missing persons to the to-do list." Seaton walked back to his seat. "That's it. Not much is it?"

"No, but early days. Okay, let's get investigating. Before we put any televised appeal together we need to know our stuff. I want every one of the witnesses found and questioned again, and any others you find along the way that had any connection to either girl. I've made a list of those we know, with last known addresses. Daisy, I want you to trawl their personal stuff. What did they like, did they have hobbies, where did they go to school, did they have a gym membership? Anything you can find at all that might be a connection, however slight. No one has looked for that because the cases didn't get connected before they both turned up dead. And if you lot find anything that Daisy can add to the list, let her know. I want to speak to the farmers who owned the land they were buried on, their staff and all surrounding properties. Depending on how far we get, we'll spread out from there. There's a job for you, Seaton, get a list of all the local shops in that patch between Swindon and Pangbourne. There can't be that many, and they might have lived further afield but it's a start. Again, we can pan out later. Anything else you can think of immediately?" Meredith nodded at the negative response. "Okay, let's get going. George, you work out who's going to do what, and dish it out. You'll stay here. You and Daisy will review and collate all the information."

Meredith walked to his desk, and Trump followed him.

"A word if I might, sir? I spoke to Linda, and she was naturally concerned, so much so that as she's seeing her counsellor Maxine today she suggested you might want to meet them together. Two birds, as it were."

"No, Trump, I don't. Me meeting with them will not help Patsy. Tell Loopy...don't worry, I'll call her. I'm grateful, Trump, but I need them speaking to Patsy, not me. Let me have a word and explain that." Meredith was back on his feet and heading for the carpark.

"He's smoking again, then." Seaton said as the door closed behind him. "Not even trying to hide it."

"Yes. He's got a lot on his mind. Now, George, where do you want me to start? Are we doing them alphabetically, or do you have a cunning plan?" Trump walked across the office. He wanted to tell the others to be gentle with Meredith but couldn't bring himself to break his confidence.

• • • • • • • • • • •

While George and Trump sorted through the list of witnesses, Meredith paced the carpark, phone clamped to his ear, puffing on his third cigarette of the day.

"Skipper, how lovely to hear from you! Are we doing lunch? You'll love Maxine, she's so down to earth and patient. Well, she'd have to be to put up with me. I'm finding it very difficult to focus. But enough about me. Is that a yes?" Linda Trump paused for breath.

"No, Loopy, I'm afraid not. I've got work to do, and what would be the point? It doesn't matter what I think, it's what Patsy does. Is—"

"Understood. I called her the other day, left a message asking loads of open questions. You know, how are you, do you fancy coming for lunch, shall we get together, and I've not had a response yet. That's not like Patsy.

Poor Patsy, I'm really worried. I mean, I was a mess. I killed someone with my bare hands! And the knife, but you know what I mean. Skipper, no one can know how that makes you feel. Not..."

Linda got choked up and took a while to compose herself. She cleared her throat. "Not unless they'd been there and done that. Maxine said...no, I won't go off at a tangent, but it's tough Skipper, really tough. Doesn't matter what anyone says, it's you that has to deal with it. Max...I'll call Patsy again now. Is she in? Stupid question, of course she is. I've not been out much either, although me and Louie...I'm not staying on course, am I? Let me start again. How are you, Skipper? Louie was a mess when I was still weeping and wailing all over the place. I think that's one of the reasons I knew I had to get a grip, you know. So, how are you? And honestly, I don't want any macho nonsense."

Meredith waited a beat to ensure Linda actually had paused for a response.

"Honestly? Shit. We both are. But we'll get there. Look, I'm sorry I bothered you, Loopy. I believed from what Trump said that you were further along the road to recovery. It's not fair to ask you to cope with our problems, too. I can't do lunch, but I promise to pop in for a coffee soon. But only if you're still baking your masterpieces. You go and get ready for your session. I'll speak to Patsy again tonight." Meredith took a deep drag on his cigarette and closed his eyes as he blew the smoke out in short bursts.

"Skipper, you're smoking again. I'm not impressed but I forgive you, as I know you have a lot to deal with. And don't think you can brush me off that easily, I'm calling Patsy, even if you tell me not to. I won't say you've called me. I'll ask where my return call was."

"Thanks, Loopy, but she won't pick up. She never does. I was going to ask you to pop in but it's too soon. You concentrate on getting you better first. I don't want to knock you off course." Meredith felt his eyes tearing up and blinked rapidly as he lit another cigarette.

"I'm going to pretend you didn't say that. Patsy is my friend, my best friend. I'd do anything for her, you know that. If she needs me, then I'll need to man up. Skipper, Maxine gets here about twelve. I can't go to her office because I won't drive. My mind wanders too much, and now Louie is back at work it was that or nothing. She doesn't mind. Are you sure you can't spare half an hour? She'll be here until two. So you could pop over when it's convenient. Please, Skipper, you know something has to be done."

Meredith closed his eyes and looked heavenward. He hadn't thought they'd be meeting at the house, he'd assumed that she expected him to discuss personal matters in public, or worse, be analysed whilst sitting on a black leather couch. But Loopy's home wouldn't be too bad, would it?

"Skipper, are you still there?"

"Loopy, I think you've proved your dedication to Patsy. Look, I'm making no promises, but if I can get away you'll see me between twelve and two." Meredith took another drag as he wondered whether he'd even try.

"You'll find the time. What do you fancy, marmalade loaf or lemon drizzle? I've gone mad on citrus fruit this week, so the choice is yours, but I've got to use them up."

"Loopy, I said I'd try. Don't go to any trouble," Meredith warned.

"You'll be here. See you later. You didn't say, oranges or lemons?"

"You sound very confident."

"Because I know how worried you are. You're calling her Patsy instead of Hodge. Don't bother answering, I'll make both. You can take one home with you. 'Bye for now, I've got stuff to do. See you later."

Meredith took the last puff of his cigarette and stubbed it out. "Much later, Loopy."

He'd decided. He had no intention of going, even though it wouldn't be as bad as discussing Patsy sitting in a café somewhere.

• • • • • • • • • • •

George looked up as Meredith entered. "You'll be pleased. We've got four booked in already."

"Good work. Book some in for me. I've got no intention of sitting behind this desk while you lot go out enjoying yourselves.

"I don't think it will be enjoyable. None of them seemed keen."

"Tough. George, let the others phone the witnesses. You get onto anyone on the job who dealt with it. Oh, Daisy looks excited."

Everyone turned to look at Daisy, who was waving a hand in the air.

"One moment, please." Daisy hit a button on her keyboard and looked at Meredith. "Jasmine's boyfriend, Carl Mason, says he's flying out to Florida tonight for three weeks. If we want to speak to him it has to be in the next couple of hours or when he gets back. What do you want to do?"

"Where is he?" Meredith asked.

"In town, he was about to go home, which is in Whitchurch."

"Then ask him to come here. It'll be quicker if he's going to be watching the clock."

Carl Mason arrived twenty minutes later.

"Kent, you can join me. Where are we going?" Meredith asked as he pulled on his jacket.

"Ground floor, room seven. They've already been taken there," Daisy replied.

Meredith stopped walking. "They?"

Daisy shrugged. "That's what Renee said. I didn't ask her, sorry."

"Then I'd better go and find out. Kent, you might have to get rid of someone."

Kent nodded and followed Meredith down to the interview room. Meredith peered through the glass panel and looked at the forty-something couple sitting at the table. Mason looked confused, his companion nervous. It was she who spoke as Meredith opened the door.

"What's this all about? Why did you need Carl to come here? We're going on holiday today."

"Mr Mason, thanks for coming in. I'm DCI Meredith and this is DC Kent." Meredith smiled at the woman. "I'll explain all in a moment. Are you Mrs Mason?"

"No. But I'm his partner. Sandra Ganley. We live together." She glanced at Mason, who nodded. "Why are we here?"

"Hello, Sandra, did you know Mr Mason back in 2002? How long have you been a couple?"

"Yes, we worked together. Is this about something that happened twenty-odd years ago?"

"It is. How long have you been together?"

"What, seeing each other or living together?"

Mason turned to look at her. "Why don't you shut up a minute and let them ask the questions? We've got to be at Heathrow by six." He glanced at his watch. "We need to get a move on." Turning his attention to Meredith, he asked, "I'm guessing this is about Jasmine, if we're going back that far. But I'm not sure what it can be."

"As you may be aware, Jasmine's remains were found last year, and we've reopened the case."

Sandra gasped. "He didn't do it. The police said they had footage of her getting into a taxi in Swindon. After all these years, what can we tell you now?"

"How well did you know Jasmine?" Meredith asked.

"I didn't." Sandra shook her head, hand on her chest. "I didn't do it. I knew who she was, but I didn't kill her."

"Okay, in which case, as we're after details about Jasmine, we won't need to speak to you. DC Kent here will take you somewhere to wait. It shouldn't take long."

"Can't I stay? Take me where?"

"I'm afraid not, and as time is of the essence..." Meredith looked at the door, which Kent had opened. "Kent will settle you down somewhere quiet with a cup of tea."

"But I—"

"San, will you just go? Phone Billy if you don't want to hang about but get a move on." Mason tapped his watch as he spoke.

When the door had closed behind them, Meredith nodded at Mason. "So, were you two a thing when Jasmine disappeared?"

Mason ran his hands through his thinning hair and shook his head. "No. She was the cause, though. Actually, that's not fair, I was the cause because of Sandra."

"You'll have to explain that."

"We both worked in the office at the distribution warehouse down in Avonmouth. Hard to believe but I used to be quite popular with the ladies. I got around. I settled down when I met Jasmine. She was...I don't know, different. Exciting. Challenging. Caring. Confident. I fell for her hook, line and sinker. If I'm honest, I didn't even recognise San when she came to work there. But she remembered me. It's bad that, isn't it, forgetting all about someone you'd slept with?"

Meredith didn't answer as there was a tap at the door, and Kent walked in.

"Sandra's going home. She called Billy," he explained as he sat next to Meredith.

Mason nodded acceptance, and Meredith picked up where he had left off. "You cheated on Jasmine with Sandra? I didn't see that anywhere in the file."

Kent's eyes widened, and he wondered how Meredith had got to that point so quickly. He'd only been gone a couple of minutes, but he stayed silent as Mason answered.

"It wasn't relevant."

"How do you know? You just said you were the cause of Jasmine's disappearance because of Sandra. It seems pretty relevant to me."

"Okay, that sounded bad. It wasn't relevant to you lot. When she started working with me, Sandra made her interest in starting something crystal clear. It wasn't reciprocal. Don't get me wrong, she was a nice girl, but she wasn't a patch on Jasmine. Then there was the Christmas do, one pint led to a...to nothing. It was a shag in a cupboard, which I regretted the moment I woke up the next morning. I couldn't remember much about it, not the sex. It was over in minutes, just remembered the jeers as I came out of the cupboard zipping up and bumped into some drivers. I made a joke about it, and San burst into tears. Such a bloody mess." Mason closed his eyes and tipped his head towards the ceiling. "One misjudgement and everything was ruined."

Meredith nodded solemnly. "How did Jasmine find out?"

"When I woke the next morning, she wasn't in bed. Found her sitting in the living room, arms folded across her chest. I asked her what was wrong, and she asked me why I did it. I asked what, and she went ballistic, and I mean batshit crazy. First, she threw my shirt at me and told me not to effing lie. I played dumb, trying to work out how she could know. It was only eight o'clock in the morning and I hadn't got in till gone one. I still don't know."

"She didn't tell you?" Meredith asked.

"No, and I didn't get a chance to ask. When I think about it, which over the years I have a lot, I'm not even convinced she did know for certain. There's a chance she might have been testing me. Or perhaps I'd been talking in my sleep, or she could smell it, I don't know. But after the shirt, it was my shoes, my wallet, a book. She threw anything she could get her hands on. She was a good shot, too. I just kept asking what she was talking about as I dodged the missiles. Jasmine kept demanding to know who it was. I was hungover, knackered, and shit scared of losing her, so I got angry, too. I told her if she threw one more thing at me, I was out of there. It had been nothing. I was drunk, she was a slapper from the warehouse, and I didn't know her name." Mason ran his hands over his face. "Then it got even worse."

Mason fell silent, blinking and swallowing as he considered this. Meredith gave him a moment to compose himself.

"What happened to make it worse?" Meredith asked.

"Jasmine just stilled and looked so scared. She ran to the bathroom and threw up, then she cried, then she took a shower, and came back into the living room where I sat on the end of the couch like the total idiot I was, and she began clearing up. She stepped on a piece of china from a broken mug and cut her foot. When I tried to help her keep her balance hopping to the kitchen for a plaster, she flinched when I touched her. Like I'd burned her. Then she cried again. I held her, I cried with her, and I told her I was sorry, and then I took her back to bed, and I thought we might get back to where we were. We didn't. I'd broken my lovely girl."

Meredith lowered his head for a moment. This sounded very familiar. It was Kent who asked the next question.

"How long after did she leave?"

Mason shrugged. "About six months. She wouldn't let me touch her, not after that first morning. We never rowed, and we talked and we talked. But it was just round in circles. Then, about three months in, Jasmine started going to this counsellor and then a women's group. I got angry then because as far as I could make out it was a group for victims, and I'd never laid a hand on her. I promise you. Not a finger. But she said it wasn't all about that. It was about helping people get over trauma and stuff, and her counsellor thought it would help. So I bit my tongue, and she started to come out of wherever she'd been. We went out, we bought new furniture, we did normal stuff, everything except sex. Then, on that last day, Jasmine made my breakfast. She'd never done that before, even before...you know. I asked her if it was my birthday or something, and she said it will be if you play your cards right."

Mason looked from one man to the other. "I won't go into detail but it was the best, the absolute best sex I've ever had. I didn't want to go to work but she told me not to be daft, she'd be there when I got home. So I went, and she wasn't. Gone. She just disappeared. No note, no anything."

"And you have no idea where she went?" Kent asked.

"None. When the police showed me the film of her getting into the taxi, she had a little bag with her, smaller than a carry-on you'd use for the airport, so she didn't take much with her. I went through her stuff. Her makeup bag had gone, but not the ton of stuff she kept in her top drawer. Her favourite perfume wasn't there but she'd left all the half bottles on the dressing table. And I couldn't find her new jeans, and a few other bits. So I thought she might be back. That having sex with me had messed her up again, and she was taking a few days and then weeks to sort herself out. After a couple of months, I knew she wasn't."

"And then you got it together with Sandra. Sad story, Mr Mason."

"No. That was eighteen months later. I wasn't an innocent in that time. I took up where I'd left off before Jasmine. Nameless women looking for a good time and no ties. But it gets tiresome, and yes, then there was Sandra. She's a lovely woman, kind, caring, a great mum to the kids, and I'll never hurt her. But I don't know what would have happened if Jasmine had ever come back. Now she won't, so I'll never have to find out. I bet you think that's weird, don't you? Being in love with a dead woman after all these years."

"No. No one can control that. Let's go back to the counselling and the women's group. What do you remember about those?" Meredith asked.

Mason shook his head. "Nothing. Not sure I knew much then, only that's where she used to go. It was a long time ago."

"You never looked into them or followed her? Where did they meet?"

"All over the place. She had to catch the bus, the train. Not far. They had it down near Severn Beach once, I had a mate down there and she let me drop her off and have a pint with him while she did whatever they did, to save catching a train, and I remember the next week I offered again but it was back in town. It was mostly in town but sometimes they moved it. I don't know why."

"Was it on the same day every week?" Kent asked. "Do you remember where you dropped her off in Severn Beach?"

"It was twice a week. Tuesdays and Thursdays, she didn't always go to both. And it was the village hall in Easter Compton. I just went down the road to Severn Beach because that's where my friend lived." Mason checked his watch. "I promise you, I don't know where she went or what she did. Like I said, I have a good guess why she did, but I didn't kill her."

"What did you do with her stuff when you and Sandra got together?" Meredith asked. "Did she keep a diary or anything like that?"

"I chucked some stuff. Her mate Kelly bagged a load up and took it to the charity shop, but I kept a little box of stuff, a shoebox. Personal stuff I thought she might want if she ever came back. It might still be in the loft somewhere. We've moved twice. I remembered it when I heard about her body being discovered but I haven't had the balls to go up there and look for it."

"I might need you to do that. Is the Kelly who cleared out her stuff Kelly Albright?"

"Yes, that's her. Look, it's not that I don't want to help but I've got two twelve-year-olds expecting to hit Disney tomorrow. Can I go?" Mason asked.

Meredith got to his feet and shook Mason's hand. "Yes. Enjoy your holiday. Can we give you a lift home?"

"No thanks. Car's outside. I hope you find who did this."

"Me too. Might take a while. When are you back? I might need to go up in your loft."

"Twenty-third. I'll be the knackered-looking bloke with no money."

Back in the office, Meredith gave a brief resume of the meeting. "So a note for the twenty-fourth. Let them have a chance to unpack, and we need to find out about this women's help group, and what counsellor she was seeing." Meredith glanced at the clock. "I'm popping out. Carry on with what you're doing."

When he'd gone, Kent looked at Trump. "Where's he going?"

"He never said. Have we managed to find out where Kelly Albright is these days?" Trump replied.

Trump had had a message from Linda. She was expecting Meredith, and although Trump had doubted he'd go, now he wasn't so sure.

Chapter Five

By the time Meredith rang the doorbell, it was almost one thirty. He'd bought a sandwich on the way and eaten it in the car outside. He'd then sat and questioned whether he'd go in for fifteen minutes.

"Skipper, about time. You've been out there for ages. I was going to come out but Maxine said you'd come in when you were ready. I've boiled the kettle three times. Come here." Linda threw her arms around Meredith and dragged him into the house.

"Loopy, unhand me, it's embarrassing. I didn't have you down as a curtain twitcher." Meredith placed his hands on her shoulders and pushed her back. "You look well." He was lying. Linda had lost weight. Her hair was almost normal, not the wild mess he was used to, and she looked drab. On anyone else he wouldn't have thought that but wearing navy trousers and a white blouse just wasn't Linda. Where were the mismatched vibrant colours that he was expecting to assault his eyes? "You've changed your hair. It's almost normal."

Linda laughed. "I didn't have time to do it, I had to bake for you. Come on in. Maxine is dying to meet you."

Taking Meredith's hand, she led him to the sitting room. Meredith felt nervous, still not convinced he should be doing this. Unable to find a smile, he pulled his shoulders back. Just treat her like a witness. But not a hostile one he reminded himself as he followed Linda into the room.

Maxine Selby uncrossed her legs, stood, and held out her hand. "DCI Meredith, nice to meet you. Maxine Selby."

Meredith assessed her quickly. A tall, attractive brunette, fortyish, with minimal makeup, jeans that showed off her shape, and a baby blue cashmere jumper. Flat shoes. Her smile was genuine. He took hold of her hand. "Call me Meredith. I'd like to say it was nice to meet you but we both know it's not." He grimaced. "I'm not even sure why I'm here. That's for Patsy to decide. Has Loopy told you? Sorry, I don't know how much you know." There were the nerves, Meredith was prattling on.

"I wasn't sure what to call you. Sit, please. Linda said no one is allowed to call you anything but Meredith if they were friends or superiors, sir or guv if subordinates, and apparently Skipper if you're Linda, but never ever John. I choose friend. So please, take a seat Meredith. Tell me about Patsy."

Meredith hesitated, and Linda put her hand on his arm. "Sit down, Skipper, help yourself to the cakes. I'll make some tea." Linda left the room, closing the door behind her.

Meredith was perched on the edge of the armchair facing Maxine Selby. He watched as she tucked in her feet, crossing one ankle over the other, then leaned to one side as she assessed him, and wondered what she thought. He didn't speak.

Maxine waited a while before she gave a nod. "Would you prefer I ask you questions?"

"Not really, I'd hate it. Why don't you tell me what Linda has said, and I'll fill in the blanks or correct you?" He watched her lips twitch as he turned the tables. There was the nod again.

"I think I know all about what happened to Patsy, including her physical injuries. I'm guessing Patsy has PTSD. How severe I can't say without meeting her. What I don't know is what's troubling you because I'm told you only ever get emotional about your wife. You never discuss your private life, even with close friends like Louie, so whatever it is, it's probably serious. I'm guessing Patsy has probably withdrawn into herself because she isn't making or taking calls. Your friends are worried about her, and you." Maxine waited a beat for Meredith to speak, she was rewarded by a slight incline of his head. "How did I do?"

"Not bad. Except the last bit, what friends, and I'm okay or would be if Patsy would accept some help. I know how victims suffer after this sort of trauma because I've seen too much of it. I know it takes time to get back to some form of normality, and that counselling helps, like you're helping Loopy. But a word to the wise, ask Loopy why she's wearing such boring clothes. Loopy doesn't do boring, she does bright and in your face." He watched Maxine write something in a notebook balanced on the arm of her chair. "Didn't you know that? How could you? Sorry, that probably sounded aggressive. But I didn't even know she owned a white shirt. And then there's her hair."

"What about her hair?"

"Back at the beginning, Patsy told me she was late for a date because Loopy had to do her hair." Meredith waved his hands around his head. "It was always wild, and Patsy told me Loopy cultivated it, spent hours making it look like that. Patsy is the opposite. Wash it, dry it, twist it up on top, do something magical to it and stick a pencil through it to hold it off her neck when she's hot. But not Loopy, Loopy..."

"What's Patsy doing now?" Maxine asked.

"Literally? Probably sitting in the living room in silence or reading a book."

"With her hair. You've noticed the difference in Linda's appearance in great detail. What's Patsy doing now that is different?"

"Oh I see. Nothing much. Her clothes are casual but then they always are when she's not working. She's wearing her hair down but she does sometimes, and she never wears much makeup, certainly not when she's at home. When she's leaving the house just enough to highlight her perfection. It's not her appearance I'm concerned about, it's..." He waved his hand in circles in front of his face. "It's here. There's no spark. Not happy, not angry, not interested in anything, nothing, although she did do sad last night. Last night she cried and let me hold her for a while."

"Why did she cry? Do you know what brought that on?"

"I told her I was going to retire so I could be with her. She said I wasn't going to pin that on her, and I wasn't to do it. Then she ran upstairs, and she was crying. I asked her why and she said I was going to leave her. She let me hold her and I tried to reassure her. I calmed her down but I don't think she believed me."

"Has she any reason to believe you'd leave her? Does she think you don't want her, or wouldn't want her if you retired?"

Meredith sighed. "Before Patsy, my track record for maintaining a relationship with women when the going got tough wasn't great, despite trying to be the man I should be. It wasn't always my fault, although it probably was more often than not. I've been totally honest about all that with Patsy, and she accepted it, even made me take my ex-wife's son in when Nicola asked me to, even though Patsy thought he might be mine, she took my ex's son in. That's what she's like. She makes me a better man. How could I leave her? Why would I leave her? She was bloody perfect. She is bloody perfect. Now she needs help. It's why I'm here."

"What if she never really gets over this, what then?" Maxine looked him in the eye. "Would you still stay?"

Meredith got to his feet and pointed at her. "Yes. Yes, I bloody would. Are you telling me you don't think you can help her because I'm me?"

"Sit down, Meredith. For me to help Patsy it's useful to know about you. How long before last night were you previously allowed to touch her?"

Meredith opened his mouth but paused, censoring what he'd been about to say. "How did you know?"

"Because you told me. You said she let you hold her. It implied the opposite had been true up to that point. How long?"

Meredith sat back on the couch. The woman knew her stuff; he hadn't realised he'd said that. "Since before the attack. Patsy now sleeps in the spare room. She says it's because she's restless and will disturb me. I know it's because she doesn't want me to touch her. She freezes if I try, I've stopped trying. Can you explain that to me, how she's so frightened I'll leave her it reduces her to tears, but she doesn't want me to show her how much I need her? Why?"

"I don't know without meeting her. It might be a man touching her, or the thought of the weight of a man's body on her triggers the memory of what happened. She would like it to be different but it's not. If she doesn't give you what you need, you will leave her, but she can't. Interesting word you chose. Need. Do you love her or need her or both?"

"What a ridiculous question. Both." Meredith considered getting up and leaving but Linda kicked on the door with her foot.

"Let me in. This tea will stew if I wait any longer. I'll put it down and go."

Meredith jumped to his feet and opened the door.

"Sorry I was so long. I got distracted again." Linda looked at Maxine and rolled her eyes. "I saw Louie had left his...it doesn't matter, but I did. I'm here now. How's it going?"

Maxine answered quickly. "Well, thank you. Meredith has some thinking to do, and hopefully persuading." Pulling a card from a pocket in the cover of her notebook, she leaned forward and held it out to Meredith. "In case I forget."

Meredith took the card. "I'd better go. I've taken up enough of your time. I'll speak to Patsy tonight and call you if she's willing to speak to you."

"Ah, Skipper, you haven't had any cake. Wait there, I'll get a tin." Linda disappeared into the hall.

Meredith looked down at Maxine. "You said I had some thinking to do?"

"Yes. Because you used the word need first, not love. If Patsy takes too long to get well, will you still need her? Will you still need her if she's not making you a better man? I've no doubt you will always love her in your own way, but I'm guessing that, in part, you've felt like that about other women. And if you don't need her, what then? Because it appears that's what Patsy is focused on right now, and her answer is that you will leave her. Think about that, and then think about how well Patsy knows you. Because if we're going to help Patsy, we might need to help you, too."

Linda returned, and Meredith, lips pursed, was staring at Maxine, and only looked away when Linda pushed the tin towards him.

"Make sure Patsy has some."

"I will do, Loopy." Meredith slung his free arm around Linda's shoulder and kissed the top of her head. "Keep on getting there, Loopy. We're missing you. And do me a favour."

"What?" Linda asked.

"Next time I see you, wear one of your bright monstrosities. Maybe the one with the hippos. I liked that one."

Linda grinned at him. "No, you didn't. But I get the message. I've got a lovely one I'll wear though. It's pinstriped, but when you look closely dolphins form the stripes."

"Sounds perfect. Maxine." With a curt nod, Meredith was out of the room but in the house long enough to hear Linda's comment.

"I told you, didn't I? He's perfect, and so is Patsy. We've got to sort them out."

Meredith slammed the door. "No, I'm bloody not." Shoving the cake tin under his arm, he strode to his car. This was why he didn't trust these people. They didn't so much sort your mind out as fuck it up. Instead of going back to work, he drove home.

Opening the front door, he called out his arrival. He'd not done that a few weeks ago, and Patsy had almost passed out with the shock.

"Only me. Where are you?" He dropped his keys on the hall table and looked at the flashing light on the answer machine, before poking his head into the sitting room. Patsy wasn't there. He was headed for the kitchen when her feet appeared through the banister.

"Are you okay?" she asked, bending down to look at him through the spindles.

"I think so. Come down, I've got a surprise for you." He watched the hesitation before she continued down the stairs. Going into the kitchen, he put the kettle on and dropped the teabags into mugs. Patsy's phone was on the counter. He tapped it to activate it. Two missed calls, one from Linda, and one from Barbara, her stepmother.

Turning around, he found Patsy standing in the doorway. "Come in. Sit down. I want to talk to you." He watched her features, first the hesitation, then the fear. "It's nothing bad, I promise."

Patsy nodded and sat stiff-backed at the table. "I thought you said something about a surprise."

Meredith held up the tin. "Not a big one but cake from Loopy. I've not tried it yet." He thought she'd ask where he'd seen Linda but she didn't.

Patsy smiled. "That's nice. How is she?"

"Getting there but worried about you. She said she'd called a couple of times, and you hadn't answered or called her back."

"Oh, I'll do that later. I was changing the beds. Took a while." Patsy held up her plastered arm. "My shoulders are aching now but the sheets are clean."

"You should have left it until I got home. I'd have done it. I'm not totally useless. Or as I suggested, as you don't seem to want me to do anything, we could get a cleaner in until you're fit and well..." Meredith winked to show he was joking as he put the tea on the table and collected the cake tin. "Neither option is a problem, you just need to say. Plates." He walked to the cupboard and his head dropped as Patsy hissed at him.

"Jesus, Meredith, it was just a few sheets. I have to do something. I'll go bloody…" Patsy looked down at her hands. "Sorry, I know you meant well. But it needed doing, and I needed something to do."

Sitting opposite her, Meredith held out his hand. Patsy knew it was there but kept her eyes trained on her lap.

"Hold my hand." Meredith tapped his knuckles on the table. "Patsy, I'm asking you to hold my hand and look at me."

Patsy placed her hand in his. She didn't return the affectionate squeeze; it was simply there. After a few moments, she looked up.

"Do you love me? Because I love you. I need you to listen to me. I. Will. Never. Leave. You. Ever. I am not known for my patience but for you I have as long as it takes. I want my Patsy back but, if necessary, you can stay put in that spare bedroom until they carry me out in a box. I won't make you do anything you don't want to. All I would ask is that you try to get better. That you try to trust me. Will you do that?"

Patsy nodded.

"Good, then let's have some cake." Meredith placed a slice of cake onto a plate and pushed it forward before cutting the second. "You first. She's never let us down but she's not been herself. Hording citrus fruit at the moment, she tells me."

Patsy broke off a tiny corner and placed it in her mouth. "It's good."

"How can you tell with that tiny morsel? Have a proper bite."

Patsy slammed her hands on the table. "I'm not a bloody child, Meredith. Please, don't treat me like one. I'll eat when I'm hungry."

"I'm sorry. I didn't mean to piss you off. Seems to be my go-to at the moment. Patsy, you're not eating properly, you're not sleeping, unless you wait until I leave the house. You say you love me, and you're worried I'll leave you, yet you won't speak to me, won't speak to anyone."

He pulled Maxine's card from his pocket. "This is who is helping Loopy. Loopy couldn't sing her praises loudly enough. If you don't trust me, speak to Loopy. If you don't trust Loopy, speak to her." He tapped the card before sliding it across the table. "Because you have to speak to someone. I won't watch you fade away, Patsy. If you don't do something, I'll bring in the big guns and call your father."

Patsy's head shot up. "You will not. You saw the mess he was in when he came to the hospital. He's too old to be worrying about me."

"And you promised him it would all be alright. It's not, is it? Is it?" Meredith demanded. "You know they tell alcoholics and the like that the first step to solving their problem is recognising that they have one. We have one. You have one."

"Do not call my father. Promise me, Meredith."

"Only if you promise me you'll speak to someone. I don't care who, and I don't mean about the weather."

Patsy nodded.

"Say it."

Patsy rolled her eyes. "I promise."

"Then so do I. Let's say you have three days to keep your promise before I call your father. Deal?"

Patsy nodded, and Meredith didn't push his luck by asking her to say it. He bit into his cake. "Thank you. Now, I'll leave you to think about it because I have to get back to work. I might be a bit late. I'll do a bit of shopping on the way home."

Patsy nodded again, and as he passed her, he leaned down and kissed the top of her head. He felt the flinch but ignored it. As he left the house, he crossed his fingers, hoping he'd not just made matters worse.

Two hours later, in the middle of sorting out an interview, Meredith's phone pinged. He glanced at it and saw he had a message from Patsy.

"Could you bear with me one second?" Placing the call on hold, he picked up his mobile.

Don't worry about shopping. It will be at home before you are. P x

Smiling, he returned to his call. "Apologies. Now, where were we?"

Chapter Six

The next few days passed quickly. The work was tedious but rewarding as the number of witnesses the CCRT tracked down grew and more interviews were booked. As yet, Daisy had found no link between the two victims, but Meredith was pleased with their progress.

Meredith enjoyed going to work and celebrating the minor victories with the team. There was a hesitant optimism that once the interviews got underway the following week, they'd inch forward towards solving the case. At home, nothing much had changed. Patsy now joined Meredith to eat dinner each night to show she was trying but they both knew it was forced and unnatural. When he left for work on Friday morning, he tapped on the door to the spare room. Patsy rolled over and looked at him. His heart lurched. She looked so lost.

"I'm off now. I'll see you later. Oh yes, I'll leave the card for Maxine Selby on the kitchen table. I'm sure you haven't forgotten that today is make your mind up day. I've not mentioned it because I know you needed time. Just remember, I love you, and I wouldn't ask if I didn't think it would help."

Patsy closed her eyes again and sighed as she nodded. She didn't speak, even to say goodbye. Meredith closed the door quietly, believing she wouldn't make the call. His sigh was deeper than Patsy's, as he wondered if he'd go through with dragging her father into the mess. He was having a hard enough time fielding calls from his daughter Amanda. And Peggy.

Peggy was the self-appointed matriarch of their family. Meredith had taken Peggy under his wing when she was a witness in a previous case, and down on her luck, or so they thought. Patsy and Meredith had taken Peggy into their home until she was well enough to go home. Peggy was forthright and took no prisoners when expressing her opinion, and she loved Patsy like the daughter she had lost. The night before, she had accused Meredith of hiding something from her and issued an ultimatum: if Peggy hadn't heard from Patsy by the weekend, she was turning up, with or without an invitation. Patsy was already in bed by the time Meredith returned Peggy's call. He'd tell Patsy tonight once she'd given him her decision.

Walking into the kitchen, Meredith looked at the card and hoped Patsy would use it. He was on his way out when he turned and went back to the kitchen, took down the number, and sent a text to Maxine.

Meredith here. It's a long story but I gave Patsy an ultimatum. It runs out today. If she doesn't call you, I have an idea I'd like to run past you. Perhaps you'd call when you have a moment. Thank you.

He hesitated before hitting the send button.

Maxine called him as he parked his car outside the station.

"It's Maxine Selby, Meredith. You are certainly an early bird."

"Apologies, I didn't mean call now. I didn't want to get distracted by work and forget to message you. But thanks for calling."

"Let's deal with the most important issue. Ultimatum? What does that mean? I'm concerned, Meredith. People who have experienced trauma will heal in their own time. Sometimes...I haven't got time now, but what ultimatum, what have you done?"

Even though she'd never met Patsy, her concern was evident and her accusation, although silent, noted. Meredith thumped the steering wheel.

"It wasn't heavy. At least I don't think so. Her father was concerned about her, and I told Patsy if she didn't accept that she needed to speak to someone in three days then I'd have no choice but to be honest with her father about her condition. He's approaching eighty, and has been in poor health recently, and he thinks I'm hiding something from him, which I am. He's the most important person in Patsy's life."

"Interesting. How did that work out?" Maxine still sounded angry.

"Well, she's not called you yet. Today was her last day. I suppose we'll both know by the end of the day. Which was why I wanted to speak to you. I know you think I'm an arsehole who likes his own way, and if I'm honest, many people would agree with you. But I'm not doing this for selfish reasons. I'm doing it for Patsy."

"For Patsy too, should have been the end of that sentence. What was your idea?"

Meredith bristled. The woman clearly didn't like him, and he wondered if asking her to help Patsy might cause him more trouble in the long run. But here he was. "Would you be prepared just to turn up? Not alone. With me, or perhaps with Linda. She's offered to help, but I don't want her to go backwards by helping Patsy. Patsy still has manners so she wouldn't refuse to see you. The only question would be whether she'd be prepared to actually talk to you over and above a polite greeting and rejection."

"And what about you?"

"What about me?"

"Meredith, I've only met you briefly but from what you said, how you've framed your statements, together with what your number one fan, Linda, has told me, I believe it's you who's contributing to Patsy's problems. Her main issue is dealing with what happened to her. I've no doubt she is having flashbacks, or nightmares, maybe both, hence the erratic sleeping pattern, but I think overriding her ability to cope with that is you. Look, I'm sorry, I have a very full day today and must get on. Text me your home number and Patsy's number and I promise I will take her call if she obeys your ultimatum. If she doesn't, I would ask you not to go through with your threat and support her in that decision, although you may state you still think it's a good idea. In the meantime, I'll give some thought to your latest idea, and whatever Patsy's decision is we'll speak next week. Now, I really must go."

"Thank you." Meredith's tone was curt. He felt like he'd just been in front of the headteacher and been given a double detention for something that he had no control over. She might be good with her patients, but their nearest and dearest got short shrift.

"I'll also need a formal letter of instruction. With Linda that's the police authority. Will it be the same for you and Patsy?"

"I don't...hang on, I don't need your help. Not with me. We're not going down that road. Patsy will be your patient. Not. Me. Don't get me wrong, I'm willing to speak to you if it will help her but about her. I don't need to be taken back to my childhood and any trauma that might have occurred. I already know all that bollocks, so if that's your plan, although God knows why, I'll need to find someone else."

"Perhaps I phrased that incorrectly. Let's speak over the weekend. I really must go. Goodbye, Meredith."

Meredith stayed sitting in his car while he calmed down. He reached the conclusion that the woman was after money, but she wasn't going to get any by having him unpack the family of skeletons in his closet. If Patsy weren't so poorly, he'd be happy as a pig in shit. He'd tell her that next time they spoke. Right now, he had work to do.

Several hours later, despite the conversation still dangling in the back of his mind like an irritating cobweb with the spider ready to dash out and trap him, he and the team tracked down the final few of the original witnesses and had them all booked in for interviews. It would take a couple of weeks to see them all, and only a few would prove to be of any use, if that, but Meredith was feeling positive. About the case, at least. He called for attention.

"Right, I know it's Friday, and I know it's almost lunchtime but we're not switching off for the weekend just yet. Now we've got all the witnesses and officers who dealt with the case booked in, we're going to concentrate on doctors and organisations etcetera." He picked up the pen and tapped the whiteboard before removing the lid. "We've got their doctors. Daisy, remind me."

"Dr Bryant, Riverbank Medical Centre for Jasmine and Dr Carmichael, Whiteladies Road Health Centre for Louise. Jasmine disappeared a long time ago, so Dr Bryant might not be around anymore," Daisy told him.

"This is true but we can still speak to someone in charge and get their records. There was no record of Louise having her broken arm treated, but we need to find out if either was referred for counselling of some description. If not, we need to continue working on that list of local support groups. How are we doing with that?" Meredith asked.

"We've got loads, Guv. A quick google brings up a shedload. It's working out which ones might be relevant," Kent replied. "I'll start making a list but that's a big job."

"And when you're not interviewing, you'll have nothing better to do." Meredith wrote *counselling* on the board, and underneath *Easter Compton*. "We've already got one dead cert, if they are still going to have records. Next?"

Seaton raised a finger. "Neither girl used their bank accounts again. We've had that confirmed. Louise bought something in the café at Temple Meads after buying her ticket but that was it. She drew out fifty of the three hundred and odd pounds she had in her account the day before. The balance wasn't touched, nor was the six hundred and fifty quid she had in her savings account. Jasmine's account was left with a balance of just under a hundred after the purchase of the ticket. Wherever those girls were going, they were either expecting to come back, or knew they had another source of income in the years before their death. Either way, they didn't spend or perhaps want that money."

"So nothing to add to the list then?" Meredith rolled his eyes, but smirked to show his amusement.

"No, Guv. But here's one for the list. Louise used to go to a keep fit class. One of our witnesses said she was surprised because Louise had said in class etcetera, when I asked what class she said keep fit, although they've stopped now because the teacher moved away. But there were other women there. Louise may have confided in one of those."

"That's better. We'll be picking up a lot more of these as we speak to the other witnesses. Don't miss them. Anything else?"

"Workplaces. Jasmine worked at the Co-op, and Louise part-time for an optician. She was one of those who allowed you to pick up an eighty quid frame before breaking the news that the specs would cost you closer to four hundred by the time she'd added everything on. From what I can see only a couple of people from where they worked were spoken to at the time."

The list was lengthy and the task of tracking down all the possible witnesses was daunting given the intervening years.

Finally satisfied, Meredith walked back to his desk. "That'll do for the time being. Let's take an hour and attack that lot in some sort of order when you get back. If anyone is going to the bakery, I'll have a chicken pie."

While his team went about their lunchtime rituals, Meredith looked at the list and made a bet with himself that the breakthrough they needed would come from the least expected source and his money was on the keep fit club or the boy that collected the trolleys at the supermarket. It had been a week since they'd been given the case and he'd not heard from the chief super. He cursed himself for tempting fate and made another bet that he'd probably turn up as they were about to go home as it was Friday. Meredith decided he'd show him the door. He needed to get home to Patsy. And then his mind was back on Patsy and whether he'd take Maxine Selby's advice if Patsy hadn't called her. A thought occurred to him and, making sure he had a lighter, he headed for the carpark.

Meredith lit his cigarette before making the call.

"Meredith, what a surprise, I have ten minutes, what do you want?" Maxine Selby asked. "Patsy hasn't called."

"I wasn't calling about Patsy. I think if she had, she would have texted me."

"Oh, so she does communicate with you during the day? She's not totally cut herself off, that's good."

"Oh shit, here we go again. No, she doesn't. She has once, to tell me she'd done the shopping online the day I gave the ill-advised ultimatum. I texted her in the first few weeks but gave up." Meredith took a long drag on his cigarette. "We're getting sidetracked. I'm calling about work. And I know time is money, so you can bill me for an hour of your time."

"I haven't got an hour. What do you need?"

"Then we'll bank the rest." Meredith explained about the disappearance of the two girls. "So we know Jasmine was attending a group, and as Louise's husband had been knocking her about and she had a restraining order against him, it's highly likely she would have been too. How do women usually find these groups? We've found hundreds online, but back when Jasmine went missing I doubt if that was her route."

"It depends whether it was an official group. Most meetings with counsellors would be on the recommendation of a doctor or perhaps an employer, if the trauma was work related, as in the case of Linda and perhaps Patsy. But not always. We are always available to members of the public who think we might be useful. They simply need to pick up a phone. Self-help groups are usually, but not always, a voluntary thing. Victims helping victims, there can be a professional presence but not necessarily. Few groups are funded by government, most are charitable ventures."

Meredith pictured Patsy sitting in a roomful of troubled women, all with opinions and advice but none of them qualified to give it.

"You huffed."

"I'm sorry?"

"You huffed." Maxine imitated the noise causing Meredith to smile. He was glad she couldn't see him, she'd probably think it meant something more than amusement.

"Ah. I huffed because I wondered how many additional issues people picked up taking advice from amateurs."

"They're not for advice, although that would normally be available if requested. They are for support. Human contact with others who have experienced similar things. Someone to speak to, even if it's about the weather. Getting out of the house. Being allowed to bare your soul, voice your fears, however unfounded, without judgement. Being allowed to sit in silence and simply listen. You see?"

"I think so. So based on what I've told you about the case, it's highly likely both women would find benefit attending such a group?"

"Yes. Think of the AA or the various men's wellbeing groups, which are commonplace these days, most people would benefit from attending, even those who think they don't have issues to resolve. And perhaps crucial for those who do."

Meredith smiled again. She thought he had issues to resolve other than Patsy, and perhaps was an alcoholic. "You tutted. Is talking to me like talking to a child who refuses to listen? Because I am. It's all registering."

"I don't think I did, and I'm sure it is. If I tutted it's because I'm going to be late for my next appointment and I haven't a spare minute today, although now I have to find sixty or so more because it's not only you who has taken me off course," Maxine explained.

"Then I apologise and thank you for your help. I hope you can find another couple of minutes should Patsy call."

"I will, of course. And no apologies necessary, I enjoy speaking to you, Meredith. And look forward to our next conversation, but for now, goodbye."

"One chicken pie." Trump held up a bag. "Was that good news? You were smiling. That's a rare occurrence these days."

"Not really. It was Maxine and she's told me that many of these self-help groups aren't official as such, and usually organised and run by people who are or were experiencing similar problems. The haystack just got bigger."

"And that made you smile?" Trump handed over the bag, a wary look on his face.

"Don't look at me like that. I've not lost the plot. It gave me another thought about how to help Patsy." Meredith jerked his head towards the door. "After you."

Chapter Seven

2023 – Brandon Farm

"Jasmine, love, have you seen my gloves? I'm sure I had them this morning." Cissy stood in the centre of the kitchen, arms akimbo as her eyes searched every available surface.

Susan waved her hands in the air. "Guilty. I had to take Mark's flask down to him. He forgot it. Here you go." Pulling off the gloves, Susan passed them to Cissy. "How's Father?" As she asked, she realised she rarely used his name. Despite having little to do with him, she had to call him Father to keep up the pretence. It seemed natural now. The same as everyone calling her Jasmine.

"Up and down. He wasn't good this morning, but he's rallied a bit. The doctor's coming in later. I don't think he's got long."

Susan hung her coat on the hook. "You've been saying that almost as long as I've been here."

"I know. His will to survive amazes me. They told me to expect the worst when he had his accident, then add to that all his other ailments since, he's a walking, or rather a lying down miracle. Bless him."

Susan hid her smile as she filled the kettle. Bless him was just a Cissy catchphrase. She used it for everyone. Susan had heard her cussing her husband and wondering if she'd ever be free of the burden. From the little Mark said, and it was very little, none of them had had much time for him before the accident. Susan would have been there for four years come August, and to her knowledge Mark had not spoken to him in all that time.

That first year, Susan had prayed for his early demise almost every day. Not so much now because she'd settled into their way of life. It could be hard, especially in the dark winter months, but generally it was acceptable. Mark might be as entertaining as a brick, but he was as passionate as a bull in a field of cows. She smiled at the comparison. She was even thinking like a farmer these days.

"What made you smile?" Cissy asked, her own face beaming. "So lovely to have some happiness in this house. That's you, that is. You make us all happy."

"Will you miss me when I'm gone?" Susan asked playfully.

Cissy's face fell. "You'll go then?"

"I don't know. I'm guessing so. It's a big world out there. Never thought I'd see much of it, but now I've got money and no problems chasing me around, who knows, I might get to see some of it." She linked her arm in Cissy's. "Once you're released from looking after father, you could come on a trip with me. We could hit Europe. Just imagine us strolling up the Champs-Élysées or wondering if we're brave enough to go to the top of the Eiffel Tower. To be honest, a glimpse of Buckingham Palace and Big Ben would be a treat. Young Thomas has seen more of the world than me. Forty-two years old and never been to London." Susan looked wistful and Cissy bumped her shoulder.

"Let's plan a trip. It won't be foreign because we haven't got passports but we could go to London, although I've always fancied Edinburgh. Perhaps we'll do both. I thought you'd stay. I thought you were happy here. What will we do without you? You've become the glue that holds us together." Cissy's mouth drooped and her shoulders slumped. "I've been relying on you too much."

Susan wrapped an arm around her shoulder. "Get on with you. You're the glue. I'd have been out of here that first time with Mark if it wasn't for you."

"Exactly. And look at you now. You've got him eating out of your hand. Even Jasmine the first didn't manage that. Why do you want to go?" Cissy pulled out a chair and sat at the table. "You could do worse, you know. This farm's worth a few bob, as is the income from the land we rent out, and if he ever gets round to kicking the bucket, I'm positive he's got money hidden somewhere. I know how we scrimped and saved when he was running things, and now we don't. Not that much has changed. The bugger was probably syphoning it off, and he can't have spent it. That'll all go to Mark, and therefore you."

"But it won't, will it? I'm not related to any of you, not even by marriage, and it's not the money. I've got my money in that account. Not a vast sum in the scheme of the farm and the rest, but more than I've ever dreamed of having. I might have done well for you but that's worked both ways. Let's not talk about it. It might be years away. But yes, I'd like to go for an away day with you. Anywhere will do, just not Gloucester or Stroud. I'll never go back there."

Cissy still hadn't perked up, so Susan clapped her hands. "That's what we'll do. Thomas is on half term soon so he can help his dad. He likes that. We can cook everything they'll need and freeze it, leave a list of instructions, and they'll be fine."

"Oh, if only. But I can't leave because who'd deal with him?" Cissy looked at the ceiling. "Not Mark, and you can't expect a boy to change beds and wash an old man."

"No, you can't but you can pay a professional to come in and do it. In fact, you could do that anyway. How old are you, Cissy? Sixty-two, sixty-three? You must be worn out. He might go on for years, and you need a break. I'll speak to Mark tonight." Susan pointed at the gloves in Cissy's hands. "What did you want those for?"

"Bugger! I was going down to the village to pick up some bits. I'm nearly out of flour. Not to worry, tomorrow will do. Thomas will be out of school in an hour, and I promised him a roast." Cissy finally found her smile again. "Now, there's someone who deserves something nice. He works so hard, both here and at school, and he's still only a baby, really. He'll go places that one. Can't see him wanting this life when he's older. He's a bright boy. Mark won't hold him over a barrel like his father did to him." Again, she glanced at the ceiling. "But what else would Mark have done? He's never been interested in anything else."

"What was he like as a boy? I can't imagine him any younger. I sit at the table and look at the pair of them, and Thomas is the mini version of Mark, but that's where the similarity ends. Thomas is so full of everything, it's hard to keep up with him sometimes, but Mark barely says a word. I know he listens, but he never joins in. I take it he didn't get on with his dad."

"Least said about that the better. His father resented him. Didn't like the attention Mark drew away from him, from the farm. Father wanted to be the centre of attention. Of my attention. He resented Mark from the day he was born. That boy never stood a chance, and all he did was get born." Cissy blinked. "But we are where we are, and things are better now. Thomas has a different life, and like I said, that's down to you, Jasmine." Placing the gloves on the dresser, Cissy walked to the pantry and lifted some potatoes from the basket inside the door. "Chatting won't put tea on the table."

Later that evening, Thomas had gone to bed, Mark was dozing in front of the television, and Susan had taken a bath while Cissy settled the old man down for the night. When Susan left the bathroom, she could hear their muted voices as she crossed the landing to her room. She stopped when she heard Cissy cry out in pain.

"Ow! You're an evil bastard. Ow! Stop it! Please, Charlie, I'm sorry."

Cissy was clearly in pain, and Susan hurried to the door and had her hand on the door handle when the old man spoke. She paused to listen because in all the years she'd been there, she'd only heard him mutter a few words before. He'd just lie there and watch her go about whatever task she'd gone in for. She hated going in there, but Cissy needed help to get him out of bed these days, even with the hoist. It wasn't hard, but the old man did nothing to help. Thomas did it mostly because the old man co-operated when Thomas was there, but when Thomas wasn't around it fell to Susan to help Cissy, and he'd just stare at her. He gave her the creeps. She pressed her ear against the door.

"I said send the boy in. I have a right to see my grandson. What you forget, Cissy, is I ain't got much to lose. But you have, you and that useless lump of a son. What would the boy think if I told him what you two did? What would she think? I hear him rutting away at her. Ha! I suppose I should give him credit for that. At least he gets that right. She likes it these days. I turn the telly down sometimes to listen to 'em. She knows how to please a man, not like you. Go on. Piss off, I can't bear to look at you. The boy brings my breakfast. Gerry's coming over tomorrow."

Susan heard movement. The wheelchair knocking against the cabinet as it always did. Crockery chinking together as Cissy loaded the tray, and she moved away from the door, tiptoeing across to her own room. Their room. The room where she had sex with Mark and the old man listened. Her nose wrinkled, and a shiver ran up her spine. She'd not known that. It should embarrass her but sod him, he was a nasty, miserable old man, and he was horrible to all of them. No wonder Mark wouldn't even mention his name. All the same, she was glad Thomas and Cissy were on the other side of the house. If not, she wouldn't be able to look them in the eye.

Whatever the old man had done to Cissy, she didn't deserve. Cissy had no life because of him. And what was it with Gerry? Telling Cissy about the visit from his younger brother sounded like a threat. Susan had to keep out of the way when Gerry came to visit. He came every few weeks. She had to leave the room and make herself busy somewhere until he was upstairs with his brother. But Cissy hovered, always on edge on those days.

Such a weird family, and despite not wanting to leave Cissy, she knew she'd go once they had what they wanted. Susan pulled on her dressing gown and went downstairs. Mark and Cissy were standing at the table. They had their backs to her, and she couldn't see what they were doing.

"I swear he gets nastier every day, and I'll tell you, Mark, if I wasn't worried about your future, yours and Thomas's, I'd be out of here like a shot. Just leave him to fester in his own mess. Ow! That stings."

"Let me finish him," Mark said, no trace of emotion in his voice.

"No! No more violence. No more or I'll go to the bloody police myself. Do you hear me? Thomas and Jasmine have no part of this. Think about them. Do you hear me?"

Mark nodded, and Cissy held up her bandaged hand. "Thank you." She placed the other on his cheek. "You're a good son, Mark. Now, turn the telly off, lock the door and get up to bed with your wife."

Susan hurried back up the stairs, wincing as the floorboard at the top creaked. Shit. Turning around, she made her way back down as noisily as possible. They both turned to look at her.

"I'm knackered, and I've got a terrible headache. Have we got any painkillers?"

Cissy's shoulders relaxed. "Above the kettle on the shelf. I'll have a couple too. Managed to stick a knife through my hand, washing up. It's aching like mad." She held up the bandaged hand.

Susan nodded and went to collect them. The sink was empty, the crockery still on the tray brought down from the old man's room. He'd stabbed Cissy. Susan popped two pills into her hand and passed the packet to Cissy.

Filling a glass with water, she took the pills, made her excuses and went to bed. She lay in the darkness thinking about what she'd heard, and wondering if Mark's offer had been serious, and what it was the two of them had done, that the old man could threaten Cissy with? Would Mark really kill his own father? She hoped not. She'd got used to being here and was enjoying her life, limited though it was. But compared to what it had been, it was idyllic. But Mark had a temper, she knew that. His hatred of his father was obvious. Perhaps that's why he never went in to see him. Perhaps he was frightened of what he might do. Although he'd been fine with her since that first time, he now never even raised his voice. Mark was besotted with her. But faced with the spite his father had dished out to Cissy, who knew what he might do if his father tried it with him? No wonder he would never go in there. The old man was violent. He'd stabbed Cissy, and who knew what else had gone on before she got here, before he was laid up in that bed. Perhaps that's why Mark was like he was. What a horrible life the old man had given them.

Mark came into the bedroom and undressed in the darkness, dropping his clothes onto the chair. He climbed into bed but didn't reach for her as he usually would. Susan placed a hand on his chest.

"Are you okay? No cuddle tonight?" she asked.

"I thought you had a headache."

"I've got a remedy for that. Painkillers and..."

Susan trailed her hand down his torso. Let the old man listen. Let him hear what he was missing. He had to die sometime but not by Mark's hand, not if she had anything to do with it. Mark would be arrested, and Cissy definitely wouldn't want her to go then. It was all too risky. She had to keep Mark happy. There was a lot of money sitting in that account now, and Susan wanted to collect it.

Chapter Eight

Meredith came home to the smell of food cooking. He smiled as he dropped his keys onto the table and pulled off his tie.

"I'm home. Something smells good."

Meredith walked into the kitchen. He saw that Maxine's card had gone from the table, but there was no sign of Patsy. He opened the oven door to have a peep, the sauce on the top of the lasagne was well browned, minutes away from burning. He grabbed a tea towel and lifted it out, cursing as the heat penetrated the towel. With the crisis averted he went in search of Patsy. She was asleep on the couch. A little frown creased her brow, but she looked peaceful. He left her to sleep and went to shower. If she'd slept through him swearing and banging about in the kitchen, she must need it.

He doubted she'd called Maxine Selby, he'd have heard, but following Maxine's advice, he wouldn't push her. He wouldn't even mention it until Sunday. The weekend would be strained enough without him making it worse.

By Sunday morning, he was finding it difficult to bite his tongue. He tried instead to engage Patsy in conversation, but after a few polite responses the weekend had been like two strangers stuck in a lift together. Mid-morning, he sat next to her on the sofa, and she lowered the book she'd been reading for the last week.

"Let's go out for lunch. Anywhere you like, pub grub, posh restaurant, fish and chips at the seaside. You choose. What do you fancy?" He inclined his head and smiled. "I think I know what you're going to choose."

Patsy looked past him and out of the window. "It looks cold. It's grey and dismal. Let's stay in, I was going to roast a chicken."

"And I was right. Shall I peel some potatoes?" Meredith was back on his feet and Patsy jumped up to join him.

She placed her hand on his arm, and static arced between them. Meredith grinned. "I'm electric, me. Remember?"

Patsy snatched her hand back and looked away. Of course she could remember. Her chin trembled, and she pulled her shoulders back. "I remember. You sit down and find some sport to watch. You've been working all week." Without looking at him, she walked away to the kitchen.

Meredith followed her and sat at the table, watching as she collected the things she needed to prepare lunch. He pushed her to one side when the chicken was ready for the oven.

"Patsy, let me help you. It looks so bloody awkward with that plaster on. Let me help you." He lifted it into the oven and went to the sink to peel the potatoes. "You chop those carrots or something."

Preparation complete, Meredith sat back at the table. "We've got an hour or more. You don't want to go out. Everything that needs to be done is done. What shall we talk about? Come and sit with me. I'll pour some wine. An apéritif."

Patsy nodded and twirled the glass by the stem while Meredith opened the bottle. "Tell me about the case. I've got no news because I'm still recovering."

Meredith paused the flow of wine. "Was that a dig? If it was, it's unfair. I'm trying to help your recovery. You, on the other hand, seem to want to wallow in your misery." Placing the bottle down, he held up his hands. "I'm not knocking that, I've never been where you are and I don't know what it's like, but I know this isn't good for you. It can't be. What if nothing changes? Are you happy to be this sad, day in and day out forever?"

Patsy shook her head. Her tears were blinked away, and she pushed her glass forward. "No. No, I'm not. It's hell, it's shit, and I want...I want to be me again. So, let's get back to normal. It's Sunday. You would normally moan about work and run wild theories past me. Go on, try me. I might surprise you."

Meredith finished pouring her wine and sat opposite. It was a start. He smiled at her. "For the record, I don't moan. I might express my displeasure occasionally, but I am not a moaner nor, for that matter, a nagger. Are you sure you want to do this? It's about the murder of two young women."

"It's never going to be nice. It's what you do, Meredith. It's what we do."

"Doesn't have to be, not if I re—"

Patsy showed him her palm. "Don't. Please let's not go there again. You don't like me when I cry. Tell me about the case."

Meredith looked at her. Was that an attempt at humour or an accusation? He couldn't read her anymore. He nodded. "If you're sure?"

When she nodded, he gave her a résumé with as much detail as he could remember.

"So, we've got all those who were questioned originally lined up for interview, and this list of stuff that we have to work through. It's going to be a long and tedious case. Maxine Selby said that anyone could run the victims' groups. That most are informal, just a collection of people needing help, company, or just someone to listen to them. I don't know where we're going to start, but Linda is making noises about coming back soon. She's usually good at those conundrums. Tomorrow, I'm meeting with Louise Marshall's landlady, she was convinced it was Louise's husband before we saw Louise skip out of that station with not a care in the world and jump into a taxi."

"You've spoken to Maxine Selby about me?"

"I was after advice on the victims' groups. She explained what they were for and how they were usually set up. It gave me more questions than answers. But she seems to know her stuff."

"Did you mention me?" Patsy's eyes stayed on him. She'd know if he lied to her.

"Of course I did. How would she know who you were when you called if I didn't?"

"Did you tell her what happened? How much does she know?"

"I didn't need to. Loopy has done the groundwork because what caused Loopy's problems is the same event."

Patsy considered this for a moment. "What did you tell her about me?"

"That I love you and I want you back, that you're lost somewhere in here," Meredith said, tapping the side of his head. "And you don't seem to want to come out."

"That is not true!" Patsy snapped.

"Maybe not. But it's how it seems. You say one thing but do another. You need help, but you won't even let me comfort you."

"Oh right, so you've told her you're not getting any, and I've moved into the spare bedroom." Patsy rolled her eyes.

Meredith rapped the table with his knuckles. "It's not about getting any, Patsy. It's about not even being able to hold your hand, put my arm around you, wipe your tears away. Jesus. Is that what you're worried about, what some stranger with a qualification to help you might think? Because as far as I could tell, you have nothing to worry about. She's a nice woman. Calm, confident, considered. She knows her stuff. I think you'd like her."

"I might, who knows, because if you like her then she must be perfect." Patsy's delivery was sarcastic, and Meredith laughed. "Don't laugh at me, Johnny, I don't like it."

"Oh, sarcastic and angry in one sentence, well, at least in her absence the woman has got somewhere with you. We have emotions out and about. And for the record, she pissed me off. She seems to think that together with what that animal did to you, I'm part of your problem. Me. I can't remember her exact words because I was wondering how this became my fault. Par for the course, I know. A relationship is falling apart, so Meredith must be responsible. So, you tell me, am I to blame? Is the reason I'm not allowed to help you somehow my fault? Because if it is, I'm sorry, sorry from the bottom of my heart, and I'll do anything to put it right, but how the fuck am I supposed to do that if you won't talk to me? I don't want to talk about work. I want to talk about getting you better."

Patsy sat stock still, hardly even blinking as he ranted at her. She watched his head fall on his chest as he pushed the chair out from the table and stood up.

"And I just fucked up again, didn't I? I'll leave you in peace and go for a walk or something. Don't forget the chicken is in the oven."

Meredith left the room, and Patsy heard the jangle of his keys as he collected them, winced as the door slammed, and then she ran as fast as she could into the living room and watched him walk away. Meredith had been close to tears. What the hell was she doing to them? Walking to the sideboard, she lifted Maxine Selby's card and stared at it. After steeling herself, she went to the phone in the hall.

"Oh, hello, I thought I'd be leaving a message. My name is Patsy Meredith, and I'd like an appointment to see you, please."

Patsy was on the phone for a while, and after an appointment had been made, she went to the kitchen and busied herself preparing lunch. She didn't know how long Meredith would be. He didn't enjoy walking for the sake of it, and although he hadn't taken the car, the pub was within walking distance, so he could be some time. However long he was, he'd have a meal waiting for him when he got home.

Meredith returned two hours later. He called his normal greeting from the hall, and to his surprise, Patsy answered him.

"I'm in here. Your lunch is on the table. It will need a minute or two in the microwave."

Meredith thanked her and went to the kitchen. It was pristine apart from his lunch and his half glass of wine still sitting on the table, which had been laid for one. He drank the wine as he waited for the microwave to ping, and gingerly took off his shoe and sock. He knew it. A blister. This was why he hated walking. He ate his meal alone, then topped up his wine and went to speak to Patsy. He was surprised to find her sitting with her laptop on her knee but cautioned himself not to query or even recognise that.

"I'm sorry. Useless words I know, but I am none—"

"Let's not start that again. Your instinct was right, concentrate on the groups." Patsy scrolled with her mouse. "And ask why Bristol, although...no, I don't know."

"Are we talking about the case again?" Meredith held up his wine. "Would you like one?"

"Not yet. Sit down. When you question anyone, ask about the victims' groups. These girls disappeared, apparently of their own free will. They survived for years without using a bank account, or contacting anyone from their previous life, and my guess is, not only did they know where they were going, they knew they would be looked after. Neither of them took much with them, possibly a change of clothes and some personal bits, so they weren't worried about what they were going to wear. Louise looked positively happy when she left the station, and—"

"Are you reading the files?"

"Meredith, you seem to be asking a lot of stupid question. Of course, we're talking about the case. Of course I've read the files. Do you want to hear my theory?"

"I do."

"My theory is that someone offered them some form of work and a fresh start. They didn't need money or clothes as that would be taken care of. Jasmine didn't even take her passport, not sure if Louise had one, did she? Don't answer that. I think both of them were recruited for who knows what, when they were at their most vulnerable. And it worked for so long but something went wrong and they were killed. I think Louise replaced Jasmine, so perhaps Jasmine's death was an accident because it takes time to find curly redheads willing to give up their current lives, so someone out there has a type. If Jasmine was killed in 2008 or 2009, and Louise went missing in 2010, she could have been her replacement. Has Louise been replaced? If she died around 2016, did any other curly redheads go missing between then and say 2018? Could be longer if she had to be a redhead."

"I don't know but I'll start looking. And I agree about the type, but perhaps they didn't take more stuff with them because they thought it was just an overnight thing. Mason, Jasmine's bloke, told me she'd taken basic makeup, deodorant, her best jeans, and that he might have a box of stuff that was important to Jasmine because she might have wanted it if she'd ever come back. An overnight, not sailing off into the sunset. But good theory, Hodge."

Patsy's lips twitched. They were working. He'd called her Hodge. But he was wrong, and she told him so.

"No, you're wrong. There's no way those girls were held for years on end without discovery or some form of escape attempt. Even if it was a phone call or a postcard. One even gave birth and required stitches after the delivery. Who was holding them, a medical professional?"

"Sarcasm again, Hodge? You've upped your game today." He winked at her to let her know he was jesting. "But I beg to differ. Louise gave birth in the last year of her life, 2015 maybe 2016. Five or six years after she disappeared. If she'd been held captive all that time, she would have been brainwashed or too scared to make a fuss, especially if daddy accompanied her to the hospital."

"So where were they held? In what condition? And before they got brainwashed, why didn't either of them run or attempt to?"

"I don't know. They might have. Or held in a dark room for three months. Allowed a light after six, and into the living room after a year. Daylight after two. Grateful for the resemblance of a normal life at the end of it. I don't know, Hodge, it's all theories at this stage but I promise you I'll follow up on yours."

"Okay, let's agree to differ. You know I'm right, you just don't want to admit it. What about Louise's broken arm? Have you got hospitals on your list? That repair was neat, so unless your medical abductor put it in plaster that was another hospital visit. And I have a vague recollection of hospitals alerting the police if they think a patient is being abused or coerced in some way. Was there any such alert from any hospitals? I'm guessing you'd check those in Swindon and Reading and work out. It's a shame Linda is off, she's brilliant with hospital records, as you know. Get Seaton and Kent to do the door-to-door. Let Louie concentrate on the witnesses you already have. I think his accent might be better suited to that. Why are you grinning?"

"Because you're being...is classist a word? You're suggesting that the farming community wouldn't respond well to a plummy accent. Don't worry, I won't tell him."

"Get a grip. There are posh farmers, you know, and ones with enough money to pull off what you're suggesting. How many people would have to keep that secret? I'm telling you, Meredith, and I will say I told you so, that those girls went and then stayed of their own free will. I doubt it was a cult because the red curls are a bit limiting. When you find who killed them, it will be interesting to find out what went wrong."

"I'll keep you posted and thank you." Meredith raised his glass.

"For what?" Patsy closed her laptop and placed it on the floor.

"For giving me food for thought on the case, and not tearing me off a strip for being heavy-handed earlier."

"You're welcome. I'm exhausted now so I'm going to have a nap. I might not get up again if I'm lucky, so I'll say goodnight."

Meredith's face fell, and he glanced at the clock. It was only half-past five. But he forced himself to nod. "'Night, Hodge. I hope you're not awake all night. Come and join me if you do wake up. I mean down here, not in bed, not unless you want to. Oh shit. Just go, Patsy, I'm cocking up again."

"No, you're not. I called her."

"Who? Maxine Selby?"

"No, Peggy. Although I must, she threatened to come round and use her key in her last message. Yes, I called Maxine. She seems very nice. 'Night."

Meredith closed his eyes. They might get there. It was only one call but it was a start.

Chapter Nine

Meredith smiled as George entered the office. "Morning, George. Did the wife kick you out? You're early."

"No. I'm guessing yours didn't either, given the smile on your face. Haven't seen that for a while. Everything back to normal?" George threw his coat over the back of a chair and went to sit on the corner of Meredith's desk.

"That wasn't subtle. If it wasn't you there might have been words. Normal? I don't think I know what that is any more, but Hodge has agreed to speak to someone. Even made the call, she tells me, although I wasn't there, so it's still fingers crossed time."

"Patsy doesn't tell lies. Well, something has changed. You smiled, and you called her Hodge. Is that because you're at work?"

"Probably because the last conversation I had with her was about work. We had words yesterday, and when I got back, she had her laptop open and had read through the files. She has a theory." Meredith explained Patsy's theory about the victims leaving and being wherever they ended up voluntarily.

"Sounds like a reasonable theory to me. And I'll get Daisy to up the misper file. But you had words? Get a grip, Meredith, the girl hasn't been well. You don't have words, and if you weren't there, I'm guessing you stormed out. Disappointed in you, Meredith, I can't lie. That girl needs your support, and you storm out having given her work to do. Unbelievable. Un-bloody-believable. I can see you've got a drink, I won't offer."

George was already on his way to the kitchen. Having originally recruited the young Meredith into the force and been his mentor, George, a uniformed sergeant for many years, was allowed liberties that no one else was brave enough to take with Meredith.

"You don't want to hear my side of this story, then? I'm automatically wrong. Don't push your luck, George. You might be old but I'm getting pissed off with always being the perceived wrongdoer. You might be the one who cops my frustration."

"Ha! I'd like to see you try. You're not that far behind me, son. I can still float like a butterfly."

George danced about on his toes, shadow boxing as Seaton came into the office.

"Alright, George? Too much coffee this morning? Do you reckon this rain will ever stop?"

"Just showing Meredith what he's got coming if he doesn't sort himself out. I'll make a trayful. The others won't be long." George left Seaton looking at Meredith.

"Should I ask, Guv?"

"No. I don't need your low opinion of me added to the list. I might get a complex."

"Couldn't have been that bad because you're smiling." Seaton sat at his desk.

"How could I not smile coming to work with you lot? Although it goes against the miserable bastard label I've picked up."

"You've had that for years. That's not new. Oh, there you go, it's gone. Your face is back to normal. Good weekend?"

"Can we just get on with some work?"

"I'll take that as a no."

The morning meeting was brief, and although Meredith didn't share Patsy's theory with the team, he took her advice and allocated the farm visits to Seaton and Kent.

"I'll do the rounds with Trump. You two had better get going. I hope you've got your wellies. Trump, what time is the first one?"

• • • • • • • • • • •

Trump held out his ID as the door opened. Meredith appraised the woman who was nodding as Trump introduced them. She was smartly presented. Her dark hair, which was starting to show grey at the temples, was pulled into a bun, and she wore a lemon shirt and navy suit, although her suit was on the cheap side and had a shiny appearance that wasn't supposed to be there. On her feet were a pair of sheepskin slippers.

"Come on in, as I explained to the girl I haven't got long. I've got to be in by eleven. I've only worked there a couple of months so I'm still on best behaviour. Take a seat." Kelly Albright waved them into the living room. "Ask away. Jasmine was a good friend, but I don't know what you're hoping to get after all these years."

"We want to know all about Jasmine. The more we know, the more we might understand her reasons for leaving, and what she might have been doing before her death. Because it was a while between the time she disappeared and the time she died. So, let's start with how you'd describe her personality," Trump asked.

Kelly nodded solemnly and pulled a vape from her jacket pocket. "You don't mind, do you? I was up to thirty a day. Gave up overnight using these but I think that was out of the frying pan, and I'm more addicted to these than the ciggies. Where do you want to start? I've known her since we were...we became friends when we were twelve. She was put in a home around the corner from my mum's at first, then was fostered by a local family, Mr and Mrs Sweet, so we went to school together. We used to think they were so strict, but now I've got my own kids I realise they were just trying to help her. We were wild back then. I'd die if my kids knew what we used to get up to." Kelly took a drag on the vape and stared out of the window. "Bloody nightmares we were."

"Why don't you tell us about that time? I've seen the arrest records. You were indeed naughty girls but you didn't end up in court, and it was trivial in the scheme of things." Meredith smiled and held out his hand. "Just talk away. We'll jump in or redirect as necessary."

"Trivial in the scheme of the stabbings and the young ones selling drugs we've got today but at the time it was scandalous. My mum gave me such a hiding when we got arrested twice in one week. On the Monday it was for throwing a bottle of cider at a copper who was trying to have a word. The bottle broke and the cider fizzed everywhere. He was soaked, and we laughed so hard, he got mad and took us down to the station. That was Monday night when we were supposed to be at each other's houses doing homework. Then on the Thursday, we got caught shoplifting in Boots. We'd knocked off school and gone into town. This new long lash mascara had come out, and we had no money, so we decided to help ourselves. That got me grounded for a month, but on the Saturday night I climbed out of my brother's bedroom window, down onto the porch and went to get her. The Sweets lived in a bungalow. We went to a party one of the older kids was having because his parents were away. My mum found I was gone around midnight when she went to bed. I was thirteen, and she was too frightened to call the police in case they locked me up. I have told her I realise that now, and I think she's forgiven me."

"Who instigated all this? Who was the risk taker?" Meredith asked.

"Bit of both, really. Different reasons though. I was thick at school because I couldn't be bothered to learn, so I was permanently bored, and Jasmine, well, poor Jas was just angry. She was mad at her mum for giving her up, then she was mad with her for dying. Then she got the attitude if no one gave a shit about her why should she care about anything? We did nothing nasty, though. We didn't bully people or beat them up, nothing like that. Then we discovered boys, and we grew out of it. Although what anyone saw in us with our attitudes, I'll never know. Actually, that's not true. We were teenagers and getting curves in all the right places. I know exactly what attracted them to us. Jas was really pretty, and I had larger than average boobs. I took it for what it was but Jas kept falling in love."

"Kept?" Trump asked.

"Yes, but obviously not really. We were kids. But she thought she was in love. Looking back, I think she just needed someone to want her and care for her. You know, given what had happened with her mum and that. She'd mope about for a week when she broke up with someone and then fall in love all over again. Don't get me wrong, it wasn't sad. We used to joke about it. Then we left school and started work. It got a bit more serious then, but I kept an eye on her."

Meredith nodded understanding and thought about his long-dead friend Simon. Simon had fallen in love on an almost daily basis. He shook the thought away. "And along came Carl Mason. What did you think of him?" Meredith asked.

"Well, he was a catch. He was good-looking and older than us. He used to know the bouncers at the clubs and get in free, and he had an office job, so he always looked smart. My bloke worked for the council on the roads and always smelled like tar." Kelly laughed. "I was worried at first, wondered how she'd take it if they split up, but he was besotted with her, and they moved in together. Never a cross word until...tell me this, when a bloke has a drink, why does his brain take up residence in his dick?"

Meredith bit his bottom lip as Trump raised his eyebrows.

"I don't think that's always the case. Most men do have some control, I believe. We've heard Carl's side of that story. What did Jasmine have to say about it?"

"Most men who don't have it put on a plate for them. But we won't fall out over it. He's married her now, so there must have been something. I saw him at the funeral. He wept like me. I don't know who was comforting who more, so I guess he settled for second best. But he didn't kill her, if that's what you think I might believe. He really loved her. He was a mess between having it off in a cupboard and her walking out."

"I didn't realise there'd been a formal funeral. Who was there?"

"Formal? Yes, I suppose that's the word. It certainly wasn't personal. It was over in minutes. But there was me and Carl, my husband Den, even though he never met her, he came for me. A lady she used to work with who was still at the Co-op, and a few girls from school. Probably eight, maybe nine of us. All female apart from Carl and my Den. Too bloody sad."

"And you knew everyone who was there?" Meredith asked.

"Yes, and none of them killed her. I reckon she met someone and fell in love with them because she was so upset with Carl. She ran off with him and something went wrong. Maybe Jas tried to leave him too, and he stopped her. She was straight down the middle, Jas. It was either black or white, right or wrong. No grey bits. It was only because she loved Carl so much that she tried. If they weren't so loved up before his escapade, she'd have been out of there the next day. She never let him touch her again. Did he tell you that? That bit shocked me because up until then, they were very active."

"She told you that?" Trump asked, sounding a little shocked.

"Yes. It's what mates do. Talk. We moan about them farting in bed, or not performing, or complaining they want it too much, or too little. You know, just like you blokes do."

"And things had been good with Mason?" Meredith asked.

"Yes. And hands up, I was a little jealous. If we'd been out for a drink, my bloke was asleep before his head hit the pillow. If we hadn't, I might be in for a treat but not if he was tired. That was a wham-bam job, and I was left wondering if I'd actually taken part. Oh dear, I think I've embarrassed you." Kelly laughed and puffed on her vape as she looked at Trump.

"Not at all," Trump assured her. "I'm just surprised you're so honest about it. I take it Jasmine didn't have the same issues."

"Hardly. With Jas it wasn't about how many times they did it that week, it was how many times she'd hit the jackpot the night before. Which makes it even more ridiculous that Carl had a quickie at the Christmas do. If he hadn't, I'd probably still be jealous, and Jas would still be alive." She swallowed and looked Trump in the eye. "She'd be sitting there telling me she'd been swinging from the chandelier onto the bed, and still had time to iron the kid's school uniform and cook a three course meal. And I miss her. I still bloody miss her. So you get and find out who did this."

"We'll do our best, Kelly. So, after Jasmine found out about Carl's fling...how did she find out, by the way?" Meredith asked.

"Because his shirt smelt different. If he'd denied it, she'd have let it drop. Put it down to him standing too close to someone or hugging them goodbye. She asked me why he hadn't done that because things would have been okay then. And I told her, at least he was honest, better that than lying to her, and she said, 'You'd think, wouldn't you?' She'd have rather he'd lied, and she didn't have to go through all that pain. Sad."

"Very. Can't be right for being wrong. So, —"

"There speaks the voice of experience. He was wrong. He just didn't need to tell her that. But in fairness, he'd have been a bastard if he'd lied and it all came out a different way. What were you going to ask?"

"What she did to help herself get over it. We understand she went to a women's group and saw a counsellor. Do you know much about that?" Meredith asked.

"Not in the beginning. She'd seen a counsellor three times and stopped going by the time she told me about it. Only stopped going because she couldn't afford it, and they told her to go to this group as they thought it might help. Jas said it did help her because compared to what some of them had been through it made her realise she was moaning about nothing."

"Do you know the name of the group, or anyone else who went there?" Trump asked.

"Not really. I just let her talk about it if she wanted to. It was mainly about what other people said. If I'm honest, I didn't get it. How can listening to all that misery make you feel better? It would have had the opposite effect on me, but I kept that to myself because she was getting something out of it."

"Do you know where they held their meetings?"

"Oh blimey, now you've asked me something. I know they weren't always in the same place because she used to moan about catching the bus. She didn't mind the train, but she hated the bus. I know one of the places was in Sea Mills, but not where. Why is that important?"

"Because we're trying to find out what was going on in her life during those last few weeks before she left. She left willingly. There was no one with her at Temple Meads or at the station at Swindon. Jasmine said nothing to those closest to her but someone knew."

"And that someone should have been me. Why didn't she tell me? We told each other everything!" Kelly blinked away her tears.

"Perhaps she didn't want to be talked out of it because if she'd told you she was going away, I get the impression you would have tried to persuade her otherwise. But she might have told someone in the group."

"Ah, yes. I can see that, and you're right, I would have. What I never understood is, if she was going to do a bunk why was she trying to get a new job? I saw her the week before and she was quite excited about it. Next time, the day before she left, she didn't mention it, so I assumed she hadn't got it. But why was she looking if she was planning on doing a runner?"

"Job? There's been no mention of a job, as far as I recall. Did she say what it was?" Meredith asked.

"No. Yes, yes, she did. She said she thought it would turn out to be a glorified cleaner but it was good money. It's funny what you've got stored up here, isn't it?" Kelly tapped the side of her head. "I only remembered that because I was mopping out the canteen at work, someone had left it in a right mess, and I said, 'A bit like me, then'. Although she didn't say where it was because I know that will be your next question." Kelly winked at Meredith.

"Actually, it was going to be: Did she say where she heard about it?" He returned her wink.

"Oh, a smart arse. But no she didn't, and I didn't have time to ask because the supervisor came in and gave me a bollocking for using my phone at work. Don't know if I would have asked, anyway. It would have been the paper, or a card in a window somewhere. That's where you get jobs like that, isn't it?" Kelly glanced at the clock. "You've got ten more minutes and then I'll have to go. Was there anything else? I think I've told you all I can."

"I think that's it." Meredith slid his notebook back into his pocket. "Thanks for your time. We'll be off now but before we go is there anything you would like to tell us, anything you think we should know?"

"Not really. Just that despite what your file might say, she was lovely. Kind, considerate, gentle, just lovely, and she didn't deserve to die like that. So you find the bastard who did it, and you throw away the key. You hear me?"

"Loud and clear. We'll do our best. Thanks again, Kelly. Give your husband my best." Meredith followed her to the door.

Kelly's brow wrinkled. "Do you know him?"

"No, but I know he's got his hands full with you." Meredith raised his eyebrows.

"You cheeky bugger. Not only do you make me late for work, you insult me too. Get out," Kelly laughed as she opened the door. "You've got a killer to catch." Her smile fell away. "You concentrate on that."

Meredith saluted. "Will do."

Once in the car, Trump looked at Meredith before starting the engine.

"Well, that job fits with Patsy's theory, don't you think? If Jasmine had applied for a job as a housekeeper, which comes with room and board most of the time, she might have wondered if she was going to be a glorified cleaner, and she would have been quite happy to get on that train."

"Yes, possibly. But that still doesn't explain only taking a few clothes. I suppose it might have been a job that came with a uniform, but she would have expected a social life or time off. Anyway, how do you know about Patsy's theory?"

"George. He was explaining to Daisy that Patsy thought it was possible Louise replaced Jasmine, and therefore someone may have replaced Louise, and then the rest of her theory. I wasn't going to mention it but how is Patsy? You seem almost normal today."

"She's made an appointment to see Maxine Selby this afternoon. But if you tell me I've been smiling, I might thump you."

"You did more than smile, sir. You flirted. Like I say, almost normal." Trump started the engine and headed back to the office.

Meredith fell silent. It was possible it had been a housekeeping job, which would support Patsy's theory. But he hadn't flirted. He'd just been him. He refused to use the word normal. Pulling his phone from his pocket, he called Seaton.

"How's it going?"

"Just arrived at the second farm. The car's a right state. Nothing doing so far. You?" Seaton asked.

"Jasmine was excited about a job she'd applied for. Possibly a housekeeper's job. Add asking about anyone getting a new housekeeper when you question anyone."

"Will do. Got to go. I need to put my wellies on."

Chapter Ten

By the end of that week, Meredith was feeling positive. Nothing much had happened to move the case forward, but they were covering ground, and he knew it was only a matter of time before they'd find the key to unlock the mystery. It might then take them a while to find the lock, but at least they'd have the key.

The main reason for his upbeat mood was because Patsy had met with Maxine Selby and booked two further sessions, one of which was that afternoon. Patsy wasn't saying much, only that she thought it was helping, and had actually thanked him for giving her the shove she needed. One more interview to do, and he'd be off for the weekend. He wasn't quite looking forward to the weekend, but he wasn't dreading it like the ones before. Baby steps.

"She's here, Meredith," George called from the other side of the office. "Trump's not back yet, do you want me to sit in with you?"

"No. You get yourself off home. I'll record it. Same for you, Daisy. It's been a long and tedious day. You were here before me this morning."

"Thanks. I'll finish what I'm doing first. I changed the filter and—" Daisy fell silent as Meredith held up a hand.

"Up to you but five o'clock is knocking off time today. Tell Trump when he gets back. I've got someone waiting. What room, George?"

Meredith walked along the faceless corridor to interview room ten. It was clean and tidy, not marked and scuffed like some of the stations he'd worked in, but it didn't feel comfortable. And it didn't fit him yet. He peeped through the small, glazed window in the door. Bernice Forbes looked back at him and smiled.

She didn't look bad for her seventy-two years, but her teeth were yellowed, probably from smoking, and she looked uncomfortable. Meredith returned her smile and went into join her.

"Sorry to keep you waiting, Mrs Forbes. Can I get you a drink before we get started?"

"Ms. I saw my husband off some years ago. Should have changed my name back then but I don't like to be reminded. And no, no drink, thank you."

Meredith took a seat and pointed to the machine fixed to the wall. "Are you happy for me to record this? Just saves time writing notes I have to decipher afterwards."

Bernice Forbes gave what appeared to be a triumphant smile and nodded. "You do what's necessary. I can't wait to get started."

Meredith started the recording. "Tell me about Louise."

"Of course. What is it you want to know?"

"Everything. But start with how you met and take it from there. I'll chip in with questions now and again."

"Ah, poor Louise. Like me, she married the wrong man, although these days I think most men are the wrong one. But we won't go there, you might be offended. Louise's husband was a controlling bastard. Pardon my language. I think they call it gaslighting these days. When she came to me, she was a total mess. Didn't know which way was up because it had been so long since she'd been allowed to decide anything. It was pure chance, too. I had a room to let and put a card on the notice board in the corner shop, and she came to see me. She was a bag of nerves. I tried to put her at her ease as I showed her around but she followed around like this." Bernice pulled her hands into her chest and hunched her shoulders.

"She was frightened?"

"Bloody terrified, as I found out." Bernice tutted and tapped the table. "Frightened of her own shadow, and scared to death that he'd find out she'd been to see me."

"She told you that, and I assume we're talking about Ricky Marshall?" Meredith asked.

"We are. She stumbled on the rug on the landing, and I instinctively grabbed her elbow to steady her. She howled in agony, and then apologised to me. I'll take out the middle bit, and get to the nitty gritting, which took three meetings, shall I?"

"If that's what works for you. I'll come back to those meetings if I think it's needed." Meredith smiled encouragement.

"I doubt it will be. Ricky Marshall had a chip on his shoulder. I don't know why. He was reasonably good-looking, had a half decent job. Perhaps his mummy didn't like him. Who knows? But a chip he had. Louise had to agree with everything he wanted, whether that was what colour to paint the ceiling, to what they would do at the weekend. And she did. Not because she necessarily agreed but because none of it really mattered. She was or had been laid back and happy to go with the flow. Little things didn't bother her. All she required from life was to be happy. Before they married she said that if she'd done something wrong, and we're talking burning toast, or forgetting to put the bins out, he'd be quite reasonable and call her woolly-headed or tell her she was away with the fairies. Her misdemeanours never went without comment, but those comments never offended her and were accepted in good heart. After the wedding, things changed almost immediately. He'd become angry if she got something wrong and go into an all-out rage if it was something to do with him. Not taking his suit to the dry cleaners or forgetting to buy a card for his mother's birthday. He was irrational."

"It sounds like it. Is that why she left him?"

"Oh no. This was early on, when she still believed she loved him. She told me she'd write lists. As soon as he passed comment or issued an instruction that wasn't to be carried out immediately, Louise would add it to the list. Every day, she'd check that list and make sure it was all done. It worked for a while, and then he started telling her she wasn't doing things that he hadn't asked her to do or that she knew she had done, and he was angry Ricky again. He told her to go and see the doctor because she wasn't right in the head. She was either losing her memory or making things up. Either way, it wasn't good enough. She refused and said she'd try harder and showed him her lists. He told her just because she'd ticked them off, didn't mean that she'd done them and was trying to make a fool of him. That was the first time he hit her properly. He gave her a black eye and told her it was her fault, and she wasn't to go to work. She was a nursery nurse, and she loved her job. As the months turned into years, she began to believe him. She became unstable, gave up her job and was at the mercy of him and his temper. He kept her short of money too, and occasionally on the days she was brave enough to answer him back, he would invite her to leave."

"Did she say why it took so long?"

"He'd taken away her spirit. Any self-worth she'd had had been trampled underfoot. Where would she go? She had no family to speak of. What would she live on? She had no money and was so useless she doubted she'd hold down a job."

"What changed her mind?"

"The night before she came to look at the room, he'd given her a beating. Almost pulled her arm from its socket, pulling her out from behind the sofa where she was hiding. Hence, she howled when I grabbed her arm. In pain, she'd woken early and found he wasn't in bed. When she went to get some painkillers, she saw him unlaying the table. He insisted it was ready for him when he got up, and it was the last job she did every night. But there he was, putting the cutlery back in the drawer. The condiments had already been put away. Louise realised she wasn't going mad or being useless. She was being tricked by a man she now hated. Knowing she had to find a way to escape, she went to the shop to look at the notice board. She wasn't sure if she was looking for someone to help her, you know, one of those battered women's groups, or a job so she could try to save some money. But she saw my room being advertised, and it occurred to her that if she could find somewhere to live, she could go to work without his permission. So she came to see it."

"And you, by inadvertently hurting her arm, heard her sad tale and took her under your wing." Meredith smiled.

"Not quite that simple. I agreed she could have the room and pay me as and when she had the money, that she could claim benefits in the meantime so she could feed herself. Unfortunately I'm not a wealthy woman or I wouldn't need to rent the room in the first place, but I also told her to go to the police. And that's when she got scared again and she got up to leave. She was crying as she begged me not to tell anyone what she'd shared with me, and I agreed on the condition that she'd meet me for coffee once a week so I could keep an eye on her."

"And she did. That was kind of you. What happened then?"

"I took the liberty of getting her forms to make a claim for some form of benefit, even drew up a haphazard agreement. I'd never needed one before. My previous lady was working and didn't ask for one. But Louise needed one for this, and she began to see a light at the end of the tunnel. She filled in the forms and all the paperwork came to my house so he'd never know. Once it was all agreed, she waited for him to go to work, packed up her meagre possessions and moved in."

"Did she find a job?" Meredith asked.

"Not then, but she was looking. He hadn't allowed her access to the internet, she had no phone because he said she didn't need one. He took his laptop to work with him, although she'd have been too scared to use it anyway, so prior to leaving she'd relied on the newspaper and the board in the shop. But she was terrified to go out, you see. Bristol is a big city but I only live a few miles away from that shop, which wasn't far from their home, so we were only two miles away from him. And then, of course, he found us."

"What happened?"

"At first, he'd sit in his car opposite the house. I didn't know this for several months. At the time, I was still working myself. But she'd taken to bolting the door behind me, so when I got home I couldn't get in, and I eventually found out why. I called the police without telling her I was going to. A nice officer came to see us and said Louise would have to make a formal complaint. She wouldn't, of course, so the officer said she would go and have a quiet word and to call her if Louise changed her mind. Well, we made that call about four hours later when he was hammering on my door. By the time the police got there, Terrence, the man next door, had seen him off.

"Then he tried to coerce her by writing to her. I'm sorry, I love you, give me another chance. Luckily, she could see through that. To my knowledge, she didn't reply. After a couple of weeks, the notes stopped. He didn't appear outside or on the doorstep and we were free of him. Or so we thought. Louise needed a photograph for a job she was applying for and had caught the bus to the shopping centre where they have those machines. When she got off the bus to walk home, he grabbed her. Tried to get her in the car. When she wouldn't, he beat her and he kicked her. A passerby called the police, and he drove off. That's when she finally made it official."

"Got the restraining order and he got a suspended sentence." Meredith smiled.

"Yes, but he should have gone to prison after what he put that lovely girl through. I'll never understand the sentences these monsters get given."

"I can't argue there. We can only put them in court. As far as you know, during all this time, did Louise join any self-help groups or see a counsellor?"

"I don't think so. She rarely left the house, although for a while she managed to work part-time at the opticians on the corner. Tell me, what's he done?" Bernice leaned forward and lowered her voice. "I know you probably shouldn't speak about ongoing cases but I need to know he'll get what's coming. I lost a good friend because of him. The daughter I never had, almost. I thought she might have kept in touch."

"Who? Ricky Marshall? Nothing that I know of, why?" Meredith asked, thrown by the question.

"Then why am I here? Why are you asking about Louise? Has something happened to her?"

Meredith knew his shock must have shown. He answered her question with one of his own. "That's an odd question, where do you think Louise is?"

Bernice threw her arm into the air. "Seeing the world, I hope, wining and dining, having fun, and...Oh no, has something happened to her? Is that why I'm here?" Bernice's eyes filled with tears.

Meredith leaned forward and grasped her hands in his. "I'm sorry to tell you this but Louise was murdered. Her body was found in farmland on the outskirts of Reading five years ago. But we think she was murdered around 2016. I thought you knew. Here."

Releasing her hand, Meredith lifted a box of tissues from the shelf and placed them in front of her. "The body of another young woman was found more recently nearby, although she'd been killed a while before Louise. Why did you think you were here?"

"Oh, what a shock, oh dear me. Poor Louise. You said you didn't know what he'd done. The question surprised you. You don't think he killed her, or I suppose them. He's capable of that. I know that much. I thought he'd done something to some other poor girl, and you were getting evidence against him. Not this. Not this. That poor, poor girl. Could it be him?"

"I doubt it. Marshall had no connection with the previous woman. He would have been very young when the first woman was killed, and we do believe the deaths are connected. He's been living in Bristol while the two women lived elsewhere for some years after their disappearance. And as you will know from when Louise disappeared, he had an alibi, despite you believing otherwise."

"Oh, she didn't disappear. I knew where she was, I was stirring up trouble for him. Letting him know she'd gone and that he couldn't hurt her anymore. You know, just wanted his ego dented, and his life made awkward. Might have worked a lot better if he hadn't been on holiday." Bernice held up a shaky hand. "And I know it was wasting police time but I was still aggrieved with the powers that be, because he'd only been given a smack on the wrist after all he'd done."

Meredith couldn't believe what he was hearing. His mouth opened and shut, and he composed himself as Bernice pulled a compact from her bag and powdered her cheeks. He wondered why she was bothering, her tears were still flowing.

"Where did Louise go? She booked a ticket to Paddington but got off at Swindon and jumped into a taxi. Why, and where did it take her?" Meredith crossed the fingers grasping his knees.

"I don't know. She wouldn't tell me in case he made me tell him. I could see the sense in that. Louise was still scared of him, and if I'm honest, I knew I wouldn't hold out for long if he started on me. But she promised to write and to call when she got the chance. All I knew was that she was going to be a live-in help with a family. She'd have her own room, the money was good, and it was miles away from Bristol with no chance of bumping into him. You know, I was so happy when I dropped her off and saw her swinging that bag as she went into the station. I missed her, but she was happy, and she was free. I suppose some people aren't supposed to get a happy ever after."

"It seems not. I know you're still reeling from all this but a few more questions and I'll get someone to take you home. Do you know where Louise found the job? Was it an agency or an ad in the paper?"

"No I don't but I know she used both in her search."

"Did she perhaps leave anything behind that you didn't hand over to the police when they thought she'd just disappeared?"

"No. She came with very little. A few clothes, that's all. Like I said, he kept her short. No phone, no passport, no anything really. I remember she told me he'd burnt all her things. She had a box with cards, photographs and mementos from when she was a child. He said they didn't need old rubbish cluttering the place up. Bastard!" Bernice drew in a juddering breath. "I don't think I can help you. Can I go now?"

"Of course. Let me make a quick call upstairs, and I'll take you."

Meredith dropped Bernice back at her house and headed for home. He'd be early, and he was feeling buoyed up. Nothing Bernice had told him would solve the case, the only thing that had changed was that Louise hadn't gone missing. She had, as Patsy had suggested, been going to a live-in job. One which must have worked for a while. They now needed to find out where she heard about the job but that could wait for Monday. If Patsy's session with Maxine Selby had gone well, this might be the best weekend in a long time. Whatever happened, he was going to visit the twins.

"Hi, honey, I'm home and I come bearing good news for you," He sang loudly, as he dropped his keys on the table.

"Oh, in here." Patsy seemed surprised and forced a smile as he walked into the living room.

"You sound...Oh, hello. I didn't realise you'd still be here. The shower beckons. I'll leave you to it." He nodded acknowledgement to Maxine Selby and with a smile for Patsy, he turned away.

"No, that's okay, Meredith. We're almost done. What was the good news, or is it private?" Maxine asked.

"No, not private. Not really. Patsy made an observation about the case we're working on yesterday, and she was right. And I still need a shower, so I'll say goodbye."

"Which part was I right about?" Patsy asked.

Meredith felt uncomfortable. It was something he'd wanted to praise her over, perhaps even celebrate, but he felt once again that he was being assessed by Maxine Selby, who was now looking at him expectantly. But he smiled at Patsy. "Louise didn't disappear. Her landlady knew she'd taken a job miles away from Bristol, and it came with room and board. A live-in job, some sort of housekeeper."

Patsy smiled. "I haven't lost all my marbles then. I'll let you update me later."

Meredith bowed slightly and took the stairs two at a time, glad to be away from Maxine's raised eyebrows. He had no idea what he'd said but the look on her face told him she didn't approve. Still, Patsy seemed happy about it.

He took his time in the shower, and still hearing voices, lay on the bed and messaged his team to make sure they all turned up for the briefing on Monday. He didn't want Seaton and Kent disappearing before they knew the landscape had changed a little. His stomach grumbled, so he risked bumping into Maxine by heading for the kitchen. The oven was empty, and on opening the fridge door he saw that there was nothing he fancied eating. Silently cursing, he went and tapped on the living room door.

"Sorry to interrupt again but this will take two seconds. Nothing in to eat, shall I order something in, or would you like to go somewhere and celebrate your breakthrough? Um...I mean on the case, not this." He waved his finger between the two women, and watched as the eyebrows rose again.

"Order a Chinese. We really have finished now. Sorry," Patsy said, standing.

"I don't know what about. So no apology necessary. Not unless you were apologising to Maxine."

Patsy frowned at him. "I'm desperate for the loo. Perhaps you'd show Maxine out." Patsy turned to Maxine with a smile. "Thanks again. I'll see you on Monday."

"You will indeed." Maxine dropped her notebook into her bag and placed her cup and saucer on the tray as Patsy left. Waiting until she heard Patsy's step on the stairs, she beckoned Meredith forward.

"What? Is everything okay?" Meredith asked, keeping his voice low.

"I don't know, Meredith. But some food for thought, I'm not sure Patsy should be working the case with you. She's not at work for a reason. Do we really want her dealing with the abduction and murder of two women at the moment? Also, try to put a positive slant on anything you might have to say. Asking what she'd like to do for dinner would have been perfectly adequate. Reminding her that there's no food in the cupboard, despite her being home all day, isn't what she needs to hear. Now, I'll leave you to your Chinese. You should put a shirt on, you'll catch cold."

Meredith took a step closer and lifted a finger as her eyebrows rose. "Thank you for your sage words of advice. Here's some for you. One, Patsy looked at the file while I was out. I didn't ask her to, nor did I in any way imply it's what she should do. Own free will etcetera. Two, I've been doing the shopping since she left the hospital. If there's no food in the house that's down to me. She knows that. And three, when I need your advice on how I should dress in my home, I'll ask for it. My wife used to like it if I wandered around naked but I thought as we had guests I'd show some modesty and put my joggers on."

"Well, one, I'm glad that's what happened. Two, keep up the good work. And three, I wasn't complaining. It was distracting. I don't think you like me, Meredith. Luckily, your wife doesn't have that issue. She's doing well. Excuse me."

Meredith stood back and allowed Maxine to pass him and go into the hall. He followed her out and opened the door.

"Have a good weekend. I'll try not to arrive home at an inconvenient moment again."

"Oh, no, don't avoid me, the interaction is useful. 'Bye, Meredith."

Meredith closed the door behind her. Distracting for whom? Was the woman flirting with him, or had Patsy been distracted? He didn't like the comment on interaction, either. Patsy was her patient. He wasn't going anywhere near her. He knew little about therapy but he wasn't convinced that Maxine Selby was the woman for the job.

The weekend passed quietly and for Meredith slowly. He wasn't used to being this inactive. By Sunday, he was climbing the walls.

"I must go and see the twins. I'd like you to come, but if you're not up to it I won't push you."

"That would be lovely but they've gone away for the weekend. A cottage in Devon somewhere. Peggy did say where but I've forgotten, it ends in Combe."

"I didn't know that. Did you call Peggy back?"

"I said I would, and I did." Patsy smiled at him. "I might have exaggerated my recovery a little, and I made no mention of needing counselling, but it's what she needed to hear to go with them with a clear conscience."

Meredith slumped on the couch. "Oh, that's nice. What shall we do then? Do you fancy a game of Monopoly?"

Patsy's smile was wide. "I do not. You almost made me laugh then. I had visions of the board being upended and having to avoid walking on little houses for a week."

"Ah, now come on, that's not fair. I know you're not quite yourself at the moment, but I don't think you'd do that." Meredith winked.

Patsy giggled. "Touché, Mr Meredith."

Meredith's instinct was to grab her hand but he held himself to a smile. "I made you smile, Mrs Meredith. A real genuine laugh, too. I can't tell you how wonderful that feels."

"I'm getting there. Give me enough space but be there to catch me if I fall. Okay?"

Now her eyes filled, and it took all of Meredith's resolve to stop himself scooting across to her.

"You need space, I'll give you space. Get your shoes, or given the weather we've had, wellies."

"Why?"

"Because, my darling wife, we are going out. Not to anywhere, not to speak to anyone, but out of this house into the outside world. I'll even let you choose the destination. Beach or woodland is about the best I can do, but out we're going."

"It sounds good, but—"

"Don't argue with me or I'll carry you to the car. No buts. Ten minutes. If you don't like it, we'll come home? Deal?"

"I suppose so, but—"

"Did we not agree no buts? I promise you I won't ask you to do anything else for a week."

Less than an hour later, they were strolling along the promenade in Weston-super-Mare. The wind was biting with the odd squall of needle-sharp rain, and the Bristol Channel was its usual grey, murky and uninviting self. Meredith had held out his hand, and although she'd hesitated Patsy had taken it. Meredith felt as though they'd reached a milestone. He didn't even care that he'd reactivated his blister.

Chapter Eleven

While waiting for George to arrive so the morning briefing could begin, Trump walked over to Meredith.

"How's Patsy doing? I'm not promising anything but Linda is indicating she's ready to come back to work."

Meredith slapped Trump's shoulder. "That's great news, on every front. Patsy's getting there, and I mean that honestly. We're still in separate rooms, but I made her laugh, and we went for a walk." Meredith closed his eyes and sighed. "I never thought something so trivial would make me so happy. Tell me, what do you think of Maxine Selby?"

"Not sure what you mean. She knows her stuff, as Linda's wish to return to work indicates. Why?" Trump inclined his head. "Please tell me you've not fallen out with her. That wouldn't help Patsy."

"No! I meant as a person. Is she a person? Can anyone who assesses and pronounces judgement on everything you say even be considered a person?"

Trump couldn't hold back his smile. "You're frightened of her. Oh dear. What happened?"

"Nothing, and yes, I bloody am. My hands have gone clammy just thinking about her. Just me then?"

"I think so, yes. Oh look, saved by the bell, or at least the arrival of George. You won't have time to tell me why. Perhaps later?"

"Take your seat Trump, I have news." Meredith walked forward, clapping his hands. "Right, you lot, settle down. We've had an unexpected revelation, so we need to tweak things a little."

Meredith ran through his interview with Bernice Forbes. "So, Louise never disappeared. Bernice was trying to give her ex as much grief as possible. I think we can rule Marshall out of any involvement, he would only have been sixteen when Jasmine went missing, but it does mean we can take the focus off the self-help, victim group element of the inquiry, and concentrate instead on looking at employment agencies that would have been around at the time, and newspaper ads. I'm favouring the latter for Jasmine, the internet then wasn't what it is now. We still had to use paper and speak to people sometimes. Another uphill struggle. Unless the house to house, and I use the term loosely given the area, turns up anything that's maybe where we'll find a link."

"I'm almost glad I'm slopping about up to my ankles in mud in my wellies," Seaton said. "What else is news?"

"Not much. Here, more of the same. I'll run back over who we've spoken to, make sure the new job aspect was covered, and if it wasn't whether I think it's worth going back. But I don't think it will be. Both those girls wanted to disappear. Talking about getting a new job might have given the game away," Meredith replied.

"Does that mean you'll get your wellies out of storage and come out with us, Guv?" Kent asked.

"Already thinking about it. But I think we need to up our game. George and I were looking yesterday, and we found over forty farms or smallholdings in the area without much trying. Add that to the small areas of housing, corner shops, vets, GP surgeries, and the number of people who would have moved on. It's a daunting task but we're the team to do it.

"Although you two have been working to a pattern, I think we need to expand the area, grid this out, and everyone hit the same square at the same time, then we'll follow any leads and then move on to the next. We thought it might be a farm, as we assumed the girls had been coerced into leaving and would therefore be kept out of sight. That's not the case, particularly with Louise. We could just be looking for a big house. I doubt anyone living in a two up, two down would have the money or space for a housekeeper. Don't look like that, Kent. They'll be big grids. It should only take a couple of months." Meredith grinned and looked at Daisy. "Get the map up."

The day passed quickly in an endless stream of maps, phone calls and internet searches. By the end of the day, every building and business in the first grid area had been listed by order of potential, and the second grid started.

"Right. From tomorrow, you work individually. Trump, I'll finish the interviews with George. You start on this tomorrow, so find those green wellies. You all leave home at eight, you aim to return by six, six thirty at the latest. There's no point in working ourselves to a frazzle at this stage, not unless we're onto something. We really could be at this for months."

"I was just thinking that, Guv. Now we know why they went, do we think we should try to get some telly coverage? Maybe the local news?" Seaton asked. "I doubt a national appeal would do anything apart from bring loonies out of the closet."

"And Facebook groups with their photos and an appeal," Daisy suggested.

"Yes. Good shout, I'll add contacting PR to my list. Now, let's call it a day."

Patsy smiled as Meredith walked into the kitchen and sniffed.

"I thought I should make myself useful. It's only a stew thing and I found some bake them yourself rolls in the freezer, and I've ordered a delivery for tomorrow."

Meredith sighed. "Music to my ears, or more accurately, my stomach. Thank you. I take it the meeting went well with Maxine?"

"I don't know, Meredith. We just talk. When it's happening you try to work out why that might be significant, or what she's after, but I can't for the life of me tell half the time. If I ask, she says things like: does it bother you talking about that or should I move on and we'll come back to it? So I try to go with the flow, but I think she's good enough to know when I censor my answers. She must think it's Christmas with Linda." Patsy laughed.

"Patsy, you're laughing, you're joking. It must be doing some good but you have me intrigued now. Why would you censor your answers? It's a doctor patient relationship. She can't tell anyone what you say."

Patsy shrugged. "I know but even us headcases have stuff we think is private, and certainly unrelated."

Meredith sat down at the table. "You are not a headcase, you're traumatised. And like what?"

Again, Patsy shrugged. "Some odd stuff, some personal. I don't want to talk about it with you either. It really isn't relevant. She likes talking about you, though."

Meredith considered his response. "I didn't know that you and me had any subjects that were off limits but I'll accept that there are at the moment. Why about me? Am I relevant to your current problems?"

Meredith resisted the urge to roll his eyes as she shrugged again. "I don't know. That's what I'm telling you. I can't second guess why she asks some of what she does."

"Give me an example. I might be able to help shed some light on it," Meredith suggested, hoping her shoulders wouldn't rise again, although he had no idea why it irritated him, perhaps because it made her appear even more vulnerable than she already was.

"Oh, bloody hell, Meredith, last question, then change the subject. Did I feel guilty towards you because I wasn't my normal self? Did I feel you gave me enough space to deal with everything, or perhaps too much space to think about stuff? Questions like that. Now, subject change, how was work?"

Meredith wanted to know the answers given to those questions, but he smiled. "This is progress, Patsy, I've only been home ten minutes and I've had laughing, joking, irritation and nosiness from you."

"I'm glad you approve. Now, what's the latest? I'm too tired to read the notes. Oh, before I forget, my plaster comes off tomorrow. Any chance of a lift to the hospital? Don't worry if not, I'll get a taxi."

"I am at your disposal. I have a couple of interviews, but I can get those covered if it clashes. What time?"

"Half past nine."

"Perfect. I can go in, set it up, sort anything out and get back for you. I bet you're looking forward to it."

"So much, just to wash my hair with two hands, to lie back and soak in the bath. I should give you fair warning, I might spend a lot of time in the bathroom once this is off. But now you go and get changed, I'll finish dinner."

Meredith thought Patsy had forgotten about the case, but she asked again before he sat at the table. He was delighted to see Patsy was joining him.

"So, did I get the appropriate recognition for suggesting the girls knew where they were going and why?"

"You did. Other than that, it was just planning our attack for the area they may have been living in. Might be folly. They might have got off at Swindon and been driven to London but we have to start somewhere. On that subject, we're not going to get more bodies to help us, so it's going to be all hands on deck for the door-to-door inquiries. I'm not having George driving up and down every day. I'm going to have to do my bit. It means working longer hours and that's without allowing for motorway hold-ups. Are you okay with that?"

"Of course, why wouldn't I be? It's my fault you're short-staffed. It's my fault I'm like this, and my fault Linda is still having nightmares. Don't start asking stupid questions, you were doing so well." Patsy dropped her cutlery on the table. Her meal was over.

Meredith pinched the bridge of his nose. Eventually, he pushed his chair out and stood in front of her until she looked at him. "That's bollocks and I think deep down you know it. You just can't convince yourself of it. I refuse to argue with you. There's only one person responsible. Ask Maxine, although she'll probably make it my fault, and I'd be happy to take the blame as long as you understand that you are the last person responsible for the actions of a madman." Meredith wished he could take the comment about Maxine back but it was too late now. He waited for the backlash.

"You've got your shirt on tonight."

"What? That's your response? I wear a shirt of some description most of the time unless I'm in bed. What...Is this because of the other day, after my shower? Did my nipples or my not quite man boobs offend you? Or perhaps I offended Maxine? In which case, tough. Tell me what's going through your mind right now? I have to try to understand this."

"Forget I said anything. I just thought it was odd, that's all. I'm—"

"I'm going to bed. I am not going to fall out with you. If I don't see you in the morning, I'll be back in good time to get you to your appointment. I love you, Patsy, don't lose sight of that."

Patsy lowered her eyes and Meredith tutted and left the kitchen. She watched him leave.

"But for how long, Johnny?" she muttered, as she lifted her napkin to dab away the tears.

An hour later, and starving hungry, Meredith assumed she'd gone to bed and went in search of food. The lights were still on, and Patsy was talking to someone. He paused by the sitting room door.

"The thing is, Maxine, I'm not sure that I can. I'm sorry, I'm rambling on but I don't know if it's the right thing to do or if it will make things worse...No, I understand that. I just wanted your opinion on whether you thought it would help."

Meredith walked away feeling absolutely dejected. He would never have predicted this situation, not in a million years. He could understand Patsy's reaction to the attack. It was horrific. She nearly died, and her best friend killed the assailant, but it was difficult to understand why she wouldn't turn to him for help. And although he was pleased she'd found someone she could talk to, even if he himself didn't like them, it hurt like hell.

As he topped up his bowl, still sitting on the table, he heard Patsy moving about. The call over, she was headed for the kitchen. He turned to greet her, to apologise, although he didn't think he'd done anything wrong. Patsy entered the kitchen, head down, and a half full mug of coffee in her hand. Her shoulders were rounded, and she looked lost. His instinct was to pull her into his arms, but he restrained himself and settled for another apology.

"I'm sorry. Can we—"

Patsy's scream was shrill, and pulling her arm back, she hurled the mug at him. Cold coffee splattered across his chest as the mug bounced off his shoulder, and Patsy flew to the other side of the kitchen, grabbing the knife from the chopping board as she went. She spun around to face him. and balanced on the balls of her feet, with her knees slightly bent, and the knife clenched in her hand, Patsy was ready to take him on.

Meredith backed away and held up his hands. "Patsy, it's me. It's Meredith. Look at me, I'm not going to hurt you."

Meredith reached the wall and stopped moving. His heart thundered in his chest as he watched her. He lowered his hands.

"Patsy, it's me. Please put the knife down. You don't need that."

He moved his finger up and down, pointing to the knife as he spoke. The hand clenching the knife jerked. She was ready to use it. Patsy couldn't see him, only danger. No wonder she was frightened to leave the house. Meredith's chest rose and fell quickly as he tried to bring his own emotions under control. Perspiration dotted Patsy's forehead and her body was tense. The arm in the cast, held diagonally across her chest, jerked sporadically.

Pressing his shoulders to the wall, Meredith slid down into a sitting position. The coffee on the floor slowly soaked into his boxer shorts.

"I'm sitting. I have no weapons, only love for you. Patsy, I think you can hear me. Listen to my voice, it's Meredith. Johnny, if you like. I'm here to protect you, only I'm not doing a very good job of it. Do you remember Paris, the old lady on the padlock bridge? She told us to get a room and then had a photograph taken with us. Do you remember the castle in Scotland? Tricking me to get on that bloody cable car and getting snowed in. Do you remember our wedding, and me ruining it because I got arrested? Do you remember our first time? I was in plaster then, not you. Still the best night of my life, though."

Meredith saw the momentary relaxation of her shoulders before she blinked and fell to her knees, head bowed.

"Meredith, I'm sorry. I'm sorry." She raised her head and looked at him. "I'm so sorry."

"No need. My fault for creeping about. It wasn't intentional. I was starving and not thinking straight. You know me and my need for food. It's me who should be apologising. But it's done now. Put down the knife and tell me what you want to do."

Patsy looked at the knife and seemed surprised to find she was holding it. With a sudden flick of her wrist, she launched it across the kitchen. It clattered to a halt in front of the oven. She looked back at Meredith. "What do you mean?"

"What would you like to do? Would you like to stay here and talk, or just sit? Do you want to go and sit in the sitting room and talk or do you want to go to bed, or have a—"

"I get it. I don't know, I just don't know."

"Then we'll sit here until you do." Meredith raised his knees, and resting his arms across them, lowered his head. His mind was spinning. If he'd been anyone else, they would probably have been injured or worse. Patsy was trained in self-defence. He'd seen her take down men twice her size but then she'd been in control. Knew when the threat to her was over. What if he'd been someone else? Someone who didn't have all those happy memories. He had to get her help.

"I want to go to bed."

Meredith raised his head. "Okay, would you like to speak to Maxine first?"

"No!" Patsy spat out the word as if it were the worst idea in the world.

"Then you don't have to. I thought you liked Maxine. I thought speaking to her was helping. Am I wrong?"

"Meredith, can I just go to bed, please? I don't need twenty questions every ten minutes."

Patsy sounded defeated, and Meredith felt much the same. He pushed himself to his feet.

"Of course. Do you need a hand?" Meredith held out his hand, but Patsy shook her head. He took a step back. "Okay, I'll let you go up and get settled and lock up down here. I'll bring you a glass of water."

Patsy nodded and walked out of the kitchen. Her shoulders were back, her chin up as she tried to pretend her world wasn't imploding around her. Meredith picked up the knife and slung it into the sink, then remembering what Trump had said about Linda and knives, he pulled open the cupboard under the sink, and collecting all the sharp knives, placed them at the rear, rearranging the other items to hide them from view. A memory of his mother and her hidden bottles of vodka flashed into his mind. It must be something to do with him. He must give off a damaged hormone that says: troubled women come to me, make me love you, then let me watch you self-destruct.

Slamming the cupboard door, he filled a glass with water and, ignoring the half-eaten meal on the table, hit the light switch and climbed the stairs. He walked to the spare room and tapped on the door before pushing it open. Patsy wasn't there. The bathroom door was open, so he knew she wasn't in there. He knew where she was but to make sure he checked the other bedroom first. Empty.

He stared at his feet for a moment. Yesterday, this would have made his heart sing. Tonight, it was the last thing he wanted. Drawing in a breath, he went to their bedroom and found Patsy peeping at him over the top of the duvet.

"Are you sure? Would you like me to go into the other room?" He placed the water on the bedside cabinet and sat on the bed next to her. "You don't have to do this. It's okay, I understand."

"I do, Johnny, I do. I don't want to be on my own, and I know you'll be there. This isn't...you know. I can't. I'm sorry, but—"

"Hush. I understand. I need to pee and then I'll be back." Meredith actually felt relief that sex wasn't on the cards. When he came back, he turned off the light before rummaging in his drawers.

"What are you doing?" Patsy asked.

"Changing my knickers. The others were wet. There was coffee on the floor. I didn't think getting into bed with you naked would send the right message."

"You called them knickers." Patsy sounded amused.

"You've brainwashed me. Just so I know the rules, am I allowed to hug you?" Meredith asked as he climbed into bed.

"No." It was almost a whisper.

"Okay. In which case, I'll try to snore. That way you'll still know I'm here. Goodnight, Hodge."

"'Night, Meredith. Thank you, and I'm sorry."

"Hush. We're not having that conversation again."

Meredith raised his arms and linked his fingers behind his head and thought about all the women who'd been in his life. The ones he'd loved. They were all damaged in one way or another, and they'd all left him.

Except Emily, she hadn't been damaged, she'd been sensible and gone when the going was good. He knew he wasn't responsible for his mother's drinking or Patsy's trauma. He wasn't even responsible for Nicola's depression, not in the beginning, anyway.

Meredith closed his eyes and sighed. He had to keep Patsy, help her recover, but he was buggered if he knew how he'd manage that, but he'd do it.

"Do you need a hug?" Patsy asked, and quickly apologised as Meredith gasped in shock when she touched his cheek.

Meredith rolled onto his side. "Stop apologising. And yes, very much so. Assume the position, Hodge and then keep very still." He hoped she was smiling as she wiggled into position, allowing him to spoon her and place his arm across her.

When Meredith woke, Patsy was still there, her breathing soft and shallow. He kissed the top of her head while he could. Craning his neck, he looked at the clock. It wasn't yet six, so he could savour this for a while. Hell, he could even stay there until she needed to go to the hospital. He'd never pulled a sicky but he might start today. He kissed her head again.

Without warning, Patsy turned to face him. "Don't speak. Just get your knickers off."

Meredith opened his mouth to seek assurance but his words were lost as she kissed him.

Chapter Twelve

January 2024 Brandon Farm

Susan smiled as Mark threw his arm around his son's shoulders.

"Come on then. We've got to move 'em up to the top field. That bottom one is waterlogged. Still, we haven't got it as bad as some, at least we're not on the river. Some poor buggers need a boat to get around their farm."

"Can I drive the quad, Dad? I can do it."

"We'll see. I don't want it getting stuck. Maybe when we get up the top."

The door closed behind them, and Susan turned to Cissy. "What do you want me to do first?"

"I don't know, Jasmine. There are the chickens, the books could do with looking at, didn't get to them last month, there's him, of course." Cissy glanced at the ceiling. "He hasn't had breakfast yet, and I think Gerry's coming today so a tidy up in there, I suppose."

"I'll do it. Just Weetabix and a pot of tea?"

"Thanks love. Yes, that'll do. But he won't finish that, his appetite has gone. He won't be long now."

"Ah, that's a shame. You've only been waiting the six years since I came, and you predict it every week. It'll be a shock when it happens." Susan kept a straight face as she poured milk into the cereal.

Cissy barked out a laugh. "Get on with you. You don't need to get him out unless he wants to. I've already sorted the other out."

Susan carried the tray upstairs and walked into Charles Brandon's room with a smile.

"Morning, Father. Some breakfast for you. Do you want me to open those curtains now? It's stopped raining and the sun's put in an appearance."

"Please yourself."

Susan put the tray on the table over the bed and pushed the table closer to Brandon. "There you go, and it would please me to open them." Walking to the window, she drew back the curtains and sun flooded into the room. She stood, hands on hips, and took in the view. "Ah, that's lovely. I love this view."

"I know what you love. I hear you rogering him night after night. Never known a woman like it. Here, do you fancy a bit more?" Brandon shoved his hand under the sheet and pumped it up and down.

Susan shook her head. "You really are a nasty old man. But I believe in second chances. Why don't you try to be nice? You haven't got long, surely it would be better to go out happy than miserable and spiteful. And you can stop that nonsense. We both know it doesn't work."

The movement under the sheet stopped, and Brandon scowled. "And whose fault is that? Lover boy, that's who. Paralysed his own father without a second thought. He's the one needing second chances."

Susan shook her head. "Settle down now. We both know it's not true. I'm not going to rise to it."

"Are you calling me a liar?" Brandon brought his fist down on the table with as much force as his wasted muscles allowed. "Let me tell you, missy, you wouldn't be riding him like that if you knew the half of it. No bloody chance. You ask him, ask him what he did to me. And I'll tell you another thing, if I could get out of this bed, I'd show you what for and make him watch. Ask him. Just—"

Having heard the shouting start, Cissy had come up to investigate, and she flew into the room.

"That's enough of that. Now shut your foul mouth, you disgusting excuse for a human being, or I'll lock that door and you can wallow in your own shit until you have the grace to die. So help me, I mean it. Jasmine, downstairs, give us a minute. I'll explain when I come down."

Susan hesitated and looked from one to the other. She'd never seen Cissy angry before, and it sounded like she meant every word. Brandon sneered at her and waved a finger at Cissy.

"And if she tells you the truth, which I doubt, ask whose fault it was. Hers."

"Jasmine. Now. Please." Cissy held the door open.

Susan stepped onto the landing, and the door slammed shut. She couldn't catch what Cissy said, as it was delivered in a hiss. She went downstairs and put the kettle on, running over the old man's words in her mind.

"I think we need something stronger than tea." Cissy walked to the dresser and pulled a bottle of brandy from the cupboard. "Do you want one? Get some glasses."

Susan did as she was told and joined Cissy at the table. "What happened?" she asked as Cissy poured.

Cissy huffed out a grunt. "I thought you'd ask me if it was true first."

"I think from your reaction, it must be true. Tell me what's happened because that's awful if true. I don't think...Cissy, just bloody tell me."

"I was poorly. I won't bother you with the ins and outs, first a hysterectomy, then an infection, then a hernia because I did too much too soon, so I was in and out of the hospital for over a year. We had a cleaner coming in, you know, to keep things ticking over, but it wasn't enough. So I advertised for a housekeeper. Jasmine."

"Mark's wife?"

"Yes, although she wasn't at the time. She was a sweet thing, like you are, but softer. We got on like a house on fire. So did she and Mark, and after she'd been here six months, he asked her to marry him. She did. You got what you saw with both of them. It was lovely to see. They were so happy. It was a sweet little service, small because I was ill, and his father didn't want to waste the money. She became one of the family. She was frightened of him, though." Cissy jerked her thumb at the ceiling. "We all were. He had one hell of a temper, he controlled us all, and he never used to be like he is now, all puny and withered. A strapping bloke, he was. We were right to be frightened. But she kept out of his way. As soon as supper was over, they'd go up to their room. He was out on the farm all day, so things worked out. Us three were happy. But not him."

"Why did you all stay?" Susan asked.

"Come on, Jasmine, you're here, aren't you? Why did you agree to that? Not many girls would. Money. Me and Mark had none, not enough to go and start over somewhere else. What would we do? Anyway, this is Mark's inheritance. My family's farm, although he changed the name. I wouldn't walk away from that. My dad should never have put it in his name. I didn't care at the time but that was before..." Cissy shook the thought away. "But you don't want to hear about that. It was a long time ago."

"I do. But you're right, I want to know about the other Jasmine. You said she died." Susan had a burning sensation in her stomach. She felt sick. Why hadn't she asked more questions? When Cissy told her Mark's wife had died, she assumed an accident or maybe cancer. It never occurred to her to ask, and it would have been rude, wouldn't it? What if Mark had killed her, by accident but he had that temper. And his father said he was stuck in that bed because of Mark. This was getting scary. She closed her eyes and braced herself. "Did Mark kill Jasmine, Cissy? Is that what he meant?"

Cissy looked horrified. "No! He loved her. It wasn't Mark who killed her." Once again, the thumb jerked towards the ceiling. "It was awful. That poor, poor girl."

"Is that why Mark hurt him? Why he's paralysed?" Susan asked, her voice barely a whisper.

"I wasn't here. I'd been into town. When I got back, I found Mark weeping on the step. His father had cornered Jasmine in the shed. She'd gone to get the chicken feed. There was only one thing on his mind. She must have been terrified. That was my fault. I'd already moved out of his bedroom, and he used to listen to them...you know. I didn't know he'd bothered Jasmine before, Mark reckoned he had, but why didn't she tell us that? She'd have been here now if she had, but he wouldn't. That's how it should have been."

"What happened?" Susan's throat was dry, but she couldn't pick up her glass because her hands were shaking.

"He had her pinned against the bench. He'd ripped her dress, and he was trying to force himself on her. She saw the tractor go by and screamed for Mark. Mark didn't know what it was, just heard a noise, so he stopped the tractor. He heard then, and he ran into the shed. It was obvious what was happening. He asked what was going on, and she started to tell him. Charlie told her to shut up and started some tale about her leading him on. Mark said it was obvious that wasn't the case. Jasmine lifted her dress and asked why she would rip it. Said he was a dirty old man, and it wasn't the first time he'd tried. Charlie told her to shut up, picked a hammer up off the bench and whacked her. Just the once and she fell to the ground. Mark ran forward, grabbed the hammer out of his father's hand and was going to hit him when Jasmine moaned. She was more important to him, so he chucked the hammer on the bench and got down on his knees to help Jasmine. Charlie ran away."

"Did Mark go after him? Is that what happened?"

"Not immediately, he was trying to help her but she died. Died on the floor of the shed in his arms." Cissy blinked her tears away and emptied her glass. Holding up the bottle, she asked, "Another?"

Susan shook her head. "What happened then?"

"Mark was in a real state when he went after him. He should have called the police really, everything would have sorted itself out, but he was so mad he wasn't thinking straight. He found him hiding in the hayloft. Stupid place to go, one of the first places anyone would look. Mark grabbed him, and his father said do your worst but they'll lock you up for it. Mark didn't care, and he chucked him out of the hayloft. That's a long way down. He thought he'd killed him, so he came looking for me. And I found him weeping on the doorstep."

"What did you do?"

"Went to Jasmine, who was dead, then went to look for Charlie. He hadn't died, just broken his back and been knocked out. He'd dragged himself halfway across that barn. I told him what I thought of him, even kicked him while he was lying there helpless, and told him that at least we'd never see him again, and he laughed at me." Cissy took a swig of her brandy. "Just laughed."

"He laughed at you?"

"Yep. Told me about the hammer having Mark's prints on it, and his version of the story. How he'd seen Mark killing his wife, and how Mark had then turned on him, that he'd taken the hammer by the head, not the handle and hidden it. Then, when he tried to call the police, Mark had thrown him out of the loft. He asked me who I thought they would believe, him or Mark."

Susan ran her hands through her hair. "Shit. That wouldn't have made sense, even if he had. This sounds like something out of a film. What did you do? How did he end up there?" It was Susan's turn to jerk her thumb.

Cissy sighed. "We left him there. On the floor of the barn. All bloody day we looked for that hammer, he was in a terrible state come the end. Told us he'd phoned Gerry, and told him where the hammer was, and that if anything ever happened to him it was down to Mark, and Gerry was to give the hammer to the police. I didn't believe him so we searched him. He had his phone in his pocket. I didn't know if he was lying. I didn't know what to do, and I said as much to Mark, and that's when Charlie came up with the plan. He said we were to get him out of the effing barn, get rid of her body, and call him an ambulance. We could say he'd fallen out of the loft, and later that Jasmine had left Mark. Like you, she had no family, no one was looking for her."

"And you did?" Susan couldn't hide her amazement and disgust. She lifted her glass but the smell made her feel sick, so she placed it back down.

"Not at first. We came in here to discuss it. Mark wanted to kill his father and then call the police, said he had nothing worth living for now because he'd lost her. He'd rather be in jail with his father dead.

"I couldn't have that. What would I have done? I'd have nothing. Like I said to Mark, if he killed him Charlie's suffering would be over, and ours just beginning. So we wrapped her up and put her in the Land Rover. Then we called the ambulance. Gave them a tale about being out for the day, finding him when we got home, and they took him away. Other than the fact we'd lost Jasmine, those weeks he was in hospital were the worst. We'd taken her miles away and buried her, so if his father changed his mind and went back to the story he told us he would tell the police, it would have looked bad for us. What innocent person would bury a girl? I have never been so scared in my life. You know I used to be chubby but the weight fell off me and I've never put it back on."

"So why am I Jasmine? I don't understand that? I thought I was being Jasmine to fool him, so Mark would get his inheritance. Shit, Cissy, this is bloody weird and, to be honest, freaking me out. You buried a girl you claim to have loved, you let that monster come back and then you got a pretend wife in? I don't get it. Why? I just don't get it." Susan got to her feet and started pacing. "Okay, I can just about understand why you didn't do what you should have. And if all this is true, I'd want to see him suffer too, but—"

"Oh, it's bloody true. On our Thomas's life, it's true. But Charlie hadn't finished playing with us. On the night before he was due to come home, I had to go and meet with the doctors so they could run through his medication and the like. We'd had the bed put in and the hoist. Taken the bath out and put the new shower in. And now he was coming home. When I got there, Gerry was there. He did this big show about how great it was that poor old Charlie was getting out, and that I should call him if I needed anything. But then he said Charlie had said Jasmine hadn't been in to see him, he was worried that something was wrong, and he hoped she would be there when he got back because I'd have enough on my plate looking after my husband. And that's when I said the stupidest thing I've ever said. I said she was too busy and he'd see her soon enough."

"Why was that stupid? I mean, he wouldn't have but you could have gone back to the story about her leaving later."

"But I didn't know that. I didn't know if Charlie remembered what was what. I didn't know if he'd said something to Gerry, who was now testing me. What if Charlie didn't remember? Because we'd never mentioned it again. Not from that night, and he was a mess by the time they took him away in the ambulance. He never asked what had happened to her or if anyone had noticed she wasn't there, nothing. He might have forgotten. Shut it out. Or perhaps it was some sort of warning. I didn't know what to think. I'll tell you, the medical people must have thought I was simple. Everyone was talking to me like I knew what was going on, and all I could think about was that poor girl wrapped up in a sheet. So I just kept nodding. I couldn't wait for them all to leave me alone with him so I could ask him."

"What did he say?"

"I didn't ask him when we were still in the hospital. I waited until we got him home because I didn't want him speaking to anyone else. Mark said to ignore him but I couldn't. I went up those stairs, and I reminded him of what he'd done and why he was lying in that bed. I left him in no doubt what I thought of him. He was evil, told me if I had been a good and proper wife it would never have happened. So not to go blaming him for my failings. Said I was useless before and now I had to look after him. He told me to replace her or Gerry would get that hammer off to the police. He said I needed someone to pick up the slack and he wasn't going to listen to any excuses."

Susan dragged her hands down her face. "So that's why you put up with him, and why Mark won't go near him. I can see that. Bloody hell, Cissy, how have you coped?"

"I really don't know. Fifteen long bloody years of feeding him and cleaning up after him. It got easier but not much."

Susan frowned. "Fifteen years? Thomas is only eight. How can that be right?"

Cissy shrugged. "We found another girl. She was nice, not like you, but she tried hard. But when the baby came, oh God, I was so happy then. It would have been perfect if not for him, but she didn't take to motherhood, depression I reckon, and she put Thomas in my arms and said she was going. Took her money, she was on the same deal as you, and left. She liked Mark well enough, but he was never like he is with you with her. I asked him what we'd do now. What if his father found out so he said get another one. So we did, and thank the Lord we got you. What are you going to do? Now you know, I mean. Are you going to go? I'd understand but you'll only get what's due, not the full amount."

"I don't know. Nothing. I don't know. You really buried someone?"

"Yes. She was dead. Nothing would bring her back. Why should Mark go to prison for something he didn't do?" Cissy looked towards the door. "They're back. Please don't say anything in front of Thomas. He doesn't need to know, not until you've made up your mind."

Thomas and Mark came in. Thomas was bouncing because he'd driven the quad and got all the sheep into the top field.

"He did well." Mark smiled. "But now he's got to wash it. Like I told him, you don't get the fun without the graft. Go on then."

Thomas didn't care. He ran off smiling.

As soon as the door closed behind Thomas, Mark looked at the bottle on the table. "Why's that there?"

Cissy's hands began to shake, and she clasped them in her lap. She couldn't cope. Not again. She looked at Susan, who patted her hands before she got to her feet and grabbed Mark's hand.

"Your dad was mean to me and Cissy thought it would help."

Leaning forward, Susan whispered something in Mark's ear, and his eyes shot to Cissy, who couldn't catch her breath.

Mark nodded at her. "She wants me to move some stuff. I'll have my dinner in a minute." Smiling, he followed Susan upstairs.

Cissy thought she would die sitting at her own kitchen table. What were they going to do? Not kill him. Mark would do so with pleasure. She got to her feet and ran to the stairs. There'd been too many killings. As she pulled the door open, she heard Susan squeal, telling Mark his hands were cold. She paused as Susan squealed again, before sitting on the stairs and waiting. The rhythmic creaking of the bed began, and she got to her feet. Susan was putting on a show. Well, good for her. Collecting the bottle, she put it back in the cupboard.

Chapter Thirteen

Meredith opened the door and only stepping onto the mat, called out, "Patsy, sorry, I know I'm cutting it fine but I'm here. Are you ready?"

Patsy appeared in the doorway of the kitchen. "Yes. Can't wait." She couldn't fit her cast through the arm of her raincoat, so Meredith buttoned it in place for her, and held the umbrella over her head as they hurried to the car. "There are floods everywhere again. I don't think it will ever stop." She ducked her head into the car and allowed Meredith to fix the seatbelt. "Thank you."

"I know you hate my driving, so I don't think you'd feel safe without."

"I meant generally but you're right. Thanks for that too."

Meredith returned her smile and ran around to the driver's side. He started the engine. "Do you know it was raining when I first realised I had to have you?" He grinned at her as she turned to face him. "You probably don't remember. I'd been called to the suspicious death of that young lad. One of the morphine killings. I told you to get the car, and you parked it miles away. It was peeing down."

"I remember that. And it was just a couple of yards. I thought you were vain and trying not to get your hair wet. You were very grumpy that day. And have me? Arrogant even then."

"Grumpy because you flirted with Sherlock and I couldn't do anything about it. Grumpy because you were driving me mad and I couldn't have you. Yes, in the sexual sense. Then, anyway. I'm only human, and you were...driving me mad. With your smiles, your wiggle, and the way you looked at me. All coy and big eyes." Meredith glanced at her and smiled.

"I think you'll find that wasn't flirting. I was just being polite. Why didn't you say anything? Not then, that would have been inappropriate, but you've never said that in all this time. I thought you didn't like me. You kept snapping at me." Patsy looked out at the rain. "That seems a long time ago."

"That was frustration. Didn't take long to realise I had to find a way to have you and keep you. But that was thirteen years ago in December," Meredith told her.

"Really? That long? Wow! You'd have got less for manslaughter, or so the saying goes."

"Did you not know? I thought that was a girls' thing, remembering dates that weren't proper anniversaries. I was showing my feminine side." Meredith shook his head.

"I just knew it was a long time. Wow, thirteen years, unlucky for some."

"Don't say that. I was trying to be romantic. Blimey, you know how to burst a man's bubble." Meredith lifted his hand from the gearstick and held it palm up. "I'm just kidding."

Patsy gave his hand a squeeze. "I know. But how do you remember the date?"

"Ah. Now I'm going to confess. Jasper James is coming up for parole consideration and I got an email for my opinion. That's what made me think of the date and of Sherlock. One thought led to another, and I realised how much had changed. My interests were purely carnal then, but it didn't take long for you to make me love you."

"What are you going to say about Jasper James? Will you tell Frankie?" Patsy asked.

Jasper James had been the chief forensic officer while at the same time killing people by morphine injection. He believed he was assisting their suicide and putting them out of their misery. He was a mentor to his assistant, Frankie Callaghan, and thought Frankie was his son. He was wrong. Frankie, however, had picked up on similarities between several deaths, and Meredith had nicknamed him Sherlock. Frankie was now living with Meredith's daughter and was father to his grandchildren.

Meredith had been hoping for a similar declaration of love but now had to talk about James. He bristled and hoped his irritation didn't show.

"I'm going to say no, of course. He killed people, Hodge. Vulnerable people and left a trail of misery for the families in his wake. If I'm honest, I can't believe you're even asking me."

"I realised it was a stupid question as I asked it. Did you get everything sorted at work?"

"Yep." Meredith watched the wipers swish back and forth. He'd hoped they were getting somewhere. But it seemed that what had been a memorable wake up call for him, Patsy had already forgotten about. "All under control. Nearly there, you'll be free shortly. Doesn't take long." Meredith turned to smile at her, but she was looking the other way, staring out of the window, lost in her own thoughts.

Less than an hour later, they were on their way home. Patsy sat next to him, flexing her fingers and lifting her arm up and down.

"Feels weightless, doesn't it? It soon gets back to normal. I'll come in and have a coffee with you, I need to pee."

"Don't you need to get back to work?" Patsy asked.

"I do. But I also need to pee. Don't you want me to come in?" Meredith sighed. He didn't know whether he was on his arse or his elbow.

"I didn't say that. I was giving you an easy way to escape," Patsy replied.

"I don't need one. I never want to escape from you, Hodge." Meredith parked next to Patsy's car. "You put the kettle on."

When he came downstairs, the kettle was boiling, and he looked at the flashing light on the answer machine. "We have messages," he called, hitting the play button.

"Hi, John, it's me. Julia, for clarification. I didn't call your mobile because it's not important. We've got to come to Bristol for a couple of days, and don't panic we don't need a bed, we're in a rather lovely hotel on the outskirts, but it's been too long, and I thought we could treat you and Patsy to a meal. It would be lovely to catch up. I'm going to drop in on Amanda, too. Anyway, I'm waffling. It's not for a few weeks. Fifteenth to the seventeenth. Don't leave it too long, I'm in demand. Love you, big brother. You too, Patsy. 'Bye."

Meredith looked at Patsy. "That sounds good. It has been too long. What do you think?"

"I think it will be lovely. You two don't get together often enough. I wish it was that easy with Steve. You've only met him once."

"I know. Look, let's get over this...little blip, and I promise you we can book to go and see him. I doubt he's ever met a man with no fingernails before." Meredith pretended to bite his nails. "If you're up to it, we can...two secs. It's George."

Meredith answered the call and listened. "Bingo. Text me the address and I'll go down there. Let them know." He hung up, promises of a trip to New Zealand forgotten. "I'm sorry, I have to go. Someone recognised the photograph."

Patsy shooed him towards the door. "Off you go. Your escape beckons." Stepping forward, she kissed him. "'Bye, Meredith."

Meredith pulled her into his arms. He felt her stiffen, but she soon relaxed against him. "I might be late, but never forget I love you," he said into her hair.

"I won't. Go." Patsy pushed him away and stood on the step to wave him goodbye as he got back into his car.

Meredith's phone pinged, and checking the address, he set the satnav. He tried several times to contact Trump, leaving a message on the fourth attempt. "Trump, it's Meredith, according to my satnav I'll be with you in twenty-two minutes. Call me back if you get this. It would be nice to know some details before I get there."

Trump called back when Meredith was five minutes from the destination.

"You shouldn't have come, sir. I've been trying to call you. False alarm."

"How was it a false alarm? How does recognising someone become a false alarm?"

"Mrs Gadding said she recognised her but couldn't put her finger on it. She called her sister, who was out on the farm working, as she had a better memory. I called it in then. I should have waited. Her sister took a while, understandable I suppose given the geography and the—"

"Trump, get on with it, am I turning back or...I'm hanging up. I can see you."

Meredith pulled over. He opened his car door, but looking at the puddle he'd need to wade through he beeped his horn and beckoned Trump to the car.

Trump sat in the passenger seat, his feet hanging out through the open door, glad it wasn't still raining.

"Carry on, she sent for her sister, and what?"

"The sister agreed it looked familiar because Jasmine looked a bit like Mark Brandon's wife. They'd seen them in town the week before. The sister had gone to school with Mark Brandon's mother. I have her name. Here it is, Cissy, and helped Cissy do a buffet for the wedding. She'd seen them regularly since. A lovely family, apparently. And for the record, they didn't think Jasmine looked anything like Louise, other than the hair. But I suppose when you can tell one cow from another, the human face makes it easy."

"And that's it. That's what you're basing it being a false alarm on?"

Trump shook his head. "It's tough times all round at the moment, sir, so I'll not take that as an insult. No, Kent was up that way, and he found Mr and Mrs Brandon in the yard, in front of the farm. He said we were searching for girls who'd gone missing, and that Mrs Brandon had been a suggested likeness. Kent showed them the photographs, and Mrs Brandon said she wished she'd been that pretty. He asked her how long she'd been on the farm, and she said twenty-two years, give or take, it was coming up to their wedding anniversary. Then she kissed him."

Seeing Meredith wasn't convinced, he added, "Perhaps we should drive over there so you can see for yourself. Stranger things have happened, I know, but given the circumstances I can't see any woman agreeing to impersonate not one, but two women who had been battered to death. Can you? She might not know, of course, but Kent said she showed no shock or hesitation. It was a standard, 'have you seen these women?' visit. Would you like to go over there?"

Meredith pursed his lips. "No. You're right, I never doubted it, not really. Why would she lie if she knew she might be the next one? Onwards and upwards. I'll head back because I didn't come prepared. No wellies. I won't be late home now. Anywhere around here we can grab a sandwich? I hate eating at service stations but I have to eat."

An hour later, Meredith was back on the road. When he arrived at the office, he reviewed the two interviews George had done and the updated map. Red dots showed the locations where the team had called. Grid one was well underway but they'd barely scratched the surface of the area they needed to cover.

"Bloody hell, it will be Christmas before we get this done. I think Seaton is right, we need to go public and see if we can jog a few memories. We can carry on doing this in the background but we need to think of something else to concentrate on. We'll still do the interviews, but my guess is Bernice Forbes will be the only one who was of any use. Daisy, what about Louise's replacement? Any missing curly redheads who might have replaced her?"

"No. And to be honest, Guv, I don't think that will work. I've concentrated on Bristol. No curly redheads. I've widened it by ten miles and got two. Wrong age and one of them wasn't a true redhead, just had it dyed that colour, and like I said to George, it only takes a couple of hours to become a redhead. And that's, of course, if they were reported missing in the first place. If Louise had had a different landlady, or one who didn't want to mess about with Louise's husband and report her missing, I'm not convinced she'd even have been identified by now. She didn't have a record. How was she identified?"

"Dental records. I don't like this case, I knew I wouldn't, it's going to drive me round the bend. We might have to open another case to keep us going. I'm going to drive out to the burial sites tomorrow. But this time I'll remember my wellies. In the meantime, I'll get back onto PR and pull something together for a media appeal. You two carry on with whatever you were doing. Every little helps, so I'm told."

Meredith called it a day at five o'clock, and George glanced from the clock to Meredith.

"Spit it out, George. You obviously have something to say."

"Not me. I'll be in the good books but you were moaning earlier that this case would take forever and then let us skip out early."

"Ah yes, sorry, take your jacket off, we'll stay another hour."

Meredith laughed as George held up two fingers before making a dash for the door.

"'Bye, all. Have a lovely evening," George called as he disappeared.

Meredith smiled all the way to the car. After this morning, and the hug he'd received when he left her, he was hoping he would indeed have a lovely evening.

When he got home, he called from the hall as usual. Dropping his phone and his keys on the table, he pulled off his tie, but as he aimed it at the newel post, he froze. Patsy's car hadn't been there. He opened the door to check he was right. Her car wasn't there.

Lips pursed, he checked his phone. No messages, and hopefully no need to panic. That was a good thing, wasn't it? She'd been more relaxed today. Hopefully, she'd gone to see Linda. He walked towards the kitchen slowly, pondering if he should call her, or if that would irritate her.

"Sod it." Meredith stopped walking and dialled her number. A phone rang in the kitchen. Meredith took the few extra steps and looked at it vibrating on the kitchen table. Next to it was a folded sheet of paper. She'd gone. Patsy had gone!

Meredith turned his back on it and leaned against the door jamb as Patsy's answer service picked up.

"Hi, sorry I can't take your call at the moment. Please leave a message and I'll get back to you as soon as I can."

Meredith lifted his phone. "Now. Get back to me now." Pulling his arm back, he launched his phone towards the front door. There was a sharp crack as the phone made contact with the glass. Meredith turned back to the kitchen and took another step forward. He couldn't do it. He wouldn't do it.

Walking back down the hall, he hung the tie, still clenched in his hand, on the newel post, and climbed the stairs. Stripping off, he took a shower and had a shave. He'd not had time that morning. Patsy had distracted him. Going to the bedroom, he pulled on his joggers and a T-shirt before going into the spare bedroom. Everything was neat and tidy but that told him nothing. Patsy hadn't moved her things. Sitting on the bed in their room, he stared at the wardrobe and dared himself to open it. It seemed he wasn't up to the job, so he went downstairs and into the kitchen.

Ignoring the table, he opened the fridge and slammed it shut when he found nothing appealing. He did the same with the freezer. Going into the hall, he picked up his phone. A crack ran from corner to corner. He tapped it and smiled. It worked. He found the number he was looking for and hit the call button.

"A banquet for two, please. Delivery...Yes, that's right...Am I? Do I get free prawn crackers or something for being your most regular customer? ...Thank you."

Meredith went into the living room to wait. If he went into the kitchen, he might be tempted to read whatever she'd written. He pondered having a drink but decided against it. It hadn't worked in the past, and it certainly wouldn't work now. Lifting the remote, he pointed it at the television. Public Relations hadn't come back to him. He must remember to call them in the morning.

Chapter Fourteen

Patsy watched Meredith drive away and stood there for a few moments, remembering the warmth of his body. She really had to get a grip or she would lose him. The thought made her shiver, and she closed the door.

Sitting on the sofa, she drummed her fingers against each other as she wondered how to pull herself together. It was just so bloody hard. What she wanted she would never have again. It wasn't possible, but could she survive with what she could have? Yes, she told herself, she could because the alternative was unthinkable. Yet here she was thinking about it. Again and again and again and...enough!

Patsy jumped to her feet. It was killing her, or it would if she carried on like this. She might be going mad, but she wasn't stupid. Going upstairs, she pulled a suitcase from the back of the wardrobe and pondered on how much to take. She wouldn't be back. Meredith was, after all, Meredith. This wasn't his fault, it wasn't hers either. But she knew that she couldn't make their demise his fault, he carried enough guilt, mostly self-inflicted and warranted, but he didn't deserve this. He didn't deserve what she could offer, and he didn't deserve what would happen if she stayed. She certainly wouldn't survive it. No, this way was better. Then neither of them would have to live through it. Live through the end of Meredith and Hodge. She smiled. She liked it when he called her Hodge, it reminded her of... She stifled her sob. It reminded her of so bloody much it hurt. Back to the plan.

The plan would work. Neither of them would be happy. It would be so bloody hard but it would be better. Better than watching it all fall apart.

Patsy packed methodically. Knickers, bras, socks. Trousers, jeans, jumpers. Shirts, T-shirts. She paused. The suitcase was filling up, and she still had coats and shoes to consider. Going to the other wardrobe, she chose one pair of boots, her trainers and her favourite flats. Placing them carefully in the case, soles facing up so as not to mark her clothes, she ran through a mental checklist. Toiletries and passport!

Her packing finished, she lugged the case downstairs and put it by the door. Placing her coat over it, she dropped her phone into her handbag and removed the door keys from her keyring. He had to know he could move on without it hurting either of them. Going back to her handbag, she removed her phone. That meant not talking, so she'd buy another, one he couldn't leave messages on.

Patsy went to the sideboard and pulled out a large notepad, and scrolling through her contacts, she wrote down all the numbers she might need, and tore the sheet from the pad, folding it neatly. She should write him a note, Meredith deserved that, at the very least. He deserved so much more, but she wasn't the woman who could give him that, which was why she had to leave. Flipping away a tear she started to write.

It was minutes before that was screwed up and she started again; it was her ninth attempt she settled on.

My dearest, wonderful, handsome Johnny Meredith,

I know you already know what this is, so I forgive you if you don't read on.

I am not the me I was, and I can't really change that, so it can never be the same again. I just can't see it getting better, how could it? I'm going now while we still love each other as we should. Now while there are only good memories. And what memories, Johnny. I'd write some of them down but I'd make you blush.

I will miss you so much, but when I think about you it will all be about the good stuff. I love you, and I know without a doubt that you love me, but I see the pain in your eyes every time you look at me, and I can't add any more to that. And I won't sit around helpless while it all tumbles down to nothing. To watch that pain turn to hurt and, God forbid, guilt, and all because I'm not the old me anymore.

I know you need to be needed but I don't need you. I need me back. Without me, I can never need you. But I don't think I can be that me for you again.

I've just read that back. All very emotional and dramatic but it's true, Johnny. True in what still makes sense in my head.

So I'm leaving. Leaving for me but, more importantly, I'm leaving for you.

I'm not planning on doing anything stupid, I'm not brave enough, and I can hear you shouting, yes you are stupid by leaving but I don't think so. Let's agree to differ. You'll understand one day. So, I will buy a new phone, and text you now and again, just to let you know I'm still alive and surviving without needing you.

They say you should never say never but I'm saying it so you won't be under any illusion that I might come back. I will never come back, and I'm sorry because I know how that bluntness will hurt you. It's even making me cry.

Another emotion – there might be hope for me yet.

Have a lovely life, Johnny, don't retire. It's who you are. Who you were meant to be. Find someone to share your life with. Eventually, that is, you don't need to rush. They will never be the love of your life. That was me, or so I'm going to tell myself. As for me, there will never ever be anyone like DCI Johnny Meredith. You're irreplaceable.

Px

Patsy folded the note and took it with the keys and her phone and placed them on the table. Then, heaving the suitcase into the car, she drove away. As she did so, she smiled. A weight had been lifted. There was hope for her now she didn't have to see Meredith.

Chapter Fifteen

At a little after midnight, Meredith's phone rang. He glanced at the screen. The number was withheld, so he ignored it for a little too long before he realised it might have been Patsy. Cursing, he dropped it back on the table, retrieving it when a message alert sounded.

"Hello you. As promised, I'm alive. Go to bed, Johnny, you'll feel like shit in the morning. Don't hit the bottle, you know that doesn't work. I love you."

Meredith listened to the message three times.

As promised? When?

Meredith knew he had to read the letter, so moving the half-full cartons out of the way, he placed his finger on it, drew it closer, and stared at the keys. He hadn't known they were there; the letter had hidden them. Resisting the urge to upend the table, he tapped the note. It didn't matter what it said. She'd gone. The phone, the note, and now the keys. It didn't take a genius.

He listened to her message again. Patsy was trying to sound upbeat but he could hear that it was forced.

Still alive. What did that mean?

Meredith picked up her letter and read it. Once, twice, and after the third time, he nodded and folded it neatly.

Fuck her! Yes, she needed him, but even if she was in denial about that, what about what he needed? Had she given that any consideration? Apparently, because he'd been given permission to find someone else, but not someone he loved with all his heart, just someone who would do. Second best. Well, fuck her. He would find her, and he would point out all the flaws in her argument and bring her home. On the plus side, she was going to message him and wasn't intending to jump off a bridge somewhere. But that wasn't enough. Enough would only be possible when she was back.

But he needed to sleep. She was right, and she was also correct that he didn't need to hit the bottle, and he wouldn't. Meredith was stone cold sober, and he had no intention of being a slob. He stacked the takeaway cartons and took them to the bin. He hit the pedal with his foot to open the lid but stopped himself dropping them in. Instead, he dropped them into the sink and pulled the liner from the bin, scrabbling around to recover Patsy's first eight attempts.

Taking them to the table, he carefully flattened them out. They all started in much the same way, but each one took a different course on how she told him she was never coming back.

Meredith surprised himself with his self-control. Instead of screwing them up, he made a pile, added the final letter and slid them into the tea towel drawer. He wanted to look at her phone, see if there was a clue as to where she'd gone but tonight was too soon to chase after her. Tonight would just make things worse, so he put the cartons in the bin liner and took it to the dustbin. He went to bed, taking his phone and the charger so he wouldn't miss another call.

There were no more calls and the next morning he got up, showered, and touched up the shave he'd had the night before. He slung a pair of boots in the back of his car before setting the satnav and heading for the motorway. Glad he didn't have to go to the station, relieved he didn't have anyone in the car.

When he reached the first farm, he'd only got his first boot on when a cheery-faced man approached him.

"Alright, governor? You can't park there. Your car will be wiped out by the tractors. There's no right of way up here, if you—"

Meredith pulled his ID from his pocket. "Where can I park safely? Police. I'd like a word with whoever is in charge."

"That would be me. Police, aye? I'm innocent. Honest. Get your other boot on and come this way. Your car's safe." Turning away, he walked over to a canvas satchel, hanging from a gate, and pulled out a thermos flask. "Tea?"

Meredith waded through the sludge. "Not for me, had a coffee on the motorway."

"Motorway? Where you from, then?" The farmer poured himself a drink the same colour as the slurry at their feet.

"Bristol."

"Bristol? What you doing down here? I know they've made cuts but that's a lot to cover."

"Cold Case Review. I'm here about the body you discovered."

"Ah, yes. I heard she was from down your way. Not so much a body, more a collection of bones. Bloody sad. Jack, he's the one who lifted the bucket and saw a leg sticking out, was right upset. How can I help?"

"Not sure that you can. I read your original statement, and Jack's, but I wanted a feel of where they were buried. Have you got time to show me? If not, point me in the right direction."

"Not unless you've got a boat in that car. And what do you mean, they? It was only the one down there."

"You didn't hear about the other body found a few years earlier?" Meredith frowned.

"Oh, yes. Never heard that much about it, and it wasn't here. It was further up the river. You got lumbered with both, did you?"

"Yes. Both girls took the same journey, got off halfway, and ended up buried within miles of each other. You can't show me where, then?"

The farmer rubbed his chin as he looked at Meredith's suit. "I can for the best part but you'll get mucky. You got any overalls in the car?"

"No. Do you have any I can borrow, or there's always the dry cleaners."

"Not without going back home, and I haven't got time to do both. You got drawers on?"

"Um, if I say yes?" Meredith had decided he was wasting his time, but it was a distraction, and he had nowhere else to be.

"Then strip your trousers off and ditch the jacket. That coat will go in the machine."

"Are we paddling there?" Meredith didn't move.

"Nope, we're taking the quad. You'll be on the back. You'll get plastered."

"Sod it. Let's do it."

"That's the spirit. I'll go and get it."

Sloshing back to his car, Meredith took off his suit and tie, zipped up his anorak, and shoved his feet back into his wellies. Zipping his car keys into his coat pocket, he sloshed back across the yard as the farmer chugged out of the barn.

"Jump on. I've given you a sack to sit on, but it's going to be bouncy so hold tight."

Meredith actually smiled as he climbed on to the rear of the quad. It wasn't a seat, just a foot square of moulded plastic covering the rear axle. If anyone had told him he'd be agreeing to this, he'd have put good money on his refusal.

Back to the farmer, Meredith grabbed hold as they set off. It was a steady pace as the farmer weaved around potholes. By the time he stopped, Meredith was indeed splattered with mud.

"This it?" Meredith called, turning around as the farmer climbed off.

"Ha! Not even nearly." The farmer opened a gate, drove the quad in, and shut the gate.

"This one's not too bad. On a slope you see, the next one will get you wet."

They took off at an alarming rate. Meredith was convinced he'd have serious spinal damage by the time they got there. Any suspension the machine offered was enjoyed by the farmer, who seemed to be having a whale of a time finding every lump and bump the field had to offer. By the time they came to an eventual stop, Meredith was plastered in mud. He slid off his makeshift seat and adjusted his boxers.

"You should have warned me."

The farmer laughed. "I reckon I did. You took your suit off. Now see that oak tree down there? The one that looks like it's floating. Follow the fence behind it along to the gate, and about a hundred yards on. Behind that hedgerow is a dirt track for the tractors. Another hedgerow, you can just see the top of it, and she was behind there. The track's not usually flooded at this time of year. November sometimes, but never February.

Global warming they reckon, don't they? Trying to blame it on the cows for farting."

"So I hear. Who uses that track? Where does it go?" Meredith shielded his eyes and peered into the distance.

"Nowhere, not unless you cut across the field at the end of it."

"Who would know about it?"

"Anyone who works here. A few plant drivers. The pickers. But not the public, had the odd car driver follow their satnav and get stuck in it, but not often."

"So you think whoever buried her there knew about the lane?"

"I reckon they knew exactly where they were going. I should have realised when I saw the tulips, but you don't think, do you?"

"What tulips?"

"We get all sorts grow in these hedgerows. Daffs, primrose, cowslip, buttercups, poppies, all the usual. But do you know what's not usual?"

"Tulips," Meredith suggested.

"Tulips," agreed the farmer. "First noticed them about ten years back, a little clump of them. When Jack showed me the remains, I said to him, the bugger planted tulips there."

"Did you tell the police? I didn't read about any tulips." Meredith's eyes narrowed as he tried to remember.

"I did."

"It wasn't in your statement. I'd have remembered. That would have been significant," Meredith told him.

"Maybe not but I told the one they sent up here when I called it in."

"Okay, so if we accept that whoever buried her there was familiar with the lay of the land, he buries her and plants some bulbs. How did he know you wouldn't be digging her up the next week?"

"Why would I? That's a grazing field. Not using it at the moment because it's been so wet. Another couple of weeks and it will be full of sheep. It would never be dug up."

"And yet it was." Meredith raised his eyebrows.

"Ah, I see what you mean. It was a one off. Jack was digging a trench. Two-fold. First to stop the bloody track flooding, but also to stop the sheep from going down there. We had to fence it. They kept finding gaps in the hedge. One of 'em must have been stuck in it for days, nearly lost her. Never got it finished, as you can see. They were here for weeks. We got on with other jobs. Jack said I had to finish it, 'cos he wasn't digging up any more bodies. You don't reckon there are any more, do you? Do you want to head back? You look a bit nippy."

"Good idea. So which direction was the other farm?" Meredith asked.

"North of here. Gerry Brandon's place. He's gone over to llamas, reckons they bring more money in than the few sheep he kept. But he's mainly arable. Now he does dig his fields over more than me. He'd have found her sooner, depending on how deep that one was buried." The farmer shivered. "Gives me the 'eebie jeebies. Poor souls. Now hop on, you're turning blue."

Back at the barn, Meredith washed off his legs under a running tap in the yard and dried them as best he could with an old jumper the farmer had on a hook. The farmer watched on with amusement as Meredith tried to pull on his socks over damp feet.

"Not funny. But thanks for your help. I'll put my trousers on back at the car. Before I let you get on, you're sure you never saw either girl before?"

"Never even saw a picture of the second one."

He walked across to Meredith and looked at the two photos as Meredith flipped from one to the other. "Nope. They do look a bit alike though. Do you reckon you've got someone who doesn't like redheads on the loose?"

"Let's hope it's just two. Thanks again." Meredith wandered back to the car in his shirtsleeves and boxers, holding his coat as far away from his body as he could.

Once in the car, he left his trousers folded on the passenger seat and headed for Gerry Brandon's farm with the heated seat both warming his body and drying his boxers. That would have made Patsy giggle. He thumped the steering wheel before bringing his focus back to the job.

When his satnav told him to take the next left and his destination would be on the right, Meredith pulled into a layby, and jarred his back trying to put his trousers on. He drove across the cattle grid, cursing as his back spasmed. Pulling into the yard of Shepton Farm, he got out of the car and looked around. Other than an old Land Rover, the place seemed deserted. As he headed for the house, the door opened.

Meredith held out his ID. “DCI Meredith, I wonder if I might have a word with—”

“Hang on. I’m just visiting.” The woman turned back into the house. “Katie, a police officer to see you. Have you lost more sheep?”

A slightly younger woman appeared, drying her hands on her apron. “No. They’re all up the top now. Yes, how can I help you?” she asked Meredith.

“I’m investigating the murder of the two women found here and down on Waldwick Farm. I was after someone who could show me the burial site.”

“I’m sorry, love, they’re all out working. I can point you in the right direction, but even then you won’t get within a half a mile. It’s mainly flooded down there at the moment. The Thames burst its banks again on Tuesday. If the forecast is right, it’ll recede pretty quickly but that will take days, not hours. There’s nothing to see, though. Your lot finished with it ages ago. It’s been ploughed over long since.”

“It was more the location I wanted to see, not the actual spot. I’m interested in seeing how they managed to get a body there and bury it with no one noticing.”

“In the dark. It’s right on the edge of our land, two fields up. If they came down Parsley Lane, or took the river track, who would have seen them?”

“Okay, who would know the lanes were there? Is Parsley Lane a public road?” Meredith asked.

“Yes, but no one uses it much. In the summer, we’ve got tractors going up and down morning, noon and night. Only a few pull-over spots, so anyone local would avoid it then. To be fair, they do most of the time, and those driving through the area stick to the main roads,” Katie told Meredith.

“What about the river track? Who uses that?” Meredith asked.

“Dog walkers, runners and the occasional courting couple. It’s not really a road. You could get a car up there but not at the moment.”

“Can you point me in the right direction? I take it Parsley Lane isn’t flooded because I’d still like to have a look. I’m quite good at reversing.” Meredith gave her a wink and was rewarded with a smile.

"I don't know. I've not been that way recently. We don't use that field at this time of year. Why don't you follow Cissy? She can go that way and point it out. Sorry, if you'd been a couple of hours earlier, Gerry would have been here. That's all right, isn't it, Cissy?"

"Yes, sure. If you come now. I've got to get back. I'll see you soon, Katie." Cissy turned towards the Land Rover.

Meredith was about to follow her when something occurred to him. "Before I go, you're not connected to the Brandons of Brandon Farm, are you?" Meredith asked.

Cissy kept walking, pretending she hadn't heard while she tried to work out why he'd asked.

"Oi! Cissy, hold up. He might want to speak to you. Cissy is Cissy Brandon. I'm Katie Brandon. We married brothers," Katie dropped her voice. "I got the happy one. Charlie is a miserable bastard."

Cissy stopped walking and turned around. "Come on then, make it quick. Like I said, I should have left an hour ago. Katie never knows when to shut up."

Meredith thanked Katie and went to join Cissy. "This won't take long. Have you ever seen either of these women?"

Meredith showed Cissy a picture of Louise first, and she shook her head. "Don't think so."

"What about this one?" As he held the phone forward, it rang. He turned it to face him and, seeing it was a withheld number, pushed the answer button and strode away. "One minute. Meredith speaking, is that you, Patsy?"

"Yes. Just checking in. I'm fine. I...I have to go. 'Bye."

"Patsy. Patsy!" Meredith cursed and turned back to Cissy. She'd climbed into the Land Rover and the engine spluttered into life.

"I don't know either of them. Sorry, but I really must go. Do you want to follow me, because I'm leaving now? It's already out of my way."

Meredith put his thumb up and jogged to his car. He'd been following Cissy about a mile or so when she slowed down, her hand came out of the window, and she pointed to her right before giving a wave. Meredith saw the turning indicated and flashed his lights to thank her as he pulled into Parsley Lane. The going wasn't too bad to start with, but as he progressed the potholes got deeper, and the lane narrower, making it impossible to continue. He turned the car round at the next spot wide enough and headed back to Bristol.

He was in a foul mood, he didn't want to go back to an empty house, and he didn't want to go to work where everyone would ask about Patsy, and he'd have to admit he'd done it again. Seaton might actually thump him this time.

His chin quivered.

"Fucking hell. I'm turning into a teenager." Meredith turned the radio on and sang at the top of his voice all the way back to Bristol.

Chapter Sixteen

Present Day - Brandon Farm

Mark put his hands over his ears and stared out at the fields beyond. His mother knocked one away.

"We can't pretend it's not happening, Mark. We can't because it is. So, we need to tell Jasmine, or she'll give it away. Even if she didn't want to, it would shock her, and she'd give it away."

"But you said you told her and she was okay. She's been nice to me."

"Because in her own way she loves you. She loves Thomas, that's for sure. I'm sure she'll help us, but we have to tell her the truth to find that out. I told her about what your father did, and what we had to do, but I said the other one went away. Baby blues. I didn't tell her...you know."

"She'll go. If we tell her, she'll go. I don't care about the police but I don't want her to go. What did he say? Tell me again."

"He said very little, really. He got a call that made him angry, so I took advantage and got in the car. But before that, he asked Katie if she was anything to do with Brandon Farm, and Katie told her. Then he showed me pictures of those poor girls when they were alive and happy, and I said I didn't know them. He asked nothing else because I was in the car and told him I was going, and he wanted to follow me to Parsley Lane. But that's not the point. Come on, Mark. Think. If they didn't know about us, what would they be doing asking Katie if she knew about this bloody farm? They know something. We might get away with it if Jasmine agrees to back us up, if she doesn't...well, you know what will happen."

Mark blinked and pressed his knuckles into his eyes. "I won't do it. I won't bloody lose her because I love her, Mum. Like I loved Jasmine, only more."

Cissy patted her son's shoulder. "I know you do, love, I know. But if we don't come up with a plan, I can't see how you can keep her."

"A plan about what?" Susan had come out to see why they were standing in the yard. Neither had heard her approach.

Cissy's hands flew to her chest. "Oh, you frightened me. I didn't hear you come out."

"I wondered what you were doing. Now I know you were making a plan. What about?"

Mark took hold of Susan's shoulders. "Do you love me?"

Susan's eyes darted between the two. "Yes. Why? What's that got to do with the plan?"

"Mum saw the police today, and—"

"What did they want?" Susan asked.

"They were asking questions about the first two girls," Cissy replied.

"Again? I wonder why?" Susan looked puzzled.

"What do you mean again?" Cissy looked like she was going to cry.

"Cissy, calm down. Someone had said I looked like the missing girls, and they wanted to know how long I'd lived here. I said twenty-plus years, and they thanked us. Remember, Mark? Is that what you needed a plan for, in case they came here? If it was, I doubt they will, they've already spoken to us."

Mark's grin was wide as he took hold of Susan's hand. "Oh yes. Told you we didn't need to worry, Mum."

Cissy followed the couple back into the house. They might not be worried but her life had been a string of miserable events since marrying Charlie Brandon, and she couldn't see it stopping, not until they were chucking earth on her. She'd keep her mouth shut for now, she'd have another think. Jasmine could be right.

Chapter Seventeen

Two weeks had passed since Patsy had left. Meredith was running on empty. He'd told no one Patsy had left him, fielding questions with vague answers about her, he was even avoiding Peggy and Amanda. But he knew it was only a matter of time before he'd have to tell someone. He needed to get his head around it before fielding questions he could never answer. So he threw himself into the case. He worked long hours knocking on doors and being given the same answers. No one had known the missing girls, no one had seen them, no one recognised them. There'd been a few 'maybe, but I'm not sure' and 'looks familiar, but I couldn't swear to it', which they'd got excited about, but all had petered away to nothing.

Mason had brought the shoebox in with Jasmine's personal things. But none of it gave a clue as to where she had gone.

Meredith had joined the local gym on the third day after Patsy left. It gave him something to do, and more importantly to him, less time to think about his missing wife. He arrived when they opened at six and worked himself so hard that all he could think about was the pain radiating from every muscle. All thoughts of Patsy faded as his body took control of his mind.

On the fourteenth day, Meredith knew because he was counting, the trainer had seen him, hands on knees, gasping for air, and slapped him on the back.

"Listen, mate, you're new to this, take it steady. At your age, your body needs a slow buildup. You'll damage yourself. Let me put you a programme together."

"It's fine. I can cope."

"For how long? Seriously, I'm not after a new client, unless you want to be one, of course, but I don't want you dropping dead on my shift. Do you know how much shit that stirs up?"

Meredith pulled himself upright and rolled his shoulders. "Yep. I'm a copper. How many have you had drop dead on you?" He looked at the fresh-faced, musclebound man and guessed he was in his mid-twenties. His upper body plastered in tattoos. It looked like his legs wouldn't be far behind.

"Two. Only one that I had to deal with and I didn't like it. So, please just ease up a little, or take more time. You can do the same amount of work, just over a longer period. Have a little break in between. And drink more water. Why are you doing it? Because I'm guessing you're not here just to keep fit."

Meredith inclined his head. Was that a smirk? "Go on, enlighten me." His thigh muscle, which he was sure had a proper name, was twitching, so he walked to a nearby bench, sat down, and held up his hands. "I'm resting. Come on, lippy, you've got all the answers. Why am I here?"

"A woman, or maybe women. I'm Jared, by the way. Give me your foot."

Meredith lifted his foot, and Jared began to manipulate and flex his ankle. "Meredith. Carry on. What's my story?"

"Other foot. I'm not a psychic. But it's one of three things. Recently divorced and you're going to put yourself back out there, but think you've got too much competition from younger men because you don't want a granny of your own age, so you need to beef up to get the young chicks. Or she left you, or maybe had an affair, and you want to show her what she's missing or what she's got. Stand up. Face the wall and put one foot about two feet in front of the other. Like this, and lunge. Not too far."

Meredith did as instructed but his thigh told him it didn't like it.

"Keep going. Do ten, hold the lunge for a count of thirty to start. And change legs and do the same again," Jared instructed.

"You said three. What's the third one?" Meredith asked, pressing into the third lunge.

"Oh, the middle-aged crisis. You're feeling your age and want to prove to yourself you can still do it. But I don't reckon it's that. You never had a belly, you're reasonably good looking for an old guy. If you didn't have a woman on your mind, you wouldn't be trying to kill yourself. Change legs."

"Close enough. You should have been a copper, you can read people. Ow, ow, ow! Bastard cramp." Meredith limped in circles, rubbing his thigh.

"On the floor, give me your foot. And this is why you warm up first, cool down last, and build steadily in the middle. And I'd hate being a copper. I know too many dodgy people, and I'd lose half my mates. I'm just an expert at losing women. Why are you laughing? It's not funny. I've already had two tats changed. Why do you think I look like this? Get up and see how that is." Jared released Meredith's foot.

Meredith smiled at him. "I suppose I should be grateful I never had tattoos, or I'd look a mess like you." He held out his hand. "Pull me up. I'm old and apparently desperate."

"So, which was it? I love hearing other people's tales of misery. Makes me feel better." Jared laughed as he hauled Meredith to his feet.

Meredith picked up his water bottle and took a long draught before pointing it at Jared. "She didn't need me anymore. But feels the need to phone me and leave messages to remind me."

"Oh. Not heard that one before." Jared looked around. "See the blonde on the cross-trainer, in the blue T-shirt. If you're looking for uncomplicated relief, she'll sort you out. Her husband left her for a younger model, although I don't know why because she'd wear me out. Anyway, her goal in life now is to have fun, naked fun, with as much variety as possible and just the once. Told me she'd never rely on a man again, not even for a second round. She comes in early too. She's choosy but I think you might do alright."

Meredith's lips twitched into a brief smile as he stared across at the row of cross-trainers. "I'll bear it in mind. And thanks for helping an old man out." He turned to look at Jared. "I might take your advice. On the training front," Meredith added, when Jared grinned.

Jared winked at him. "You can book me on reception. I do Tuesday to Saturday mornings, not in on Sunday and Monday."

"I'll think about it. Now, if you'll excuse me, I need to have a word with someone." Meredith glanced back at the cross-trainers.

"Ha. Good luck." Jared slapped him on the back, and watched Meredith walk across the gym towards the woman in the blue T-shirt.

"I don't need luck," Meredith called without looking back.

The woman in the blue T-shirt smiled at Meredith as he approached. "Morning."

"Morning." Meredith nodded.

"I thought you'd already been on these," she said as he came level with her.

"Yes. I have. I needed a word."

The woman smiled. Good old Jared. She'd been getting the measure of this one for a few days. "Oh, really...oh. Ah well."

She increased her speed as Meredith walked past her towards the woman on a running machine further along.

Maxine Selby had already slowed to a walk, and seeing Meredith approach, hit the stop button.

"Meredith, I haven't seen you in here before." Maxine tucked her hair behind her ear and lifted her water bottle from the holder.

"Nor I you. A word if I might."

"I wondered how long it would take. I'm not sure if I'm disappointed or not, but first I need to shower. Let's meet in the café. I can spare you twenty minutes." Maxine walked towards the exit.

"You know?" Meredith grabbed her shoulder and spun her to face him. "You know?" Aware that he'd raised his voice, he lowered it and stepped closer. "Where is she?"

"I don't know. The café, Meredith, I'll be fifteen minutes. Don't grab me again."

Maxine walked away, and Meredith watched her go. He should have guessed. Why the hell hadn't he realised? Maxine hadn't called to say Patsy was missing appointments. Perhaps she wasn't. Perhaps Patsy was still local. He'd just assumed she wasn't. He headed for the showers, and hurrying across the gym, Jared caught him at the door.

"Meredith, hold on." Jared held up his hands and took a step back. "Tell me to mind my own business and I will, but if she's the one who doesn't need you it might be the other way around. You don't need her."

Meredith was intrigued. "Meaning?"

"Ah shit, this is embarrassing. She's not as bad as Sophie, the woman in the blue T-shirt, and I don't have personal experience, so there's that. But she might have been more than friendly with a couple of the blokes in here. So, if she's the one who doesn't need you, like I said, you might not need her. If she's not the one, carry on. Am I blushing? I feel like I am. I'll just go. 'Bye, Meredith, don't forget, you can book me on reception." With a curt nod, Jared turned away.

Meredith was in and out of the shower in ten minutes and was sitting in the café holding his coffee when Maxine arrived. He got to his feet. "I got you a coffee. Black but a pot of milk in case." He pointed at the table.

Maxine thanked him and sat down, adding a splash of milk to her drink. She didn't speak. After a minute, she looked at her watch.

"I thought you'd be bombarding me with questions. I don't have long," she told him.

"Are you going to answer them?" Meredith asked.

"If I can, without overstepping professional boundaries. Ask away." Maxine lifted her coffee and looked at Meredith over her cup.

"Did you know Patsy was leaving? Did you encourage it?" Meredith asked, holding her gaze so he could gauge her honesty.

"No, and no."

"So you knew after the event. Are you still seeing her?"

"Yes, and no."

"Will she be alright? Are you happy that she's gone who knows where, in her condition? And please give me the courtesy of more than a one-word answer." Meredith drew in a breath. The woman was good. She hadn't even blinked. Perhaps he was losing it. "I'm very worried about her, and I need you to help me here."

Maxine nodded and brought her eyes back to his as she tilted her head. "Interesting. You say you are very worried, and yet if we hadn't bumped into each other here, you wouldn't have called me. Why?"

Meredith sighed. "Can we not do this? Would you please just answer my questions? I don't need to be analysed. I'm a fucking mess. I always have been, and no doubt always will be. Please, just concentrate on Patsy. Are you sure that she is not a danger to herself, leaving when she was in that state?"

Maxine's eyes narrowed, and her brow creased for a moment as she considered this.

"Patsy called me rather than turn up for our meeting. We talked. She told me she'd left home two days before and she was well. She's kept every appointment since, albeit via telephone. Patsy didn't appear to be in a state. What did you mean by that?"

"You said she'd left home, not left me. Is there a difference? Will she come back? Has she said?"

"We're not going to get very far answering questions with questions."

"But at least we're now using words with more than one syllable." Meredith laid his hands on the table. "Look, much as you must be itching to get inside my head, can we save that for another day? Just answer the bloody questions. Is she coming back?"

"I don't know. My guess is possibly. We don't talk about it. At the moment, we're concentrating on her. Talking about you or home is off limits."

"What does that mean? She said you had plenty to say about me before?"

"God, your arrogance." Maxine held up a hand. "I'm sorry that was unprofessional. Yes, I really would like to get inside your head, but as this is about Patsy that's who we talk about. Of course, you are part of the reason she left, a large part, but when I asked what you had said when she told you, she said she'd left a note, and she didn't want to talk about you. Your name has cropped up occasionally, but we mainly talk about Patsy. How she feels, how she felt, how she can help herself cope. I really can't say more than she's doing well. I don't think she's a risk to herself or others."

Meredith lifted the spoon and stirred the coffee he had yet to touch. "You're sure about that? Sure she won't do anything...to hurt herself?"

"As much as I can be. She wants to get better or she wouldn't be speaking to me. Do you think differently? I'm not asking about you, just for your opinion. You said the state she was in, and now you want confirmation she won't harm herself. What happened on that last day? I'm guessing you weren't concerned then or I'd have heard from you sooner."

Meredith thought back to that day and closed his eyes. In any other circumstances, he'd have smiled. Now he wanted to damage something. He looked at Maxine. "Do you smoke?"

"No. Is that relevant?"

"Only because I want one. She said goodbye, but not in words, and the notes came later. I realise that now, I didn't at the time. I thought she was getting better. On that last day, she was happy or at least happier. She was very...affectionate. But once I'd left for work, it took her nine attempts to tell me she didn't need me, and she packed a lot of her clothes, and left, leaving her keys and phone to show me she wasn't coming back."

"When you say affectionate, do you mean intimate?" Maxine asked.

"Very."

Maxine looked away, but her head jerked back at his next words.

"But that was because of the case. I realised that almost immediately. I didn't miss that clue, so I'm not totally losing it."

"The case? Explain, please." Maxine pushed her cup to the centre of the table and leaned forward.

"One of the missing girls couldn't cope with her partner's infidelity. They tried to work it out, but she couldn't get past it and wouldn't let him near her. Not until the day she left, never intending to return. She didn't return because she was murdered, but on the day someone caved her head in she'd been gone for years. She was never intending to come back, didn't want to be found. Another sign from Patsy. She'd know I'd work that out." Meredith sighed. "That's why she was intimate, as you so delicately put it. She was sending me a message. Jasmine's bloke, who by the way has since settled down and had kids etcetera, has never forgotten that last day, he still pines for her, and as good as said if she wasn't dead and walked back into his life he'd take her back. And now I understand that. I wonder if Patsy realises that, too. If she knows that it doesn't matter how long it takes I'll still be here?"

He flinched when Maxine put her hand on his. He'd been staring into space.

"Meredith, I understand you need time to process your thoughts but I really have to go. However, I have more questions. How do you know Patsy took nine attempts at the letters? Do you have them all?" Maxine got to her feet and lifted the strap of her kit bag onto her shoulder. "If you do, it might be useful if I could see them."

Meredith considered this quickly. They were personal to him. Even if Patsy came back, he'd never get rid of them but perhaps this might help. He nodded. "I do. Would you like me to bring them to you? I have to be at work now but I can drop them off later or over the weekend."

Maxine hesitated. "I've got a full day today, so I'll pop in and collect them over the weekend. I have your number. I'll give you a call to make sure you're in. 'Bye, Meredith." Maxine hurried away.

When Meredith approached the exit, she was standing hand on hip waiting for Jared to release the non-working turnstile. Eventually, she asked him to step aside and climbed over. Landing on the other side, she noticed Meredith watching and smiled.

"Very late now. I'll call you."

Jared turned to see who she was speaking to and grinned. "Have you booked me yet?"

"Not yet. Come on then, show me where I pay to be tortured."

When Meredith arrived home that night, he was tired, and he was hungry. Jared had given him a diet sheet of foods he should eat to supplement the training. He didn't have the heart to tell him he wasn't interested in either; it was the pain he was after. Nor did he put him right about Maxine Selby. What was the point? He wouldn't have listened. But the diet sheet remained crumpled and damp in the kit bag at his feet, and there it would remain. Tonight, it would be curry with all the trimmings. He knew from the notches on his belt he'd lost a few pounds, so pigging out with a curry wouldn't do any harm.

He went to the kitchen and pulled the menu from the drawer. Unable to decide what he wanted most, he ordered the meal for two. He could have what he didn't eat tonight for breakfast. Order placed, he headed for the shower. The doorbell rang as he towelled himself. That was quick, or was it? He asked himself as he wrapped the towel around his waist and headed downstairs. When he was alone at night, he lost track of time. Perhaps it had been a long shower. Grabbing a fiver for a tip from his wallet, he opened the door.

"At last. I thought...Oh. I wasn't expecting you. Did you call?"

Maxine Selby looked him up and down. It was subtle, but he noticed.

"I didn't. I was passing and saw the light on. May I come in?"

"Yes. Of course." Meredith grabbed the top of the towel. "I'll get some clothes on."

When he returned, Maxine was standing in the kitchen.

"Apologies. I should have called."

"It's no problem. Have a seat." Meredith pulled open a drawer. "I can't let you take these."

"I won't need to. Do you mind if I read them and ask questions?"

"Not if you'll also answer some. Do you want a drink? Tea, coffee, wine?"

"A glass of water will be fine. I'm driving."

Meredith busied himself fetching the water and pouring himself a glass of wine. The woman made him feel nervous. He glanced across as she shifted Patsy's words around on the table.

"Are you putting them in some sort of order? They all say much the same thing." He walked to stand behind her and scanned them quickly.

"But not exactly." She swapped the second and third around. "I think that's it. Two moments, let me read them."

Meredith went and collected his wine, and not wanting to reread them, leaned against the sink watching her. A pad was pulled from her bag, and she filled a page with neat notes quicker than he'd ever seen anyone write. She read through her notes, and then lifting the sheets made a neat pile in the centre of the table.

She looked at Meredith. "You can put them away now. Are you ready to talk about them?"

Meredith nodded. He placed his wine on the table, and returned the letters to the tea towel drawer.

"How many times have you read them?"

"The final one three, the others once. I'm not a masochist."

"Yet you didn't get rid of them, I—"

"Don't say you find that interesting. It's irritating because it's only interesting for you. I know you're trying to get in when you say that." Meredith tapped the side of his head before sitting opposite her.

Maxine grinned. "Not true. Apologies if that's what you thought. What I was going to say is when she wrote these, Patsy wasn't sure why she was leaving, and the various versions are her explaining it to herself, not you.

She realised that, I think, and settled on the last version because that one explained it to you. So, let's start there."

"Fire away." Meredith pinched the bridge of his nose, and although he knew the answer, wondered why he'd agreed to this.

"Why do you think Patsy would think you'd feel guilty about not making her better?" Maxine asked.

"Because she knows I love her, and I was trying?" Meredith shrugged, and Maxine glanced at her notes.

"I quote: 'And God forbid the guilt'. Why was that more important than making you feel pain and hurting you? I think I understand but I'd like to know from your perspective."

"Ah, that's different, and not related to the question, and I doubt you do. Go on, give it your best shot," Meredith said, and laughed at Maxine's expression. He leaned forward a little. "Your eyebrows do a lot of talking, and whilst you are very good at asking questions, you don't enjoy being challenged."

"Oh, but I do. And you, Meredith, would be a challenge for anyone. All my patients are a challenge. In different ways. My eyebrows, aye? I'll have to learn how to keep them under control. They were telling you I didn't think that was wise. What I think isn't important to you. Not at this stage. What did you mean by a different question? This isn't trying to catch you out, it's because I don't understand how you are processing what I'm saying."

Meredith leaned back in his chair and sipped his wine. "I process words efficiently. The master of hearing the unsaid, or so I'm told. You asked why Patsy would think I felt guilty, and my answer was sincere. However, that's not what she meant when you quoted what she wrote. That guilt wouldn't be because she'd made me feel it, it would be because I'd have put it there, and she was telling me she couldn't know what I'd done, and she would if she stayed."

Maxine's chest rose. "Meaning you'd have cheated on her."

"Yes. You can hear the unsaid."

"Was she right to think that?"

"No. Yes. Possibly. Honestly? No, I can't see it but I don't have a great track record. Which I'm not prepared to discuss because this is about Patsy, not me. So no but I couldn't swear to it. And that makes me feel like I already have." Meredith held his hand up. "Do not analyse that, get back to Patsy."

"Who were you expecting when I arrived? It was someone. Someone you didn't mind opening the door to almost naked."

"Oh, you think I was...that, lady, is what's called saved by the bell. And now you will see for yourself. Although it might make me feel guilty, so you're welcome to join me, providing those eyebrows behave."

Meredith went to the door and collected his curry. Maxine watched as he unloaded the cartons onto the table.

"This might make you feel guilty because you've purchased enough for four, I take it?" she asked, with a smile.

"Are people with your qualifications allowed to exaggerate? This is the standard meal for two. Shall I get one plate or two? That wasn't a catch question. Your eyebrows are at it again."

"I wondered whether it would be appropriate but I don't think you care. So yes, Meredith, I'll join you for dinner."

Meredith put two plates into the microwave to heat them and went to the cutlery drawer. A voice called from the hall and his head fell on his chest.

As he put his finger to his lips and dashed forward, the door opened, and Peggy walked in.

"Come here and give me a hug. At least you're sober and eating, I was...For God's sake, Merriwinkle, she's only been gone two minutes." Peggy pointed at Maxine before jerking her thumb towards the hall. "You. Out! I don't know what you were expecting, but it'll end in tears, probably yours." Then she turned, and slapped Meredith, hard, across the face. "I told you what I'd do if you ever did this. You swine. What will I say to Patsy? Jesus! You're making me want to swear. Did you not think of the twins?"

Meredith burst out laughing while rubbing his cheek. He pointed at Maxine who had got to her feet. "Sit. Peggy, this is Maxine Selby, Patsy's counsellor. Maxine, this is Peggy Green, self-appointed busybody, and much-loved member of our family, despite not being related. Peggy, would you like to join us? We're trying to work out how to make Patsy better and come home. You think you know everything, so perhaps you can help.

I know what you thought, and I'm ashamed of you. But whatever your answer, what would the twins have to do with it?" He glanced at Maxine. "The twins are my grandchildren. They're not even a year old yet."

Peggy took a seat, and Meredith put another plate in. "Lost for words, Peggy? I should have this recorded."

"Okay, clever man, you want both barrels? If it came to a contest between you and Patsy, Patsy would win. She'd be the one we looked after, not you. You'd get all hurt and sulk and stop seeing us because it wasn't fair."

Meredith juggled the plates to the table. He'd left them too long and they were burning his fingers. "Not true because I never sulk. I love the twins too much to stop seeing them, whatever the provocation, and you would never abandon me." Meredith's chin quivered. "She's gone, Peg."

Peggy jumped back to her feet and wrapped her arms around him while he composed himself. "That's better. That's what I expected." Peggy glanced at Maxine, who smiled at her. "I'm sorry. When Merriwinkle pulls himself together, we'll have a chat."

When Meredith showed them out, it was almost eleven. Maxine was driving Peggy home because she'd taken a taxi to Meredith's, as she didn't like driving in the dark, and between them Peggy and Meredith had emptied two bottles of wine.

As Maxine started the engine, Peggy placed her hand on Maxine's arm.

"I think you'll need to stick around. I don't think she intends coming back. How do I tell him that? How will he cope?"

Chapter Eighteen

The next morning Meredith drove to the gym and wished he'd dreamt the conversation the night before. Knowing full well he hadn't, and how much it would have mortified Patsy, the three of them discussing their love life because he hadn't been too chuffed himself, and he was there. A smile crept to his lips. He knew full well it was Peggy's way of putting a shot across Maxine's bow. Maxine was attractive and unattached, as Peggy had found out within minutes of sitting down. It was just as well Meredith wasn't interested because Peggy would certainly have put a dampener on it. Despite all that, he was glad Patsy had phoned Peggy and told her. Now he wouldn't have to tell the family, so he could see them tonight.

Now, all he had to do was survive his first session with Jared and tell everyone at work. If he didn't they'd find out another way. And he didn't want the whispering and the conversations which ended abruptly when he entered a room to be any worse than necessary. As it was Friday, they'd all be there.

Jared was chatting to the receptionist when he arrived.

"Good morning, Mr Meredith," Jared greeted him. "Hang your suit up, I'll meet you in there. Did she call?"

Meredith presented his membership to the scanner and walked through the now working turnstile.

"She did. We had a curry."

Jared followed him into the changing room. "*And?*" he asked, wobbling his head from side to side.

"And there's a reason you don't know from personal experience. You'd never cope with her." Meredith winked and held his hand towards the gym. "Shall we?"

"Yep. You're not going to tell me, are you?" Jared pulled the door open.

"A gentleman never tells. But don't mind me, fill your boots, if you think you're up to it."

"Is that a challenge?"

"Nope. I'm amusing myself. Where do you want me?"

"What is it you're hoping to achieve? You didn't fill that bit in on the form."

"Pain. There wasn't a box for pain."

Jared looked at him for a moment. "That bad? We'd better warm up first. I'll give you pain but not any lasting damage."

"Good man."

Two hours later, Meredith looked up as the door to the office opened. Seaton called a greeting.

"Morning, Guv. I've bought doughnuts. How's Patsy?"

Meredith had considered telling them individually, it would be easy to speak to Seaton. He'd been through this with Meredith before. But the questions, the bloody questions.

"Give me five minutes, let me just get this done." Meredith clicked his mouse several times and stared at his screen intently. It worked, and Seaton went in search of coffee.

Fifteen minutes later, everyone had arrived except Trump. Meredith glanced at the clock and decided doing it twice wouldn't be too bad. Trump knew when to shut up. He got to his feet and called for attention.

"Listen carefully, I'm going to tell you this and then we're going to get on with some work. This case is irritating enough without adding to my irritation, but this needs saying so you lot will stop asking."

Seaton had been organising the papers on his desk, and his head jerked up to look at Meredith. He tutted and ran his hands over his face. He was too old to be dragging Meredith out of pubs. Kent glanced at him and looked back at Meredith, wondering what was coming.

"Yes, Seaton, you're right. Patsy has left."

"What do you mean left? You or the job?" George asked, folding his arms across his chest.

Meredith ignored the gasp from Daisy. "Me. Perhaps both. Time will tell. Now, just let—"

"Well, if she's left you she won't be coming back here. How could she?" Daisy asked.

"Will you lot bloody shut up and let me finish?" Meredith held up a hand, and when no one commented, he nodded. "Thank you. Patsy hasn't been doing too well. There have been ups and downs, and she's decided that the only way to get herself sorted is to leave me. I understand that. I accept that."

He held up a finger when George opened his mouth. "I want her back. I hope she comes back, even if only to work. But at the moment, she's saying no, and I accept that because above all else I want her to get better. In anticipation of any questions which I won't be taking: No, I don't know where she is. No, I didn't try to stop her because I didn't know she was going. Yes, plenty of people have heard from her. She calls me every few days, she's spoken to Peggy, and she's still speaking to her counsellor." Meredith passed a flat hand through the air. "That's it. Now, back to work. They're doing an item on the local news tonight. Hopefully, someone will pick up the phone but in the meantime can we please get on with...Oh dear God. Loopy, you look well."

"I feel it. I'm only here for a day to see how I cope. You know, make sure I don't wipe the system." Linda laughed and took off her coat. "How's Patsy doing? She's still not called me. Do you think I...what? Why's everyone looking at me? Is it this? I wore your dress." Linda held out the skirt of her pinstriped dress and did a twirl.

No one spoke, and Meredith stepped forward. He put his arm around her shoulder.

"You look fabulous. Let me show you the lounge. We have a lounge here, did you know? Trump, you'd better come as well."

An hour later, everyone was settled at their desks. Linda had insisted she was well enough to stay because she'd only make up what Patsy was doing if she stayed home alone, and made Meredith promise to get Patsy to call her next time she phoned. Meredith didn't have the heart to tell her he didn't actually get to speak to Patsy, so agreed he would.

Linda distributed the baking she'd brought with her and looked at Meredith. "Let's get on with it, Skipper. I'm not having you blaming me for things going off schedule."

Meredith winked at her. "Thank you. Now we have the dynamic duo back together, we're going back to square one. Not with the knocking on doors but running through who said what. By the end of the day, I want those two to know as much as we do. Then they can run back through it and find out what we missed while we get on with it. So, Daisy, show her what you've got so far, explain why we've changed tack several times, and the rest of you get your notes up to date. In detail. Linda's back and she won't accept abridged versions. Get on with it."

Meredith went back to his desk and breathed a sigh of relief. He knew they'd all have something to say but it was done. Everyone who mattered knew. As that thought entered his mind, he closed his eyes and hoped she'd been in touch with her father. That was her job, not his, and as she'd spoken to Peggy he'd assume she had. He needed a cigarette, and the team needed to gossip. Picking up his cigarettes, he headed for the carpark. Pulling out his phone, he called Amanda, his daughter.

"Dad, how are you? I've wanted to phone you a million times, but Frankie and Peggy said I had to give you space. Have you had enough space because I have a hug with your name on it."

"That would be most welcome. Are you in now? I don't want a fuss, I don't want to be fed, but I can spare an hour for a hug and some baby dribble." Meredith smiled at the thought.

"I'm at work. I'll get home about three," Amanda replied.

"Work? Why are you at work?"

"Dad, you knew I was going back. It's only part-time. In case you hadn't heard, there's a bit of a crisis in the NHS at the moment. I'm doing my bit. How embarrassing was it having Peggy slap you across the face in front of that woman?"

"It wasn't. It was good that there was a witness to see what I have to put up with."

"Ha! I don't believe you. So, are you coming to dinner?"

"I doubt it. I'm up to my eyes here, so I'll pop round in the morning. Is that okay or are you working?"

"I'll be home. Don't forget or we'll turn up on your doorstep."

"I won't." Meredith couldn't face the thought of polite conversation around the dinner table, or worse, pointed conversation. Add to that, the twins would be in bed. Stubbing out his cigarette, he headed back to the office, wondering if he'd go home to a message from Patsy.

Chapter Nineteen

Brandon Farm

Cissy folded the tea towel and hung it on the handle of the oven. "Thank goodness for that. Is it just me, Jasmine, or did that seem like the longest day?"

"No, it was a bugger. But it's done now. Put your feet up, Cissy. Would you like a Baileys?" Susan patted the sofa next to her. "Sit here. I'm going up in a minute, there's rugby on tonight and I'm not sitting through that. I've found a book to read. I don't know where Mark has got to, he better not have used up all the hot water."

"No drink for me. Tempting though it is. What's on now? Anything worth watching?"

Susan stood and passed the remote. "No idea. Find something before he comes down. You might get half an hour in."

Cissy took the remote and began flipping through the channels. "Oh, the news. Let's see what today's dose of despondency has to offer."

"Rather you than me. I'll say goodnight. Oh, here he is. I hope there's some hot water left."

"There is. Mother, there's rugby on. Don't get too comfortable."

Cissy patted the seat vacated by Susan. "Jasmine warned me. Come and watch a bit of news with me, then I'll make you a sandwich for your supper before I go up. But I need to keep the weight off these feet for a few minutes."

The national news ended, and the local news came on. Cissy's eyes had closed but they opened wide as the words penetrated. Mark leaned forward, elbows on knees, and looked at the faces of the two women he'd buried.

"...brutally murdered. So if you recognise either of these women, or have any information at all, please contact the police on the following number."

As the presenter read out the number on the screen below the photographs, Susan skipped into the room in her dressing gown.

"It was bloody freezing. I forgot my...Oh, bloody hell, they're serious then. I wonder why they're looking for them after all this time. Did they say why? Why did you turn it off?"

Cissy handed the remote to Mark and lifted the book from the arm of the chair. "Hit the wrong button. Come on, I need my bed." The hand holding the book was shaking as she thrust it towards Susan.

"You are tired, you're shaking. Come on. So, why are they looking for them? What was that about?"

"I don't know. I'd nodded off. You go first."

In his bedroom, Charlie Brandon sat staring at the television. He couldn't make sense of what he'd seen. Charlie rarely watched the news but was glad he had tonight. If they'd found the body, bringing in this new girl had worked because there was no one hammering on the door. But who was the other girl? The other body? Grabbing his stick, he lifted it into position to bang on the floor and summon Cissy but changed his mind. This needed careful consideration. Pressing the remote, he dropped it onto the table as the room went dark.

Staring at the ceiling, Charlie Brandon wished, as he did several times a day, that he could get out of this bloody bed. He'd confront them then, but he couldn't, so he had to play his cards carefully. Smiling, he closed his eyes. He might be stuck in a bed but there were still games he could play. What he needed to know was how much the girl knew. If he called it wrong, the shit could hit the fan.

The next morning, Cissy was up first. It was usually Mark but the tossing and turning was making her nerves bad. Better to be busy. She was laying things out ready for breakfast when Mark appeared.

"You're up early."

Cissy screamed, and the mug in her hand hit the tiled floor and shattered. "Bloody hell. You always did creep about, big as you are. Get the brush. My nerves are shattered."

"Why?" Mark lifted the broom from the cupboard and passed it to her.

"What do you mean, why? Think. Mind you, if you had used your brain then we wouldn't be in this mess now." Cissy was repeatedly tapping the side of her head. "If Jasmine had been in the room and heard what happened to poor Jasmine, or whatever her...Louise, that would be it. If she'd heard, what then? What would have happened then? Dear God, Mark. We should make plans. I reckon we're on a countdown to disaster. I don't know how they'll find out, but they will. What will happen to Thomas then?"

"Why would something happen to Thomas?" Susan asked.

Cissy screamed again. "Will you two stop bloody creeping about! Stamp your feet, whistle, anything but bloody creep. My heart won't take much more."

Susan grinned at Mark. "I've told you about creeping up on people. It must be catching. Cissy, you look knackered. I slept like a log. Two pages and I was out for the count. Go back to bed. I'll take care of things here."

"I'm okay. My back hurts if I lie down for too long, and you don't want me with a bad back." Cissy rubbed her back for good measure.

"If you're sure. I'll tell you what, I'll take Thomas down to the supermarket and you stick to light pottering. You do too much. Tell her, Mark."

"I am not a bloody invalid just because you two creep around scaring me. I'll go to the supermarket. You can see to the washing and keep Thomas occupied. Mark's got a lot on today."

"No, I haven't. No more than usual. He can come with me, you know he likes it."

Cissy rolled her eyes. "Fine. Everyone bloody ignore me. I'm just a stupid old woman trying to keep everyone safe and happy. Do what you bloody well please, but start by clearing up this mess because it was your fault." She threw the broom at Mark and stomped upstairs.

"Is there something more bothering her, do you think?" Susan asked, taking the broom from Mark.

Mark shrugged. "She said she was okay. Don't make a fuss about it. She'll get angry. Mum doesn't like a fuss."

"Yes but if she is ill or something, she'll need to see the doctor."

In one stride, Mark was standing before Susan. He gripped her upper arms, his fingers digging into the soft flesh. "Leave it. Just bloody leave it. Nothing good comes of poking your nose in. Do you hear me?"

"Mark, you're hurting me. Mark!" Susan tried to jerk her shoulders free, but his grip intensified.

"I asked you a question. Do you understand?" Mark spoke through gritted teeth.

Susan nodded, wondering what had sent the pair of them into a tizzy. Mark hadn't hurt her since the first slap.

"Say it. Say it and promise you'll just get on and leave Mum alone. Come out with me and Thomas."

"I understand, and I promise. And I might come and help you two, but I need to make sure everything here is sorted first, or Cissy will have to do it when she gets back. I'll leave it, Mark, but I'm telling you there's something wrong. Now, please, let me go."

"Good girl."

Mark released his grip and pulled her to him. Tilting her chin, he kissed her. Susan returned his kiss, she could now switch it on and off as easily as he could, and she wondered what that said about her. And for the first time in a while, she hoped Cissy was right and the old man was going to die soon because she had to assume it was him that was upsetting the applecart. If it wasn't, then she needed to get out of here before she was as mad as the rest of them.

Chapter Twenty

Meredith combed his hair, looked at his reflection, and nodded. Not bad. He'd never been in bad shape, not really, but now he almost had a six-pack if he held his breath, tensed himself and turned in the right direction. Jared was most impressed. Not that he wanted it, it was just the result of the exercise, a chain reaction in his body. What would Patsy think of that? Would she expect him to maintain it when she got home? Would he bother?

He slung the comb into the sink and stormed downstairs. Patsy wasn't coming home; he was only kidding himself. Other than Peggy, no one even mentioned her name in his presence. It had been seventy-nine days. Seventy-nine days of pain, confusion and frustration since she'd gone. Frustration in all aspects of the word. He'd watched the woman in front of him on the cross-trainer a little too closely this morning. She wasn't even his type, and he'd asked himself if that mattered. Then nearly killed himself trying to work off that train of thought. Whatever Patsy thought of him, he wouldn't give her the satisfaction.

Lifting the phone from the charger, Meredith lay out on the sofa with it on his newly discovered muscles and stared at the ceiling. She wasn't coming home. He'd never get the opportunity to tell her he'd waited. But he wouldn't give in. Not yet. The twins, the gym and work were keeping his mind occupied, almost, although he doubted they'd ever solve this case. The television appeal hadn't brought a single response. On Monday, they'd be starting on the last grid, and then it was a brick wall.

His mind wandered back to Patsy. Would she call today? It had been over a week.

Patsy's calls were becoming less frequent. The first couple of days had been twice a day, then once a day, and in her call at the end of the first week, she said she'd call in a couple of days. Then it was next week, and now she never said when. He'd hurry into the house praying the red light would be flashing on the answer machine because she had never called his mobile again after that day he answered while speaking to Cissy Brandon. Now Patsy called the house when she knew he would be unlikely to pick up.

Meredith thought back to that day. What had she said? Had she said anything worth hearing? He closed his eyes, trying to picture the scene. She had, he thought. That day kept coming back to him but he couldn't remember what she'd said.

The phone rang. Meredith's arms flew into the air in shock, and he snatched it up.

"Patsy?"

"Afraid not, John, it's Julia. I take it Patsy isn't around, will she be back this evening?"

Meredith hadn't told his sisters. Mainly because he hoped he'd never have to. They only saw Julia a few times a year, and Ann, who now lived in Canada, a few times a decade. He closed his eyes, wishing he had his cigarettes handy. There was no need to tell her now. He'd do it next time.

"No, afraid not. You didn't want to speak to me, then? I'll try not to feel wounded." Meredith swung his legs off the couch and went in search of a cigarette.

"Yes, I wanted to speak to you. That's why I tried the mobile you never answer. Anyway, it's good in a way because I wanted to run it past you first." Julia sounded hesitant.

Meredith drew in a lungful of smoke and stepped out into the garden. It was fresh but bearable. He stared at the daffodils in bloom, and the tulips yet to open, which Patsy had planted. She loved seeing them reappear each year.

"John, are you still there?" Julia asked.

"I am. Just stepped out into the garden. Run what past me first?"

"Emily is moving back to Bristol that's why I'm meeting her. She's got a job, and she thinks a flat, but she doesn't know many people anymore. She—"

"My Emily?"

"No John, not your Emily. You have your Patsy. Dear God."

"Julia, would you just spit it out? Who is Emily, and what did you need to run past me? You're making no sense, which isn't like you. You're the sensible one, as you like to tell people." Meredith took another drag on his cigarette.

"You're smoking again." Julia huffed out a sigh. "Emily Andrews, as was. Emily Matthews now, although not sure she'll keep his name."

"So, my Emily. Is she getting a divorce? What did you need to run past me?"

"Well, I didn't, not really. Emily will soon make friends, she's that type of woman, but I thought it might be nice if she had someone to have dinner or drinks with while she settles in. I'll come to Bristol as much as I can but I thought of Patsy. I was going to call her and invite her out with us tonight, and if they got on well, Emily would have someone close by. Then I wondered what you'd think of that because you two always cared for each other. But talking to you now, I realise that was stupid. It was years ago. We were kids. Mum was even alive. Emily was good with Mum, do you remember? Anyway, Patsy's not around, and you're on your own. Would you like to come? I'm sure Emily would love to see you. Or have you got a boozy night with the boys planned as Patsy is away?"

Meredith took another drag and blew the smoke towards the daffodils. Could he be bothered to bat away unwanted questions that he didn't want to answer? Would there be any? He doubted it. Those two would just chat away like he wasn't there. That had been what usually happened back in the day. Julia thought Patsy was away. He hadn't been out for months, not since before the attack. Meredith counted on his fingers. That had been over six months ago.

"Sod it. Why not? Just remember I'm there occasionally, so I don't get too put out," Meredith replied.

"Can't promise that, John, but I'll try. Do you want me to pick you up? It will be early. I have to drive home because...Oh, I can tell you when I see you. Right, get off the phone. I've got things to do before I head your way."

"You didn't say what time you'd be picking me up, or where we're going so I know what to wear. I don't want to spend hours tying my dickie bow if I could have worn jeans."

Meredith knew Julia was smiling. She'd always teased him about being more worried about clothes than her and Ann put together.

"I'm meeting her in the Italian on Park Street at six, and as we're too old to go dancing, and no one dresses up these days anyway, I'm sure jeans will be perfect. You're the only man I've ever met who asks what he should wear. I love you, big brother, but you are weird. Do you know that?"

"I do. Love you too."

Meredith stubbed his cigarette out and returned to the sofa. Something had occurred to him before the phone rang, and thoughts of Patsy had banished it back into the recesses. Perhaps lying on the sofa would bring it back.

He tried to think about the case but he couldn't find anything to latch his mind onto. They were getting nowhere slowly, and he wondered if he'd eventually have to admit defeat. That brought his thoughts back to Patsy. Would he admit defeat over her? He didn't know; he hoped not. How long would be too long? Closing his eyes, he wondered if he should tell Julia. Probably but not tonight.

Tonight, he would try to enjoy himself. He smiled at the thought of Emily. Or the Emily he'd known. He should have married her, young as they were. They'd still be together, probably broke with half a dozen kids and even more grandchildren. His first love, his first broken heart. He'd had a few since then. It would have avoided all that mess, all that sorrow. But if he'd done that, he wouldn't have Amanda, and he wouldn't have had Patsy.

Patsy!

And there he was, back to Patsy again. Five thirty couldn't come quickly enough. He needed a distraction.

Lighting a cigarette, Meredith wondered what Emily was like now, whether she'd been happy. Obviously not at the moment, not if she was divorcing her husband but he hoped she had. Her childhood had been almost as bad as his own. Had the years been kind to her? Or would he be meeting a chubby, middle-aged woman? It didn't matter, it would still be

Emily. No one could change the essence of a person. And Emily was or had been, he eventually conceded, essentially perfect, even without her good looks. He was doing okay, especially now he was developing a six-pack, and Julia didn't look old enough to have her second grandchild on the way. But that was the Meredith gene. At least his father had been good for something.

At five o'clock, he went up to get ready. He applied a liberal dose of deodorant and patted his favourite aftershave on his freshly shaved cheeks. Pulling on a clean pair of jeans, he found they now sat low on his hips. Belt or no belt? He'd choose a shirt first. Collared shirt or T-shirt? He tried on four, and eventually settled on a lightweight, wool sweater that buttoned to a collar. Now he needed a belt.

"Bloody hell. I'm regressing. That's Julia's fault," he muttered as he laced his shoes.

He went downstairs and stood in the bay window looking out for Julia and thinking about Patsy.

"What are you doing now, Patsy? You should be here."

• • • • • • • • • • •

Patsy was standing at the pickup point at Auckland International Airport. She pulled up the collar of her coat. It was chilly out here.

Steve would be another fifteen minutes, he'd got stuck in traffic. She fingered the phone in her pocket, wondering if she should call Meredith. It was Saturday teatime in England. He might be there. Patsy wrinkled her nose. Meredith would be okay. She'd leave it until she settled in and started her job. Meredith needed to move on. He'd get there. She had to stop worrying about him, and herself. There was no going back.

The sound of the horn made her jump, and she waved as Steve jumped out of the car. It had been too long. He ran and pulled her into a hug.

"I can't believe you're here, it's been so long. Martha can't wait. She's been complaining about getting someone to help her out for ages. How was the flight?" he asked, releasing her and grabbing her suitcase.

"Okay, I slept most of it. Still exhausted, though."

"I'm not surprised. It's a bugger. You are sure about this, aren't you? What I'm trying to say is, come and at least have a holiday and see how you feel. Your options are open."

"I'm more sure than I was when I first phoned. If you're happy, I'm happy."

"Does Meredith know?" Steve asked.

"No." Patsy looked down at her feet.

"Is it Meredith's?"

"No." Patsy shook her head and blinked rapidly. "No, not Meredith's. It's mine. This baby is mine. That's why I'm here. Let's get going before you make me cry. This is the first day of my new life."

"Fair enough. You can tell me when you're ready. Have you told Dad? He won't be happy."

"No. I know. I'll call him in a few days when I'm settled." Patsy buckled the seatbelt. "Now let's go, I haven't seen Martha for five years, and I haven't even met Joseph."

"You're looking rather handsome. You look very distinguished in a raincoat. Ooh, and you're going grey."

Meredith rubbed his temples before leaning across and kissing his sister. "You look rather lovely yourself, if a little windswept."

"At least it didn't rain on us. The deal's done, and Emily can move in whenever she's ready. It really is a lovely flat. Sort of overlooking the Downs, but really just a bit of green and some trees. We parked miles away. It was a bit breezy on the walk back. Don't worry, I'll put a brush through it before we get out of the car."

"Where is she?"

"I dropped her at her hotel so she could check in and dump her suitcase. I offered to go back and get her but she says she'll walk, which to be fair is probably the safest option because I'd probably have to park further away than the hotel. Bristol is a nightmare for parking."

"Tell me why you aren't staying the night. You could have stayed at mine. Or perhaps shared with Emily and giggled all night like you used to."

"Ah, John, it was such fun, wasn't it? If it wasn't for Mum, I'd go back to those days tomorrow. Ooh, before I forget, Ann sends her love. She's coming over this summer, said she'd be after a bed for a couple of weeks. I told her we could do it between us and she'd have the best of both worlds. And what do you think about going away for a few days, just the three of us. We'd have such a laugh."

The ten-minute journey was filled with similar chatter. No mention of work, and no mention of Patsy. Meredith began to relax.

When they arrived at the restaurant and were waiting to be seated, Meredith took Julia's coat and went to hang it up with his. When he returned, she squeezed his bicep.

"Are you having a mid-life crisis? Have you been working out? You look good, by the way, but what have you done with my brother? The one who avoided exercise, remember him?" Julia asked.

"I do. I miss him most mornings. But it keeps me out of trouble. And, for the record, I've decided to give middle age a miss. I'll go straight to doddery pensioner when I think it's appropriate," Meredith replied.

"About eighty-nine then." Julia nudged him. "I can get you one of those buggy things, and make sure it's got a mirror so you can check your hair."

"Why? What's wrong with my hair?" Meredith pretended to check his reflection in the window. "Bloody hell!"

Julia stepped closer. "Ah, here she is. Go on then, open the door."

Meredith nodded and allowed the door to close behind him. Stepping into the street, he smiled at Emily. Emily stopped walking and grinned before she looked away. Spotting Julia, she shook her fist.

"Is that all the greeting I get after all these years?" Meredith asked.

Emily lifted a hand and gave a weak wave. "Julia never told me it was you. She said it was an old friend. You don't really fall into that category. She said I'd be pleased, though, and she was right. Oh my god, Meredith!"

Without warning, Emily launched herself at Meredith. He caught her and hugged her tight. Kissing her temple as they rocked from side to side. Emily laughed when Julia tapped on the window. Meredith blinked rapidly and cleared his throat.

"She's hungry. She gets angry when she's hungry. Come on." Meredith grabbed her hand and led her towards the door.

"I think you'll find that was you."

"You remember then," Meredith joked, as they joined Julia.

"Everything," Emily said, before turning her attention to Julia. "That was unfair. You could have said."

"I thought a surprise would be nice. It was, wasn't it? That was reminiscent of his twenty-first. Do you remember, he made you dance with...them. Poor old Tony. I told you about Tony, didn't I?"

"Yes. I've just told Meredith I remember everything. Oh, I think our table's ready."

They spent the next two hours chatting much as they had all those years ago around the Merediths' kitchen table, Meredith finishing what the girls couldn't eat. Meredith was unnerved. It was like the years had been wiped away. Emily was back. What the hell was he supposed to do with this new situation? She still looked like Emily. A few lines at the corners of her eyes, a little more padding on the jawline, a little curvier everywhere else. But there she was, essentially Emily. He shook the thought away as Emily got to her feet.

"Excuse me. I shall return."

Meredith busied himself topping up their glasses so he wouldn't be tempted to watch her. He held the bottle towards Julia. "Are you sure? Just a little one?"

"No. I'm fine. Are you?"

"Dandy. Why? Did I say something inappropriate or rude?" Meredith asked.

"No, Meredith, you laughed in all the right places but you aren't fully in the room. Emily won't have noticed but I have. I also noticed you got emotional when you greeted her. I thought I was going to have to escort you home to save you from yourselves but I can see that's unnecessary." Julia winked at him to show she was almost joking. "What's the matter?"

Meredith grabbed her hand and squeezed it. "Just work, it's hard to switch off. Tough case. You know what I'm like. I promise to pay more attention."

Julia checked the time. "It's fine. She wouldn't have noticed. Get the waiter. If I can't drink, I am going to have a pudding."

The next hour also flew by with Meredith making sure he stopped thinking about everything other than the conversation.

"It's weird, isn't it," observed Julia, "we all had shit childhoods, one way or another, and yet here we sit reminiscing and giggling like we had the time of our lives, when in reality we were propping up the adults who should have been looking after us. Do you remember the night your dad took an overdose, and our mum insisted on swapping bedrooms so you could stay with us, then got so blind drunk she tried to get in bed with us? Wasn't sure who screamed the loudest, you or Mum. Do you remember?"

Meredith looked at Emily, and his eyes twinkled. "We do." He looked away as his arousal made itself known.

Julia looked from one to the other. "You didn't." She wagged her finger at them. "In our house, with us all there trying to ignore Mum? Why don't I know this? Meredith, Emily was vulnerable."

"I think you'll find that it was the other way around. She took advantage of me." Meredith smiled at Emily. "Am I lying?"

"Nope. It was all down to me in the beginning. Maybe. But yes, I did force myself on you." Emily giggled and covered her face with her hands. "Don't look at me, I'm blushing."

"And so you should be." Julia tutted. "You've never told me that, either of you. Not that I would have believed Meredith's version. I still don't believe it. Oh blimey, I wish I was staying the night now. What other secrets would be unearthed I wonder. But I must go or I might finish that bottle for you."

Meredith collected her coat while she said goodbye to Emily. "I'll walk you to your car."

"Ever the protector, my lovely brother. But it's only yards away." She looked at Emily. "He never changes."

"Even so." Meredith smiled at Emily. "I'll be back."

Julia linked her arm in Meredith's. "Walk her back to her hotel, Meredith. She'll refuse but ignore her."

"I will."

When Meredith returned, Emily had reapplied her lipstick. Meredith sat down opposite her and raised his glass.

"Hello you. That was a lovely hurtle through, what? Better times? I'm not sure but it was certainly fun."

"It was. It was also excruciatingly painful. How many times did you think what if?"

"Tonight, or generally?" Meredith asked.

"Oh, Meredith, every bloody day. I'll never admit it, but I never should have left, and after I did I should have come back. But what can you do? I seem to be the master at making poor decisions."

"No, that would be me."

"I don't think so. How many times have you made the same mistake over and over?" Emily challenged.

"I could list them for you, and I promise my list is definitely longer than yours, but I'm not going to because then I'd become maudlin, and I was having a good time. Correction, am having a good time."

"Me too. Let's drink to that." Emily raised her glass.

"I think I've had enough. Anymore and I might lose control of what few faculties I have left. Here, you carry on. I'm happy to watch until you're ready to go."

"Ah, that could be a long night. Won't your wife be waiting on the doorstep with a rolling pin?"

"Nope." Meredith shook his head and watched the surprise register in her eyes.

"Hang on, will your wife be waiting in front of the telly?"

"Nope."

"No wife waiting? And by that, I mean waiting anywhere."

"Nope."

"I won't ask why but I do have a question."

"Fire away."

"Would you walk me back to my hotel?"

"With pleasure. I've paid the bill. I'll get our coats."

They walked down the hill to the hotel in silence. No hand holding, just the odd bump of elbow or shoulder.

"Posh hotel," Meredith said, as he allowed her to enter first. He nearly admitted he'd almost spent the whole of his wedding night there. But he kept that information to himself.

"Yes. One off treat, what with today being the first day of the rest of etcetera."

"Good enough reason."

"I thought so."

They went straight to Emily's room. Once in she switched off the lights.

"Have you become shy?" Meredith asked, his heart beating so fast he wasn't sure he'd survive.

"Yes and no. I need sex, Meredith, sympathy sex, if you like, and you've always helped a damsel in distress. And I'd like it tonight. With you. But let's get on with it before anything sensible happens to stop it. And, because it will be like the first time. Creeping into your bedroom in the dark. God, I still remember your every move. Strip off and get in bed. Pretend we're back in your bedroom."

"I don't want to burst any bubbles but I don't think a repeat performance is on the cards. I'm getting old." Meredith laughed, but still pulled off his jumper as he kicked off his shoes. "Shall I pretend to be asleep? Oh."

Emily was lying next to him, naked. She ran a hand down his chest before pressing her lips against his. "Love me, Meredith. I need you," she whispered.

Meredith forgot everything. Emily needed him. He was the old Meredith again, he was free, he had the rest of his life in front of him, and a beautiful woman wanting nothing but his attention, and he gave her it. But having thoroughly aroused the pair of them, he rolled away. "I'm sorry I can't do this."

Emily could still feel his erection. "I think you can. You just need to put this—"

Meredith grabbed her hand. "It's not—"

Emily sat up and hit the light switch. "Do not give me the 'it's not you, it's me' crap. Do not do it." Her breathing still ragged, she looked down at his naked body, and he pulled the sheet to cover himself. "Bloody hell, Meredith, that was not the time to change your mind. And judging by the tent you've made, you haven't. What's going on?"

"Do me a favour and cover up. You look even more beautiful, all angry and flushed, and I don't want to ruin us." Meredith cleared his throat. "I don't want to take what you're offering, which, by the way, would be gratefully received, and ruin us because she still might come back. And then what happens to us? Both of us. Me and Patsy, me and you? And if you stay there looking like that, I won't say no a second time, and I'll never be able to hide the guilt, not from either of you. Jesus Christ! Is there any alcohol in this room?"

Emily got out of bed and walked naked to the fridge. "Too late for brewer's droop, Meredith. But to be on the safe side, I'll only let you have one. Wine or whiskey?"

"Both, they're tiny. And put something on. Look, a fluffy robe." Meredith pointed to the robe hanging in the open wardrobe.

"I'm good." Emily tossed him the little plastic bottle and got back in bed, allowing him to cover her with the sheet. "Who goes first?" she asked.

"Me. Because if you do, I might feel sympathetic." He leaned down and kissed her forehead. "Sympathy sex? Is that a new thing?"

"I made it up. Bugger. I should have been bigger on the talking and less on the bodice ripping. Who knew? I mean, you're Meredith, even I can't blame me for getting that wrong."

"I will never not love her. Just like I will never not love you. The difference is you left and never came back. Patsy might still come back." He sighed. "I'm lost. Absolutely fucking lost. But on the bright side I haven't hit anyone, and I've not hit the bottle. Much."

Meredith poured half the bottle into his mouth and grimaced. "It's that simple. I never expected this." He lifted the sheet and peeped under it. "But I was nervous. Do you know I changed my shirt four times, convinced, absolutely convinced it would never leave my back. I was wrong, and I'm sorry. I hope we don't both regret this night. You for making the offer and me for refusing. I have a lot of regrets, I just hope this isn't one of them."

"Apology not accepted. I now have another memory to keep me going. It's all educational. This one tells me to make him talk to you first. Don't let him do that thing and then...I won't spell it out or the sheet will be off again."

"I won't ask what thing, or you'd be right. Bloody hell, Em, I've got to put some distance between us. Tell me why you're getting a divorce." Meredith swung his legs off the bed and hunted for his boxers while trying to hide his erection.

"No. It's depressing. I should have done this years ago but I was too sad and too lazy. He only hit me once, when I got back to the hotel after your twenty-first. He'd seen us on the taxi rank, so I probably deserved it, because if you'd asked I'd have left with you, but I wanted you to stay for your baby. I didn't want that on my conscience, whatever Karen had been up to."

"He hit you and you stayed?"

"Get off that tall horse, Meredith. You cheated on her and she stayed. You were married, and she knew what you were up to. Don't look all hurt, although I'm sure it does. Why have you developed morals? Tonight, of all nights! Fucking hell. Look, you're even making me swear, I don't swear! Yes, I stayed. I felt guilty. It wasn't his fault I still loved you. It was okay. I thought I'd have a couple of kids and settle for being Mrs Average. That would do, because if you can't be Mrs Special what choice have you got? But I couldn't have kids, or he couldn't. We never bothered to find out, it just didn't happen. We just bumbled along. But here's the question, do you think that's because, in my mind, I was never really with him? Don't feel sorry for me, I was as good as lying to him. Feel sorry for him, I do."

"Keep kicking. The pain helps." Meredith zipped up his jeans and went to the fridge. "Wine, beer or, yes, we have brandy."

"Wine. I don't love you, Meredith. Not anymore. That faded away a long time ago. But I loved the sex, which is why I was so brazen tonight. I knew what was coming. I'm not a loose woman. I'm almost fifty-one years old and I've only ever slept with two men. You and him. How sad is that? All those men out there and I picked you two."

"It's sad if you didn't love him. You should have stayed. Here, I mean, not with him. We'd probably have hated each other by now. But whatever happened to us, we wouldn't be sitting in a hotel room wondering why we weren't having sex."

"I don't think that's true, do you? We could never hate each other. Look, I'm going to ask you to leave now. Much as I'd like to sit up all night and discuss how fucking, oops, there I go again, miserable our lives have been. This is supposed to be day one. And you haven't ruined it. Not yet. I wasn't even expecting to see you, so, it's been a weird sort of bonus. Almost a spectacular one, I'd like to think."

Meredith nodded agreement. "I think you're right." He tied his shoelaces. "Put the robe on and give me a hug."

Emily didn't move, but held out her arms, and Meredith walked into them, resting his forehead on hers. "You might not love me but I will always love you, and I will always be there for you. If you want me to be. But not in your bed. Not until she doesn't come back." He kissed Emily's nose. "If you need someone to talk to, someone to have a rant at, or someone to take you for a drink or a pizza, miles away from anything comfortable, and everyone being fully clothed, call me."

"What if Patsy comes back?" Emily asked, rubbing her nose against his.

"I'll still be there. Patsy will like you, you'll like her, and I'll feel very awkward for a while. Or you can dump me, your best friend, all over again and I'll be sad because I like having you back in my life." Meredith ran his finger down her back, causing it to arch. She pressed her body closer to his. "But you have to be wearing clothes."

"Bloody hell, Meredith, will you just go?"

"Not willingly, not really. But yes."

Chapter Twenty-One

Brandon Farm

Susan looked at the ceiling as Charlie Brandon banged for the fifth time in the last two hours.

"Have you unplugged his telly again? If not, what's wrong with him? Is he ill?" She looked at Cissy, who was rubbing her fingers over her forehead. "I'll go."

"No, it's..."

Susan had already started up the stairs, and Cissy didn't have the energy to argue, so she slumped into the chair next to the fire.

Upstairs, Susan bustled into Charlie's room. "What is it? Why don't you let us bring you downstairs? You could just ask then instead of all this bloody banging."

Charlie laughed. It was genuine amusement that ended in a coughing fit. Susan patted his back and handed him a glass of water.

"You think I want to be with them? Not in a million years. You leave me up here."

"Then go into a nursing home. Now, what do you want? Mark's expecting me to help him with the sheep."

"Doing what?" Charlie demanded. "We don't shear until May."

Susan knew he missed the farm, and she found a smile for him. "Come on, Charlie, what do you want?"

Charlie glanced at the door. "Shut the door and I'll tell you a secret."

"Don't muck about. Look, here's the deal, you tell me what you want and I won't take that bloody stick away. You carry on and she'll unplug that telly again." Susan had her hands on her hips. It wasn't only Cissy who was tired.

"Did she tell you why she pulled it out? Because I watched the news, that's why. I hadn't realised, I know now. No mole." Charlie tapped his collar bone. "Just here."

Susan touched her collarbone. Perhaps her predecessor had a mole, but why would that matter to him? This was all his fault. Or the start of it was. She shrugged. "No, but I've got one on my back. What do you want?" Reaching across the bed, she pretended to make a grab for the stick, and was surprised when he grabbed her wrist.

"Get out while you can. You've been good to me."

"Charlie, what do you want? That's it. Let go of me, I'm off." Susan yanked her arm free, and despite her brave words, she was frightened. She needed to get out of the room and work out if he was just trying to scare her or if she needed to leave.

"Ever wondered what happened to the first two? If not, start wondering that's all I'm saying." Charlie's eyes shot to the door. "Don't tell them I told you. Now bugger off before they come looking for you."

"I have no idea what you're on about. But, yes, I'll go."

Charlie could see she was thinking about it. "Gone." He clicked his fingers. "Just like that. Don't forget."

Susan went to the bathroom and sat on the toilet. Charlie was mean and miserable. Was he trying to scare her? She didn't think so. How would he benefit? What was in it for him? Two minutes of excitement in seeing he'd scared her? Cissy had admitted what happened to the first girl, the real Jasmine. Cissy hadn't needed to do that. She could have made up some story about how Charlie ended up in that bed. But that was what worried her. Charlie hadn't made up that they had disappeared. What had been on the news that she hadn't seen? Perhaps he was on his last legs and wanting to get stuff off his chest, and Cissy had turned off the television when she'd come into the room. The next day she'd unplugged Charlie's television, so he was up there with nothing to do. That had been a week of hell with non-stop banging from Charlie.

Susan screwed her eyes shut and groaned. She had three choices: go, while she was still able to, although she'd be penniless and homeless; ignore

Charlie and pray to God he was trying to wind her up; or ask Cissy. The last one was risky because Cissy had already told her why the second woman had gone, and if Charlie wasn't lying what would happen to her then?

It hadn't been too bad living here. She was fond of Cissy, and Mark too, in a way. Thomas really was like a son to her, but she wasn't leaving penniless. She wasn't going back there. Just the thought made her feel sick. No, she'd have to try to find out some other way. She had to find out what had been said on the news. Susan wasn't very good on the computer, none of them were, but the internet was supposed to know everything. She'd offer to do the books more often so she could try to work it out, and she'd get out and about more and see what everyone had to say.

A sudden thought occurred to her. It might have been in the newspaper. There was a stack of them in the parlour. They were used for lighting the fire. Susan could look there too.

She pulled the flush. Cissy might be looking for her. As Susan unlocked the door, she told herself to act naturally and wondered if that was even possible now.

"What did he want?" Cissy asked, as Susan walked into the room.

"He'd dropped the remote, and when I gave it to him he didn't want the telly on. I told him to stop being a nuisance. We'll see." Susan hesitated, wondering what to do next, and decided to let Cissy decide. "What do you want me to do? I've got an hour before Mark will need me. Shall I do the books, or perhaps give the parlour a once over?"

"You're such a good girl. Don't worry about the invoices, there's not that many. Do the parlour. The grate could do with clearing out."

"Will do." Susan collected the little plastic tray of cleaning materials, and a bucket from the cupboard. She held it up to Cissy. "Wish me luck, I may be some time."

Susan had spoken in a deep voice, and Cissy laughed.

"I'll send out a search party if you're not out by lunchtime. Don't forget to cover that rug, or better still, move it. Only cleaned that a few weeks ago. And if our Thomas has left that Lego in there, try not to break it. He worked for hours on that."

"I know. I'll be careful."

Susan took a cursory glance around the parlour. A quick flick around with the duster would do. Then she could concentrate on the fire, or more importantly, the newspapers. In ten minutes, all surfaces had been dusted.

She knelt on the rug in front of the fire and began to scan each double page back and front, before laying the newspaper out to cover the rug. She continued to repeat the process. If Cissy came in, she'd say she was being doubly careful with the rug. She grunted as she pulled out the basket. Sweeping out the soot and embers, she emptied them into the bucket and wiped everything clean before pushing the basket back in. Scanning each page again, she then rolled up the newspaper sheets and tied them in a knot, placing them in the basket ready for the next fire.

"What are you up to?" Cissy asked from the doorway.

Susan yelped. "Bloody hell, Cissy, and you moan about us creeping about. I was just getting it ready for the next one. Do you need me?"

"You've done enough for the next ten. I was worried about you. Leave that now. I've made a fresh pot. Here, let me take the bucket."

"Thanks. I'll clear the rest of this away."

As Cissy left the room, Susan folded the paper she'd been checking. As she placed it on the pile, a headline caught her eye. It was a brief article.

Buried Remains Connected

Thames Valley Police have confirmed that remains found on Shepton Farm have been connected to those found nearby in 2018. The case has been passed to the Bristol Cold Case Review Team, who have promised an update shortly.

Susan's hand covered her mouth. Shepton Farm was Gerry's place. This was no bloody co-incidence. She needed a plan. The newspaper was months old. Had there been an update? Was that what the television appeal was about? Finishing her tasks, she carried the plastic box out and put it away.

"You took your time. What's wrong?" Cissy asked. "You don't look right."

"Headache. I'll be better once I've had a cuppa and some fresh air." Susan poured herself a cup of tea and then lifted down another mug. "I'll take misery guts one. Might stop the bloody banging." Her hand shook a little as she spooned sugar into the mug.

"Don't forget the paracetamol," Cissy commented, frowning.

Susan took a sip of her own drink and headed for the staircase.

"He won't thank you," Cissy told her as Susan opened the door.

"No. I know, but still."

Susan climbed the stairs and paused outside Charlie's door. Taking a deep breath, she went in, closing the door behind her. Charlie was asleep. Placing the mug on the table, she shook him gently.

"Charlie, wake up. Charlie!" Her whisper was harsh, and Charlie opened his eyes. He looked confused. "Charlie, I need your help."

"Ha! I wish. I'm no good to you now, girlie."

"Charlie, I'm serious. What did they say on the news? Was it about two bodies? Did they say what happened?"

"Oh. So now you believe me. Get out. Get out. Go on, go. They had their heads smashed in. One of them had had a baby. I said GET OUT."

Charlie began thrashing about, flinging his hands towards the door, before cursing as the door opened.

"What's going on in here?" Cissy asked.

"Nothing. No, nothing. Charlie was cross because I woke him up. Weren't you, Charlie?"

Charlie seemed to shrink into his pillows. "Yes. Sorry, I spilled my tea." He looked at the table and kept his gaze there.

"You haven't apologised to me since the day we were married. Jasmine, get his tray. I'll clean this up."

Susan picked up the tray on the bedside cabinet, and Cissy added the tea to it before mopping up the spillage with tissues. She then replaced the tea and looked at her husband.

"I'll be back to sort you out later." Turning, she pointed at the door. "Go on then, Jasmine, our Mark will be waiting."

Susan nodded and stepped on to the landing with the tray. As she passed her own bedroom, Cissy gave a shout and pushed Susan hard in the back. Susan flew into the bedroom, losing her footing. The tray flew into the air and crashed onto the dressing table. Susan landed on her hands and knees and, turning, saw Cissy pull the key from the lock.

"What are you doing? Why did you do that?" Susan pulled herself to her feet as the door slammed. She whimpered as the key turned in the lock. "Cissy, don't do this. Why are you doing this?"

"Don't be smart with me, Jasmine. I'm sorry to lock you up, but I need to speak to Mark. What a bloody mess, I thought this was over. I thought you were the one."

Susan ran to the door and hammered on it. "Let me go, Cissy. I won't tell anyone, I promise."

"Calm down, Jasmine. Everything will work out. Let me speak to Mark."

"No! Cissy please! Don't get Mark."

"Don't be daft, I have to tell Mark. Settle down now."

Susan heard the door at the top of the stairs close. They never closed that one. What the hell was she going to do? She ran to the window. Perhaps she wouldn't hurt herself if she jumped. She released the catch and tried to raise the sash, but it wouldn't budge, and her feeble thumps did nothing but hurt her hand. Running around the bed, she searched for the knife which had been on the tray, discarding it quickly as it was only a butter knife. She picked up the fork and sat on the bed, her back pressing into the headboard. If she could stab him in the eye, she might have a chance. Her hand shook as she waited for him to arrive.

Chapter Twenty-Two

It had been ninety-two days. No message from Patsy, no nearer to solving the case, and only a little of the final grid left to cover. Instead of going home, Meredith drove back to the office. Nothing was likely to come up now that would help solve the case. He would leave the grid to the others to finish and double check the paperwork. Much as he hated admitting defeat, there were other cases to be solved.

Meredith had taken Emily to dinner the night before. It was their third outing and it had been fun. They talked about everything except Patsy and them. Emily was enjoying her job, and the freedom her new life had given her. He smiled when he thought about her telling him of her latest adventure.

"So, I signed up. Talk about in at the deep end. Someone called Lexi had broken her leg, so I was handed a script. The cheeky devil, who reminded me a bit of Ben, said they needed some old blood, and I could have the part of old Mrs Maxwell, the nosey landlady. Old! Probably just as well it's not pantomime season, or I'd probably be the dame." Emily had giggled. "Oh, Meredith. That's it. They need old blood. You should join us. You know you like to be in the spotlight, and Ben's not around to steal your thunder."

They'd been walking back to the car, and Meredith paused for just a moment, before pushing her into a hedge.

"Take that back. Jacobs never stole my thunder. And thank you for remembering I have a great presence on the stage, but I shall have to refuse."

Emily was laughing and shaking her head. "But why? Have I got leaves in my hair?"

Meredith pulled out a twig. "Because I do a job that doesn't allow for showtime. I'd let everyone down, and good as you might be as the nosey landlady, there's no understudy who would want to step into these shoes. Get in the car and stop talking nonsense."

Then Meredith drove her home. Leaning over the handbrake for a chaste peck on the cheek, and waiting for the door of her flat to close before driving back to the empty house he was getting used to. Just like old times but without the string of women.

Linda tapped on the window, and Meredith turned to face her. He smiled. Her hair was back to normal, and her psychedelic blouse hurt his eyes. He climbed out of the car to join her.

"Where are you going? he asked. "It's not half four yet."

"Maxine. She couldn't fit me in otherwise. I think I might stop seeing her soon. Seems like a waste of money. Although I love our chats, and she does too. Are you okay, Skipper? You were miles away then."

"As I'll ever be, Loopy. I had dinner with a friend last night, she wanted me to join an Am Dram group. And—"

"You were considering it? Oh, my. DCI Meredith on the stage. But if I'm honest, I can't see it. But more importantly, she? No one would blame you, Skipper. You have fun and enjoy yourself." Linda patted his arm. "I'd better go. I might get lost even though this will be my fourth time at her place. You know what I'm like."

"Not so fast, Loopy. What do you know that I don't?"

"Nothing. See you tomorrow, b—" She stopped speaking when Meredith grabbed her hand.

"Loopy, you are a lousy liar, and I will apologise to Maxine if necessary. But we both know if I was seeing someone, which, for the record, I'm not, you would be mad at me. Unjustified as you pointed out but you would be mad, or sad, or both. And definitely not telling me to have fun and enjoy myself. So, I'll ask again, what do you know?"

Linda rested her head against his arm so she didn't have to look at him. "Nothing. Not really. I asked Maxine if she'd heard from Patsy, and she said yes. She never gives much away. So I said when they next spoke, would she please tell Patsy I was now begging her to call me. And she did this thing with her eyebrows and said she would if Patsy called. Naturally, I asked why wouldn't she call? And she just smiled and told me to stop trying to get confidential info out of her. She said she would pass on the message if she could. Well, it doesn't take a genius, does it? Patsy has probably told Maxine she thinks she's better. I hope she is, but she's not here, is she, so how can she be? I wasn't going to—"

"Okay, I get the picture. Go off to your appointment. And, Loopy, I want you in bright-eyed and bushy-tailed in the morning. You're taking me through your maze of information, and we'll try to find what we've missed, if anything, because another couple of weeks and we'll have to admit defeat for now, and get on to something we can solve."

Loopy saluted. "I'd forgive you, you know, if she was more than a friend. So would Patsy come to that. See you tomorrow, Skipper."

Meredith waited for her to drive away before getting back in his car and heading for home. He'd only been going in to see Linda, and as she wasn't there, he'd go home and wallow in his own misery for a while.

Unable to settle, Meredith considered calling Maxine to demand she told him what she knew. But not knowing how long Linda's session was, he flipped through the hundreds of channels available on television, finding nothing he wanted to watch. He thought he'd been coping well, but right now he wished he was the old stupid Meredith, the one who'd be working his way through a bottle and waiting for the barmaid to knock off. But he wouldn't do that to Patsy. An hour later, he considered calling Emily. It was that or another takeaway. But then he'd tell her Patsy seemed to be getting further and further away, and it might raise Emily's hopes.

Cursing himself for being arrogant, he snatched up his cigarettes and went to stand on the doorstep. He'd barely had the first puff when the phone rang. Taking his cigarette with him, Meredith ran into the hall, and snatched up the receiver before snapping his name.

"Hello, John. Jim Hodge here, I'm sure I'm the last person you want to hear from, but I just wanted to make sure you were okay, and I'm sorry I've not been in touch sooner. It's just—"

"I'll stop you there. It should be me apologising for not calling you. I didn't want to worry you." Meredith took a drag of his cigarette.

"Barbara, he says he didn't want to worry me." Jim Hodge returned his attention to Meredith. "You're a good man, John Meredith, and although it means nothing in the scheme of things, I'm sorry. When Steven told me, you could have knocked me down with a feather."

"Steven?" Meredith frowned. "Oh, Steve. Jim, are you telling me Patsy is in New Zealand?"

"Yes, didn't she tell you?" Jim relayed this to Barbara and Meredith relaxed a little.

"No. She just left. Have you got his number handy?" Meredith pulled a pen from the jacket hanging on the newel post.

"Yes. Why? Oh, are you sure? She seemed determined."

"I'm sure. The number?" Meredith was repeatedly tapping the pen on the hall table. When Jim read out the number, he jotted it on the back of the gas bill. "Thank you, Jim. You're a star. Speak soon but now I've got a call to make."

Meredith tapped in the number and dropped his cigarette into a sickly-looking plant. Pulling the packet from his pocket, he lit another while listening to the elongated tone telling him it was an international call. His brother-in-law answered.

"Hi, Steve, it's Meredith, can I have a word with Patsy?" Meredith asked, flicking ash into the plant pot.

"She's not here, she's at her place, and she'll probably be in bed, although she might be up and getting ready for work. But for what it's worth, I don't think she'll speak to you. I take it you've heard from Dad. He called earlier. He forgets about the time difference."

"Yes, he called me. I didn't know she'd come to you. Thank you for helping her. How is she?" Meredith leaned his head against the wall.

"It's not a problem, that's what family is for. Yes, she's fine. Finding her feet, liking the work, and settling in."

"Work? You said that just now. Has she got a job?" Meredith took another drag.

"Yes, she's working with Martha for the time being. I'm sorry, Meredith. I don't know you well but you seem like a decent bloke. Thank you for caring about her."

"What? Of course I care about her. Steve, I know what she's probably saying but she will come home. Just look after her for me in the meantime, and tell her I love her, and I want her to call."

There was silence on the other end, and Meredith thought he'd lost the connection.

"Steve, are you there?"

"Yes, buddy, I'm here. Look, Meredith, there's no easy way to say this, and it was Patsy's job to tell you this, not mine, but she won't be back because the baby isn't yours."

Meredith stubbed his cigarette out on the table as he considered Steve's words. The hand holding the phone was shaking, and although he opened his mouth several times, he wasn't convinced he could speak. It was Steve's turn to check the line.

"Meredith, are you there?"

"Yes. Get Patsy to call me. Pronto. Interrupt her at work, if necessary, and tell her you told me."

"Will do but I don't think she'll call. Her mind's made up."

"Just tell her to fucking call me! I'm sorry, I shouldn't have shouted. This isn't your fault. Get her to call me. Please."

Steve agreed he'd try, and Meredith hung up, resisting the urge to smash the phone into the wall. He set it back in the cradle and the second cigarette joined the first. Carrying the pot into the garden, Meredith dropped it in the dustbin and pulled his mobile from his pocket.

Maxine answered on the second ring.

"Meredith, I wondered if you'd call. Linda told me about your conversation. I can't discuss Patsy with you, either."

"Let's see how far we get. Did you know she was in New Zealand?"

"Yes."

"Why didn't you tell me? At least I'd have known she was relatively safe with her brother." Meredith pulled out the cigarettes again. His last one. He pushed the packet back into his pocket.

"It wasn't my place. I suggested it to her, of course."

"Whose baby is it?" Meredith demanded.

"What b...if you're telling me Patsy is pregnant, I didn't know that. If she is, I'm sorry."

"Why? Why are you sorry?"

"Because I know how much it will hurt you. Because now it will be the two of them that you are waiting for. Look, Meredith, would you like to come and see me? We can go through—"

"No. You don't want to know what's on my mind at the moment. In your professional opinion, was Patsy mentally stable enough to leave home? To make long-term decisions about her future?"

There was a brief silence before Maxine spoke. "Please come and see me, Meredith." Maxine spoke softly. "It would be better that way."

"Answer the question. I'm a big boy and my shoulders are getting broader by the day."

"In my professional opinion, Patsy appeared to stabilise quickly once she'd left you. It's impossible to be certain, of course, because I couldn't read her body language. Many people rehearse before seeing me. Did you know that? That's even easier over the telephone. But they have little tells as to the truthfulness of their responses. Since Patsy left, particularly since she's been in New Zealand, she has appeared positive. Very positive. She talks about what she's been doing, and what she's planning on doing. She's enthusiastic. Loving being with her nephews and nieces."

"But never once mentioning the child she's carrying?"

"No."

"Never mentioning me?"

"Yes, Meredith, she has mentioned you, and I don't feel it would be inappropriate to tell you that Patsy told me she was going to break contact with you. That she hoped you'd moved on and accept her choice to do the same. She also asked me to check in with you from time to time to make sure you were okay."

"But you haven't, did you tell her that?"

"I didn't need to check in, Meredith. I see you exercising yourself to death in the gym most weeks. Physical exercise is good for the mind, and you didn't appear hung over. Starting a conversation was pointless because you seem to think I have an ulterior motive every time I speak to you."

"That's because you do. Did you tell Patsy you saw me at the gym?" Meredith asked.

"I did."

"What did she say?"

"Meredith, this isn't doing you any good. You have to look after you, and the whys and wherefores need to take a back seat for a while. Shall I make you an appointment?"

"Will you speak to her again?"

"I don't know."

"Can you contact her? Do you know how?"

"Meredith, I'm going to go now. This conversation isn't getting you anywhere. Give me a call when you're ready to talk about you because I'm not going to answer any more questions about Patsy."

"Okay, okay. Received and understood. One last thing and I'll let you go. Given Patsy's mental instability before she left, despite the fact you thought she was better away from me, would you have thought the same if you knew she'd wandered away and was pregnant?"

"Had I known we would have had different conversations."

"What if I tell you I know for a fact that the baby isn't mine and has been conceived since she left?"

"You can't possibly know that."

"Yes, I can."

"Meredith, you can't—"

"Yes, I fucking can. I had a vasectomy over a year ago. I've had all the tests, I'm firing blanks. The baby isn't mine."

"Oh, I'm sorry. That's unexpected information. That must be difficult for you. Did Patsy know? What I'm asking is, when she fell pregnant would she also have known it couldn't be yours?"

"That's not what you're asking. You're asking if Patsy would cheat on me. The answer is no. Okay, that does sound like I'm losing my marbles. I'll rephrase. Whilst she was living here she wouldn't have cheated on me. But she's been gone months, and as she's pregnant she's obviously been with someone else since she left. What I'm trying to work out is: was she in her right mind at the time; did she pick up some stranger in a bar because there are few men who would refuse; or has something worse..." Meredith's voice croaked and he coughed. "I don't need to spell it out." He waited for Maxine to answer. "Talk to me, Maxine, I'm dying here."

"You didn't answer my question. Would Patsy have known that the baby wasn't yours?"

"No. I didn't tell her about the vasectomy. Patsy lost a baby a while back, and it was devastating, although neither of us knew she was pregnant. She was told she might not be able to carry another child but she decided she didn't want one. I'd been there and done that. I wasn't going to live through it again, and certainly wouldn't let her, so I took care of it. It's amazing what these walk-in clinics can do these days. But what relevance whether I told her has, I don't know."

"Oh my goodness, Meredith, you're placing me in a very difficult situation. But I'm going to tell you this because I don't want you to do anything silly. I want you to come and see me. Patsy has never given any sign that anything untoward has happened to her since leaving home. If she had been attacked, given her history, I think she would have gone into a downward spiral and needed more than a chat with me. She would never have coped. Therefore, one has to assume that any intimacy was consensual. I don't know that, I'm—"

"Just making assumptions. Thank you, Maxine. Wave next time you see me in the gym."

Meredith hung up and saw he had two missed calls. He hit the play button to listen to his messages.

"Hi. It's me. I'm sorry I missed you. I was hoping to speak to you, to explain, but it's probably for the best. You gave me the happiest years of my life, you were my life, and now it's time for us to move on. I have and you should. I won't be calling again. Please don't bother Steve, it's not his fault, he's just trying to protect me. 'Bye, Johnny. I do love you, but...you know."

Meredith kicked the dustbin over and lit his last cigarette as he listened to the second call.

"Hi, Meredith. It's me again. I'm not being needy, although I am needy but only because I'm hungry, and my landlady has given me a voucher. Two for one at Giorgio's. Two for one! I can't eat enough for two, but thought, hang on a minute, I know a man who can. But it's for tonight. So here I am. Do

you fancy it? Let me know, because if not I'll have to chuck something frozen in the microwave before I chew my arm off."

Meredith wiped his cheeks. That would normally have made him smile. He walked into the kitchen, locking the door behind him, and splashed water on his face. Then sat at the kitchen table with the bottle of whiskey he'd been avoiding. He looked at it for a good ten minutes.

"Fuck it." He picked up his phone and called Emily.

"I knew you wouldn't be able to resist. How soon can you be ready? I am really, really starving."

"Really, really, or exaggerating as only you can? Because I'm in desperate need of sympathy."

"Oh."

"Was that a yes?"

"It was. Shit! Should I be nervous?"

Meredith grinned. "Oh yes."

When she opened the door, Emily was wearing a robe, and her smile faltered. "You look very serious. I haven't got a fluffy one. Not my style, but if it helps..." She opened the robe to reveal her nakedness.

Meredith nodded, and his lips twitched. "Before I come in, I should—"

"Bloody hell, Meredith, I don't want you to move in, I NEVER want to be married again, and I don't want your babies, I'm—"

Meredith's kiss stopped her speaking. He kicked the door shut as he pushed her into her flat.

• • • • • • • • • • •

"Good as that was...several times, I really was hungry, and I'm even more now as I've worked up an additional appetite, but I am happy to settle on a delivery because that way you won't have to get dressed. I want pizza. That okay with you?"

Meredith held up his thumb. "Perfect. No pineapple. Fruit has no place on a pizza. Large. Stuffed crust."

Emily placed the order. "I'm going to shower while we wait."

"Was that an invitation?" Meredith asked.

"Bloody hell. Really? If you like. Have you taken one of those little pills? I'm not complaining but I'm seriously worried about your heart. I don't want you dying on me, Meredith."

"No, no little blue pills, but if you wanted another round already perhaps I should get some. What I meant was, is that a hint for me to shower? I didn't have time before I came out and," said Meredith, sniffing his armpit, "I really do need one."

"Walk this way. You first." Emily sat on the toilet in her gown and watched Meredith shower. "I think you've improved with age. You obviously keep yourself fit. I love the lines around your eyes, and the grey bits make you look...not sure of the word but it suits you. And I suppose the sex was okay, so all in all, good job, Meredith. Apologies for my cuddly bits. At least I haven't got stretch marks, and I know my boobs should only be displayed while supported by a bra, but what can a girl do when Meredith offers himself?"

"Once again, I plead innocence. I think I was taken advantage of." Meredith stepped out of the shower and kissed her forehead. "Your turn, and I shan't say this again, so take heed, there is nothing, absolutely nothing wrong with your body. Oh, the doorbell. I'll go. Don't be long. I have also worked up an appetite."

Meredith was sitting at the table eating when Emily came out.

"You look very serious. I know how much you like your food, but are you going to tell me why tonight?" Emily asked.

"Not unless it's crucial to your survival. Is it?" Meredith stopped eating and watched her carefully.

"No. I can survive without knowing. But I was only with you last night. I got a peck on the cheek. Something's happened." Emily sat down and opened her pizza. "You don't have to tell me but now the deed has been done, you can give me the speech you'd prepared on the doorstep."

"Okay. Because it needs saying, although you covered most of it. I don't want a serious relationship, and yes, I know you lived through that with me the first time but this is different. Very different because I am. So, I don't want us to move in together, I don't want to marry you, and I absolutely can't provide you with children." Meredith looked away and took a bite of his pizza.

"And. Because there is an and."

"And, because of that you can do whatever it is you want to do. Which again, I know I said the last time, the difference this time is I won't be." Meredith held out his hands as if that explained everything.

"You mean I can go out and get my jollies, while you'll be staying in watching the telly?" Emily was shaking her head as she spoke.

"Is exactly what I mean. I don't need more. I'm not looking for more. We're good together, we always were, I just couldn't see it. It's a win-win for me. I want to make sure it is for you because that's only fair. I had my cake and ate it for too many years. It's stale." Meredith shrugged. "But I can't give you any more than that. It won't happen."

"So you're telling me that it wouldn't hurt you? Not even make you a teeny tiny bit jealous, if I was entertaining myself elsewhere, and you were home alone? No one changes that much, Meredith."

"Yes, I would hurt, and probably be very jealous, but if I ask you to keep yourself only for me, you might miss out on the opportunity of finding the man you might want to spend the rest of your life with. That's not fair."

Emily started laughing, then choking, so much so, Meredith jumped to his feet and pounded on her back. When she recovered, she wiped away tears of merriment with a soiled napkin and smeared sauce across her cheek. Meredith didn't tell her.

"So, I'm good in bed and thoroughly amusing. What did I say?" Meredith asked.

"First, you're still very arrogant, we'll have to work on that, but it was you giving me my freedom to find someone to settle down with. Like I would! That worked well the first time, didn't it? And second, these things take time, there's a courtship process you're unfamiliar with because you're Meredith, but what man have you ever met, except you, of course, who would accept that? Who would say, 'Fancy coming out for a drink tonight, Em? Oh, you're shagging Meredith. Not to worry. See you tomorrow'. Who? What man in his right mind, Meredith?" Still laughing, Emily threw a pizza crust at Meredith. "You have seriously got to get a grip. Shall we now get to the real reason? I'd like to because I don't much like cold pizza and it's lukewarm already."

Meredith took a bite of his pizza. "I'm eating. You tell me."

"Because you want to be free if she comes back. You've not given up hope."

"Not true." Meredith took another bite. "Have another slice. I'm in no hurry."

Emily brooded on this while she ate. Meredith watched her. "You have a very sensual mouth, did you know that? More so than when we were kids."

"Why, thank you, kind sir. Yes, I know. It's my best feature, and why I wear lipstick most of the time. It draws the eye," Emily joked.

"If you've only had me and the husband, whose eyes have you been trying to occupy?"

"And I'm done, you can finish what I haven't. Don't change the subject. Are you going to tell me?"

"No, because it's messy and sordid, and no, because I don't really know but can imagine, and no, because I don't want to talk about it."

"Well, let's call it a night, then. It's been bloody fabulous, Meredith, but we'll go back to the friends without benefits arrangement. If you can't be honest with me the deal's off."

Meredith knew he couldn't cope with that, not tonight, so he pulled his phone from his pocket.

"This was my message tonight. It came in while I was speaking to her counsellor, asking if she knew Patsy had settled in New Zealand, and even had a job there. Oh, and did I mention she was pregnant? No. Don't say anything, just listen."

Meredith played Patsy's message. Emily heard everything Patsy didn't say. She'd been that girl. The girl saying what needed to be said and meaning the opposite. She lowered her head.

"I'll take two questions. Only two because I know what they will be."

"How do you know?" Emily asked.

"First question, who's Steve? Answer, her brother. Second question, is it mine? Answer, no. Okay, I'll allow you a third. Am I sure about that? Answer, absolutely, I've had a vasectomy."

"Oh boy. And yet you aren't angry. Sad, but not angry. So, Mr Meredith, now I understand why you came, but I still say you are waiting for her to come back. Now what I have to decide is, is that good enough?"

Meredith grabbed her wrist and pulled her onto his lap. "No. It's not, but Patsy will not come back, and I will never mess you about. You don't deserve that."

"Oh, Meredith, you think you're so bloody clever. But you're not. This thing between us is her punishment. If she comes back, she'll find out, and you won't care because you won't feel guilty. Your actions justified. But you would take her back if she came. What happens to the child takes a bit of getting my head around, but that's the truth of it, even if you don't admit it. I'm shocked that you would but also proud of you, and very jealous. Patsy must be some woman. Just because you're not jumping on a plane to drag her home doesn't mean you don't want her to come voluntarily. And I noticed she's allowed to call you Johnny."

"I don't think she will." Meredith shrugged.

"But you're not sure and, more importantly, you hope so, and here I am practically begging for sex."

Meredith rested his head on her shoulder. "You did actually beg. It wasn't practically, it was absolutely. But I won't argue, I should have taken you up on the offer the first time. I told you I'd regret it. But depending on how you feel, we could make up for lost time."

Emily put her finger under his chin and raised it so he'd look at her. "Now?"

"Yes."

"Okay, tonight we will call a 'getting the cards on the table' night. Tomorrow, in the cold light of day, we will both rethink it and meet up again. You will tell me what you really want to do because I have some pride. Is that a deal?"

"Yes."

"Are you going to cry?"

"I hope not."

"Then let's get into the bedroom before I do."

Chapter Twenty-Three

Brandon Farm

Susan heard the key turn in the lock, and jumping off the bed, pushed herself up against the wall furthest from the door, wondering if her legs would hold her.

Mark stepped in and locked the door behind him. The key now on a piece of string was hung around his neck. He held out his arms.

Susan's nose wrinkled in disgust as she shook her head and held up the fork.

"I'm sorry, Jasmine. I really am sorry, and I can see you're upset. We'll get it sorted, don't worry."

"Don't worry? Are you totally mad? And my name is Susan. Susan! Say it."

"Susan. But it doesn't sound right." Mark shrugged.

"That's because you and your family are totally mad. Lost all sight of sense and decency, if you ever had any. You've killed and buried two women, Mark. Two women are dead because of you and your family. I'm going to be the next if you don't let me go. Stay there. Don't you come any closer." Susan screamed as he stepped towards her.

"I won't hurt you but stop shouting. He's done enough damage." Mark jerked his head towards his father's room. "Ah, don't cry."

Susan's shoulders bounced up and down as her tears flowed. The fork jerking around as she fought for control. What the hell was she going to do now? Sod the money. She just needed to get out of here. She sniffed back her tears as she looked at Mark. If he was going to kill her, it wasn't now.

His arms hung loosely at his sides, and he looked sad, defeated somehow. Probably knew there'd be no more sex until they'd replaced her.

"Let me hug you, please."

Susan stilled as she watched him raise his arms again. His eyes had filled with tears and his voice betrayed just how upset he was. Perhaps she still had some control over him. She pointed the fork towards the bed. "Sit down."

Mark obeyed.

"Give me the key, Mark. Give me the key and I'll go. I promise I won't tell the police. I won't even ask for the money in my account. I'll just disappear."

Mark shook his head, and a tear escaped. "No. I can't let you go. I don't want you to go. I want you to stay here with me." His arms opened again. "Please don't go, Jas...Susan. Please."

"Mark, this is insane. I can't stay here, it's not safe for me."

"It is. I won't let anyone hurt you."

"What? Mark, think about the others, about what you did to your father. How can you say that? I might do something wrong, and then you'll get mad, and..." A thought occurred to Susan and she changed tactics. "Look, I know it wasn't your fault. It was them. And because I know that I won't tell. I'll just go. Let me go now before you get mad."

Mark shook his head. "I can't. Dad deserved it. Look what he did to Jasmine. I should have killed him there and then."

Susan closed her eyes. That hadn't worked. His fists were now clenched. "Maybe you should have, but you didn't and so now we're in this mess. But if you let me go, no one else will get hurt. Your dad will die, hopefully sooner rather than later, and you'll get the farm, you and Thomas. You'd like that, wouldn't you?" Susan felt guilty even saying it because the old man had tried to help her, but this was about her now, her survival.

"You, me and Thomas," Mark replied. "Why not you, me and Thomas?"

"Because I'm scared, Mark. And you know why, you must know why. Can I speak to Cissy?"

"No!"

In one swift movement, Mark had catapulted himself off the bed and engulfed her. He held her tight, squeezing the breath from her, and ignoring the fork jammed into his ribs.

"I would never hurt you. Do you believe me?" he asked, as he stroked her hair.

Susan was trembling and knew her voice would betray her, so she nodded against his chest.

Mark sighed, and keeping her body trapped next to his, he walked her to the wardrobe. Opening the door, he pulled the solitary tie from the hook and walked her back to the bed.

"Lie down."

"Mark, please." Susan was crying again. "Please. Let me love you. Please don't kill me."

Mark smiled as he threw the fork to the floor. He tied her wrists to the bedstead before stroking her face. Susan relaxed a little. He wasn't going to strangle her. At least that was something. He looked down at her.

"Stay quiet. I can't love you now, but I'll be back later once Thomas is in bed."

Susan closed her eyes and nodded. He'd actually thought she wanted sex. She was scared for her life, told him she'd known what he'd done, and he thought she wanted sex. He really was missing a crucial element somewhere.

"Why are you tying me up? You don't need to do that. I can't hurt you."

"I know. But you might try to escape. That wouldn't do. Do you trust me?"

Susan nodded. She wanted to scream at him, tell him what a stupid question it was but what would be the point? He only heard what he wanted to.

Mark leaned down and kissed her. "Good girl. Thank you, Susan. Just be patient, I promise it will be okay." Walking to the door, he patted the key hanging on his chest. "I'll keep this with me. Stop crying."

And then he shut the door. The key turning in the lock.

When he returned that night, he untied her and took her to the bathroom, waiting outside until she'd relieved herself and showered. He put his arm around her shoulder and pulled her closer as they walked back to the bedroom. Slipping the robe from her shoulders, he hung it on the back of the door.

"Get in bed, you'll get cold."

Susan scooted into bed, pulling the covers over her naked body. It wasn't the cold making her shiver; it was the look in his eye. She watched him lock the door and put the key around his neck. When he undressed, she closed her eyes and wondered if she could do this.

In the next room, the old man lay there listening to the bed creak. She wasn't so vocal tonight. Poor girl. He rubbed a hand over his face. Whatever happened to this one, it wasn't his fault. Not his fault.

Mark pulled Susan into a hug and whispered into her hair.

"Can you keep a secret? It's very important."

Susan nodded against his chest, wondering what other nightmare was about to be unleashed on her.

"Say it, or it won't be true," Mark whispered.

"I promise," Susan told him.

"Hush. Keep your voice down. This is a secret." Then he drew in a breath, blew it out softly, making her hair lift, and he told her his secret.

Susan was right to think she was in danger, but it was far worse than she had thought. She lay deathly still, unable to speak in case she uttered the wrong words. All she managed was a nod when he asked if she understood.

How the hell could anyone understand that?

Chapter Twenty-Four

Meredith walked into the gym and nodded as Jared held up five fingers before returning his attention to the man he was speaking to. Jared would be more than five minutes because he had verbal abilities to match Loopy's.

Meredith went to the cross-trainer. Perhaps if he did a bit on this first, Jared wouldn't push him so hard. He was exhausted. Between the talking and the sex, he'd not managed to get much sleep. He was surprised he had even come here today but smiled as he slotted his water bottle into the holder and set the machine. Emily hadn't even bothered lifting her arm to wave, so he promised to call her later so she wouldn't be late for work.

Meredith had a decision to make and a promise to keep. As he forced his legs to begin the climb, he had no idea which way he would jump. He could only hope it was the right way for Emily. It was times like this he wished he had a best friend. One who would give sound advice based on the facts. Trump and Seaton adored Patsy and didn't know Emily. There was Ben Jacobs, he knew both, liked both. Perhaps he'd give him a call. Meredith's smile was back as he ran through how that conversation might pan out. No, he was on his own. Again. If he could only get on a plane, disappearing himself seemed like a positive move.

"Meredith, I don't think that's enough." Jared had arrived unseen and tapped the screen of the machine. Causing Meredith to groan as he pushed against the change in resistance.

Meredith set the machine back to where it had been. "I'm only here so you get paid. I'm knackered. Be kind to me or you really might kill me."

Jared leaned an elbow on the handlebars. "Rubbish, I'd get paid, anyway. Twenty-four hours' notice of cancellation. You don't look rough, maybe a bit tired, and you look happy. Late night? We can always go and have a coffee instead, and you could tell me all about it."

"Very late night. And you wouldn't believe me if I told you. Just be gentle with me."

"I thought you wanted pain to make you forget. Because I'm not stroking it, so you remember. We need to get that clear from the get go." Jared made a meal of stepping away from the machine, hands up and a look of horror on his face.

Meredith threw his head back and laughed. "If you were a bit more worldly-wise, I might run a conundrum past you. But you're not, and you'd give your opinion from the wrong part of your anatomy."

Jared now rested both elbows on the handlebars and looked up at Meredith. "Okay, fair enough, you're entitled to your opinion but you're wrong. What if you tell me your conundrum, and I won't pass comment but will store it for future reference to draw upon should the situation arise?"

"You wouldn't be able to keep your mouth shut. You'd think I was mad for even having questions." Meredith shook his head. "Too young to understand. Shit, you really make me feel like an old man."

"On a plate for you then? Ooh, this sounds interesting. I know, I'll leave the setting there if you answer my questions honestly."

"No."

"Ah, Meredith, you don't strike me as a killjoy but I'm right, aren't I? Someone's offered you rampant sex."

"Possibly."

"I knew it. But you're not sure because there are strings and having just come out of one relationship you don't need more strings."

"The opposite. But as I won't discuss it with you, I'm going to say, yes, you're right. What's next?"

"Weights. I'll tell you what, just to help you out, I'll take care of the no-strings sex and leave you to concentrate on why the right part of your anatomy isn't working."

Laughing, Meredith pulled Jared into a headlock. "It's working just fine. You wouldn't be able to cope, my friend. But thank you for the offer." Meredith released Jared, who was also laughing.

"Meredith. A word if I might."

"I don't think so." Meredith turned to face Maxine. "Not unless you have news I want to hear."

"Since last night? No, Meredith, but I do think you should speak to me, although you seem to be coping."

"That's what I do. A lifetime of experience. Now, if you'll excuse me, young Jared here wants to inflict pain on me."

Jared's head was following the conversation like a tennis match, wondering if Maxine had made the no-strings offer, and if that were the case why did Meredith want pain to forget?

"Replacing one pain with another doesn't work. Come and see me, Meredith. Please." Maxine turned and walked away.

Jared clapped his hands and pointed at Meredith. "That's the bit I didn't get. You like it. You like pain. Does she whip you? Can't see evidence of nipple clamps. I bet they smart."

Meredith put his palm over Jared's face and pushed him away. "Session over. I can't do pain while I'm laughing." He was still laughing as he stripped off and threw his clothes into the locker. Walking into the shower cubicle, he looked up into the spray and refused to cry. If it had been any woman other than Emily, he wouldn't even have a conundrum. There again, if it hadn't been Emily, he wouldn't have been in a situation to make such an offer. "I hate my fucking life."

• • • • • • • • • • •

First in the office, Meredith made a coffee and opened all the files he wanted to look at. His eyes skimmed the board. It may as well have been empty for all the use it was.

Sipping his coffee, he called Emily with her wake-up call.

"Good morning, Meredith. How are you? Are you also having trouble walking?"

Meredith could hear the laughter in her voice, and his heart sank. "Yes. I've just been to the gym."

"You're joking, right? Honestly?"

"Not joking. Although if honesty is required, I worked at novice speed for twenty minutes. Wasted my time trying to teach a horny, young trainer the error of his ways and had to convince him I've never worn nipple clamps. How's your morning been? I was expecting to find you still in bed."

"Your gym sounds interesting. I'm up and almost awake. I thought I'd better escape the flat in case you came back. An almost cold shower twenty minutes ago, one and a half cups of coffee, and now I'm headed for a very hot shower because I'm bloody freezing. Other than that, wondering how I'm going to stay awake once we get past ten o'clock."

"Okay, so you're up but maybe not for long. I'd better get some work done. See you later."

"You certainly will. Where?"

"I thought I'd be coming there. Would you like the meal I promised you but you didn't get to eat because you wouldn't let me out of the bedroom?"

Meredith heard a cough and looked up to see Seaton had come in and was standing with his head cocked to one side, with a half-smile on his face, which he was trying to hide. Seaton mouthed sorry and pointed to Meredith's mug. Meredith nodded and Seaton picked it up.

"I think that's a splendid shout. Giorgio's . I'll meet you there. What time?"

"I don't think I'll have much on here, shall we say half six?" Meredith looked at Seaton, who hadn't moved, and offered Meredith a smile.

"Can we do eight?"

"We could but for some reason I think I need an early night. Have you got something on?"

"A robe but not a fluffy one. Oh, you meant later. Ah, Meredith, I made you laugh."

Meredith was laughing, "Oh my, Emily An...Do you know something, I don't even know your name these days. Anyway, whatever your name is, you made a joke. It was funny, and I'll buy you a fluffy one for your birthday."

"Don't you dare. No, nothing planned. I was hoping for a nap first."

"You can nap after. I'll pick you up at six thirty."

"Okay. Being serious for a moment because I feel we must. I know you have murderers and fire-breathing dragons to catch but thinking cap on, Meredith, I need you to think."

"I know. Rest assured I will think of nothing else. The dragons will get away with it. See you later." Meredith hung up. "Was there something you wanted, Seaton? Only you have my mug."

"Ah, there he is, back in the room. I was reminiscing, Guv. It took me back to the old days, when I wasn't a taxi driver for my daughter and could afford my mortgage. I don't know who she is, but for what it's worth I'm glad you're back on the horse."

Meredith folded his arms across his chest. "I never fell off. Why glad? I was expecting a lecture."

"Why would I lecture you? You're as good as a single man, what with Patsy not coming back. We were worried about you."

"And because I got my leg over, everything is fine in the world? It's not. I don't know who 'we' are, but you can tell them from me nothing could be further from the truth. They can stop worrying about me because I'm a big boy now, and people shouldn't go poking their nose in because it pisses me off. AND just so you know, she will come back."

Seaton perched on the corner of Meredith's desk. "Okay, I'll agree with you because I don't want you pissed off and because I like happy Meredith. But I don't reckon you believe that, or you wouldn't be making second dates and buying fluffy stuff. You'd be in, out, move on to the next until Patsy came home. Anyway, who was it on the phone? Do I know her?"

"Before your time. A very good and very understanding old friend, who I am trying not to destroy. Patsy's pregnant."

"But you had the snip, so...Oh."

"So you see, I slipped in the saddle a little last night. It was better than coming in with a headache. Much better. Too much better. So now I have a problem because Patsy will come back, and I have to be able to deal with that without hurting Emily. I have the next ten hours to work that out."

"Emily knows all this?" Seaton asked.

"She does, but as I can tell from the look on your face she agrees with you and thinks Patsy won't be back. And get this, because it gets better, she's had a shit marriage, and the thought of living with someone, let alone marrying them, makes her feel sick. And she doesn't want babies, which I couldn't cough up however hard I tried. And she loves me, and only wants me for her carnal pleasure."

Seaton hoped his mouth hadn't fallen open. "You're serious, aren't you? No, don't answer, of course you bloody are. And you're undecided because you don't want to break Emily, and you don't want to hurt Patsy, but you don't want to have to go out looking for it again."

"Bloody hell, Seaton, you've become psychic in your old age. If you know all that, tell me how long I've got to wait. That might concentrate the mind."

"Before I tell you it's unlikely, what about the child? If Patsy comes back, she will have a child. Another man's child."

"But Patsy's child."

Seaton rubbed his hands over his face. "It's not Emily you need to speak to tonight. It's Patsy. You need to tell her that. If she knew that, she'd be home like a shot."

"And that's the one thing I can't do. Not at the moment. I haven't got her number. She leaves me messages when I won't be around to pick up. If I could speak to her, I could explain all that."

"When did you find out?"

"Last night. Hence the slip. Although, to be honest, it was on the cards. I was just hoping I could resist, but at least Emily knows me well enough to know there would be rules."

"Last night! Last night? You found out Patsy was having someone else's baby last night, so you find yourself a distraction, and all night by the sound of it, but have already decided you'd take on another man's child? Guv, come on, get a grip. I love Patsy. I don't know how she managed to get herself up the duff because I know she loves you. But no, Guv, don't call her tonight, think it over."

"I have." Meredith flexed his shoulders. "But even if I get to tell her that, will she come home?"

"Properly? You think you've thought this through properly? What if you say come home because I'll cope, and then you can't? The best you could try for is, come home and I'll try my best. That would be honest but then she wouldn't come. Bloody hell, Guv, I used to envy you, you know."

Seaton got to his feet and patted Meredith's shoulder, leaving his hand there. "I don't have any advice, Guv. All I'll say is, take your time. Don't rush into anything and try to keep perspective. It seems to me that you're all caught between a rock and a hard place, and through no fault of your own it's you who's been given the power to stop the rocks from crushing you all. Surprising but true."

"Bloody hell, Seaton, that was deep. I think you should make the coffee and calm down. Your brain must be hurting."

"It is. How yours isn't fried is beyond me. Nice and slow, Guv. Nice and slow."

"Not a word, Seaton. I know you lot love nothing better than gossiping about me, and usually I'm happy for you to get on with it. But this is Patsy, you're not going there."

"There was no need to say that. Who else knows you went for the two-brick option?"

"You, me, and the bloke with the scalpel."

Seaton pursed his lips and nodded. "My lips are sealed."

The door opened and Linda bustled in, wearing a yellow dress, printed with what to Meredith looked like little green aliens, red tights and matching shoes. She did a twirl.

"Morning, what do you think? I chose this one for you, Skipper. Frogs. Because they're bouncy like me. Where are we going to start? I've been thinking it should be the beginning again, and I'm going to have to bite the bullet and go through the little we have now the newspapers have sent over the floppy discs. I've sent Jimmy in search of the hardware. Have you met Jimmy? He's a nice chap. He'll be here in a minute. Such a boring job without the date but better than going to the archive. Tom, you can make coffee. Fresh cakes here, bit wonky, but they'll taste fine. Tom, why are you here? I thought we only saw you wanderers on Fridays?"

"Dentist. I wasn't going to cancel it, almost as bad as getting a doctor's appointment. I'll be here until ten, then depending on what the guv wants, back on the road." Seaton grimaced. "Can't wait."

"What the guv wants is to get on with some work. I'll think you'll find they're aliens, not frogs, Loopy. Pull up a chair, and let's get on with it."

"No briefing?" Linda was already wheeling her chair towards Meredith's desk.

"About what? I don't think anything has happened overnight." Meredith caught the glance from Tom and ignored it.

After an hour, Meredith was frustrated. He'd read and re-read everything too often for anything new to jump out at him. He pushed his chair away from the desk and clasped his hands behind his head.

"So your cross-checking contaminator thing didn't spit anything out, Loopy?"

"Not that we haven't checked. Do you want to look?"

"Not at the moment. It's nine o'clock. I need to make a phone call."

"You mean you want a cigarette," Linda tutted. "Shall I carry on, or shall me and Daisy start on the floppies?"

"Yes, do that." Meredith pulled on his jacket and headed for the carpark. Once there, he lit a cigarette before crossing his fingers and making the call to New Zealand. It was nine in the evening. He doubted Patsy would be in work or bed. It was worth a shot. A young boy answered, and Meredith listened to him being shooed away to bed by Steve Hodge.

"Don't you try that one, Buddy. Bed now. Patsy isn't here, no more stories. Go. Hello, sorry about that."

"Well, that answers the first question. Does Patsy have a telephone wherever she's living?"

"Hello, Meredith. No, she's in the loft above the garage. She uses this one or her mobile."

"Will you give me her mobile number?"

"I can't, mate. That wouldn't be fair, would it? Look, I'll pass on a message."

"Will you do that now before you go to bed?" Meredith asked. "You've only got to go as far as the garage. I think she'll want to hear it." He listened to the sigh before Steve replied.

"I will if she's awake, otherwise it will have to wait until morning."

"What time is that likely to be?"

"What do you mean? Sorry, Meredith, you're going to have to spell it out. It's been a long day and the kids have been particularly annoying tonight."

"I need you to give Patsy a message, and it's important I hear back from her as soon as. I'm on a timer, which I won't explain. So, if you won't wake her now, should she be asleep, what time will you see her in the morning?"

"Oh, sounds odd. Around seven, I guess. Maybe earlier, depends on whether one of the kids sneak up to her."

"She's popular with the kids, then?" Meredith smiled at the thought.

"They worship her. But they're using her as a bargaining chip. You know, Aunty Patsy said this, Aunty...Sorry, Meredith, you don't want to hear about that. What was the message?"

"I did actually. Tell her I don't mind about the baby. It's not a problem. I want her to come home. No, tell her I want them to come home. Tell her she might see pain, but no hurt and no guilt."

"Okay, I'm guessing that will mean something to her."

"Yes, emphasise the no hurt and no guilt. I know you won't want to, but I'd really like you to wake her up if she is asleep because it's very important I hear from her before eight tonight, or eight tomorrow morning your time. Tell her I want to speak to her, but because it's urgent a text will do if she doesn't feel able to talk. I know I sound like a madman, but could you repeat that? Jesus, I am a madman.

"It's okay. So you want them both, no hurt, no guilt. Or do you want it in full?"

Meredith laughed. "Thank you."

"You know, I could give you our address and you could write to her. Email. Bloody hell, you could just email her. I'll text you her email address."

"Thanks. But do me a favour, give her that message yourself. She might not read an email, but she's got to listen to you."

"Will do, Meredith, if my opinion counts, I'll tell her I think she should go home. And that's shooting myself in the foot with the kids."

"Thank you. Don't forget that email address."

Meredith texted Emily, telling her he'd pick her up at eight, and strode back into the office and looked at Seaton. "I'm trying."

"Yes, you are...oh, the talking to the right person thing. Just kidding, Guv. Well done, and good luck."

Meredith's phone pinged, and he glanced at the screen. It was the text from Steve. Why was he texting first? He should be waking her up. He looked at Seaton. "I'm going to need it."

Sitting back at his desk, Meredith started the email six or seven times, deleting each attempt, knowing now how hard it must have been for Patsy. Shutting down his screen, he looked across the office. Linda and Daisy were glued to their screens, their fingers continually scrolling through pages and pages of old newspapers.

Linda glanced across the office at him. "Are you okay, Skipper? You're staring but look miles away."

"Frustrated. I need something to work with. We've got the key. The key was the job. We have to find the bloody lock, Loopy. I thought it would all fall into place once you were back. You always find that one thing. Not to worry, it might happen but I'm not holding my breath." Meredith looked around the office. "Did Seaton go?"

"Yes, you said goodbye, and made a telephone with your hand to show you would call him. Blimey, Skipper, you are in a dream world today. It's just us three. George is on his day off. Louie, Will, and Tom, when he's done, will be knocking on doors."

Meredith nodded. He needed a distraction. Perhaps he should go home. Patsy would leave any message there and he might be able to intercept her call. But she might not know yet. Aware Linda was still looking at him, he smiled at her.

"In which case, lunch is on me, and I don't mean a sandwich from the shop. Where shall we go?"

Linda clapped her hands. "Ooh, lunch out. I don't mind. But I should point out it's only eleven thirty."

"I know that but depending on where we go we might need to book," Meredith lied. The morning had disappeared, and he'd achieved nothing. Yet. But there was always hope.

"Oh, a posh lunch out. Daisy, what do you fancy? You choose, I'll dither."

They settled for Greek at the new modern restaurant as it was within walking distance, and Meredith booked the table for twelve thirty. He and Daisy stood waiting at the door to leave, and Linda asked them to wait while her fingers flew over the keyboard.

"Okay, we can go. I've set the search slightly differently but I'm running it for links again. We've gone over this so many times, I don't think we'll get different results, but I need something to keep you busy, Skipper. Your tapping and fidgeting is driving me mad."

The girls decided they wanted a meze, and as plate after plate of food was placed before them, Meredith was glad he now had a gym membership, otherwise Patsy wouldn't recognise him when she came home. His diet, now consisting of takeaways and restaurant food, would be adding an inch a day to his waistline if not.

The food was good, even though there was a lot being put into boxes for the girls to take home. Throughout lunch, he'd tried to stay on track with their conversation, nodding and grunting in the right places to keep his mind occupied on anything but Patsy and his meeting with Emily. Perhaps Linda's computer program would spit out the distraction he needed.

"Skipper, are you listening to me? Where are you today?" Linda elbowed him as they walked back.

"Miles away. Miles, and miles, and miles. I'm sorry, Loopy, what did you say?"

"I asked if you were sure you didn't want to take any of this home with you, as it would save you bothering to cook."

"No thanks. Anyway, I'm eating out tonight."

"Again? Where are you going, anywhere nice?"

"Giorgio's . Do you—"

"I love it. Have the cannelloni. I know it doesn't come with chips, but you'll love it."

"I'm not a total heathen, you know. But I will take your recommendation. Thank you."

"Who are you going with?" Linda stopped walking and held up a hand. "Too nosey. You don't have to answer."

"I do because otherwise you'll just make something up. An old friend."

"Ah, that's nice. It's not Ben, is it? If it's Ben, I think me and Louie should have an invitation." Linda turned to Daisy. "Ben is like the skipper but without the irritation. He sings, he dances, he's got a twinkle in his eye too. So the skipper but a bit—"

Meredith was laughing, and he pulled Linda into a hug. "Don't you dare say better. I'd never live it down. Sorry to disappoint, not Ben. I don't even know where he is at the moment, probably in the middle of an ocean somewhere, singing to adoring women who should know better. I'll give him a call and tell him you're pining for him. It would be nice to catch up."

"Don't you dare. I'm a happily married woman. Come on, let's go and check the results, you obviously don't want to tell us."

Meredith ignored the unasked question and pulled open the door. "I thought you said it wouldn't find anything new."

"I did. But we have to have hope."

That was all Meredith felt he was living on. Hope. Sitting at his desk, he opened his emails again, closing them before they'd even uploaded. If this was anyone else, he'd be giving them a bollocking or sending them home until they could concentrate on what they were paid to do. He watched Linda walk across to her desk.

"That's that lot stored in the fridge. I warned Jimmy it's off limits, now let's see what, if anything...Oh there's something new. There are three results. Two seconds, and...Oh. More of the same."

"Humour me. What were the three results?" Meredith asked.

"Top of the list is Jasmine, with three hits. That's new. I set it for three hits. Jasmine Jones, Jasmine Brandon and Jasmine Sealy. Sealy is new because Jasmine Brandon was new. I'll just check, and yes, she's a girl who works in a chemist. In second place, we have Brandon Farm but we know all those because someone mentioned our Jasmine looked like Jasmine Brandon, who lives on Brandon Farm. Will went to Brandon Farm and spoke to Mark and Jasmine Brandon. And you spoke to Cissy Brandon, who also lives at Brandon Farm. Nothing new."

"That's a lot of Brandons. You said three hits. We've had Brandon Farm, Jasmine, and what?"

"Oh, that needs more thinking about." Linda looked at Meredith. "I mean, it doesn't, not on the face of it but it could, couldn't it?"

"I can't answer that unless you tell me what you're looking at." Meredith stood and walked to Linda's desk.

"Broken arms. Specifically, women between the ages of twenty-five and thirty-five between 2012 and 2016 I chose those years because Louise had broken her arm in the last two years of her life. She was found in 2018 and—"

"Daisy, tell me what she's looking at before I say something I'll regret. Headlines, Loopy, headlines. We can do the rest after. Because girls it's never let me down before, I don't even know what you're going to say, but we're off and running." Meredith pushed a finger into his now flat stomach. "My gut is telling me we've done it. I think you found the lock."

Linda looked at his stomach and back to the screen. "I'm not asking what lock, you'll go all huffy again. Four results, I'm surprised at that, you'd have...okay. Sorry. Focus, Linda Trump, focus. Jasmine Brandon. Jasmine Brandon broke her arm in 2014..." Linda clicked several links. "When a cow trapped her between the gate and wall. Clean break, plaster removed on—"

"And we're off. Stand up, Loopy."

Linda did, and Meredith grabbed her face and planted a kiss in the centre of her forehead.

"Now sit down. I want to know everything about that family. Who lives on that farm?"

"Skipper!" Linda saluted and sat back down as Daisy raised a finger.

"I can see where this is going. The dates, the broken arm, the farm, etcetera. But wouldn't you and Will have noticed their reactions, or do you think they are that good at covering up?"

"Reactions? Cissy Brandon was like the rest of the people we saw. A shrug, a shake of the head and then showed me to the lane where the body was found."

"Wow. That's one cool customer. So, you think Katie Brandon is also in on it?"

"No, why would you say that? Shit. You're asking, did she react when I said, 'Do you know these two girls who had their heads smashed in?' I didn't ask her because I was there to ask for access to the burial site. I only asked Cissy because she lived on Brandon Farm, because that was where someone thought a lookalike lived. Shit, shit, shit. I dropped the ball there. Surely they would have asked Katie when they first identified them Find out." Meredith tapped Daisy's screen. "What? You've got that look like I'm missing something."

"What about Jasmine Brandon? Will showed Mr and Mrs Brandon the photos. Surely, if she was Louise's replacement, then she must have known what happened to the other two? If she didn't, why did she kiss him? Hang on, look." Daisy clicked away until she had Will's report on the screen. "Look. She said blah, blah, wedding anniversary coming up, and kissed him. You wouldn't do that if you didn't know, you'd be shocked, terrified even. I think we're getting excited about it for nothing. I don't believe there are two women living on that farm who would accept that, lie to the police, and get on with their lives as though nothing was wrong."

"And you may be right. But we need to get excited about something, so humour me. Find out who lives in that house, where they came from, where they went to school, where they shop, anything that you can. Humour me, Daisy, because I'm rarely wrong, even without evidence, and in normal circumstances I would be kicking arse for missing this months ago, including my own. But I'm not because at least we got there. Now we have to prove it and find the evidence. You two work on that. I'll speak to Will and see if he was as sloppy as me."

Daisy and Linda exchanged a glance as Meredith walked back to his desk. Will was in for a serious earache if he had missed something, but they busied themselves looking for information. Meredith called Will.

"Yes, Guv? One more and I'm calling it a day."

"You went to see the Brandons when someone said there was a likeness to Jasmine Jones. Talk me through it."

"Hang on, let me get in the car. I'll need my notebook."

"You don't take your notebook with you when you're speaking to people?"

"Yes, I do. But I've taken off my jacket, and it's in the jacket pocket. Wellies go in the boot because they're mucky. Have I done something wrong? You don't sound very happy."

"I hope so."

"I won't ask. Right. Blimey, that was weeks ago. Got to farm, Mr and Mrs B in the yard. Asked how long she'd lived there, Twenty-odd years, wedding anniversary soon. Didn't recognise girls. She said she wished she was that pretty."

"So you did show them the pictures, how did he react?"

"From memory he just shook his head. She did most of the talking. And of course I showed them. That's the whole point, isn't it? What's going on, Guv?"

"I cocked up and didn't show someone I think will be a crucial witness. I was hoping you'd done the same."

"Afraid not. Do you want me to backtrack for you? Who's the crucial witness?"

"Katie Brandon, who would be aunt by marriage to the bloke you spoke to. Close your eyes."

"What?"

"Close your eyes and put yourself back in the yard. Picture them if you can. Any twitch of the jaw, any sharp intake of breath. Did they make eye contact? It's at times like this I wish we wore bodycams." The thought took him back to the footage of Patsy's attack, and he fell silent, wondering if there was a message waiting for him at home.

Will wondered if Meredith had been drinking, and although Meredith couldn't see him, he closed his eyes. They'd been happy, they were laughing and joking. He got the photos ready...

"I think I cocked up."

"How? What did you miss?" Meredith gave Daisy the thumbs up. He knew she'd been watching.

"I missed the crucial bit. Shit! I'm so sorry, Guv, don't know why, probably because they seemed all loved up."

"Are you going to tell me or keep apologising? You are forgiven as will I be if I'm right." Meredith tried to keep the anger from his voice. It was unnecessary.

"I didn't say how they died. I'm not convinced I even said they were dead. Guv? Are you there?"

"I am. We might be onto something. I need the girls to finish what they're working on, and I need to think. I'll keep you posted."

Meredith walked to his whiteboard and wiped it clean. He wrote the heading: Brandon Farm and listed the three names he knew were there: Cissy, Mark and Jasmine Brandon.

He spun round to face Linda. "Linda, do you still have access to the hospital records?"

Linda gasped and looked up. "Guess what?"

Meredith rolled his eyes. "Am I going to have headlines?"

Linda poked her tongue out. "Our Jasmine Jones married Mark Brandon on the third of January 2003. That's a big headline."

"It is. Why have we not found this before? Has everyone in this department lost the plot, including me?" Meredith waved the pen in his hand as he spoke. "Don't answer, it's because we didn't look. We knew when they were born, they wouldn't have been pronounced dead until they were dug up. I'm guessing you did a births, deaths and marriages search."

"Yes because you wanted to know who, when, and where about the people in the house. Cissy and Charles Brandon were married in 1978. Mark was born in 1983. No one has died there since 1980. I've not found anything else as yet."

"Keep looking. Actually, answer the question, have you still got access to the hospital records?"

"Yes. What am I looking for?" Linda clicked away from the screen she was on.

"Maternity records. Jasmine Brandon 2014 to 2017. Start there. Louise Marshall had given birth in the last, let's say, year of her life. She died around 2016. We'll start there and work out. To be on the safe side, look up Louise Marshall and Jasmine Brandon."

"I can't. We don't have access. We only have access to orthopaedic records."

"Bugger. Okay, search again. Just put the name Brandon in to start with. Let's see if anyone else crops up. If the child survived, they might have broken something too."

Meredith wrote the information they had on the board and paced while the two women continued to search.

"Got a hit," Linda called. "Charles Brandon broke his back falling from a hayloft in 2009. Doesn't say much else. He's paralysed from the waist down."

"Might be relevant. Jasmine was killed around that time."

"What if she pushed Charles out of the loft, and Mark or Cissy killed her?" Daisy suggested.

"It's possible. Anything is possible with this lot if we're right. How the hell do they persuade them to become other people? Not Jasmine Jones, she married into it, but both Louise, and whoever it is living as Mark Brandon's wife now, chose to do so."

"Perhaps he looks like George Clooney but is evil," Linda suggested.

"Good theory but I won't write it on here, if you don't mind." Meredith glanced at the clock. "Okay, I'll get everyone back in here tomorrow. If necessary, we'll go out to the farm and bring them all in for questioning. I'd like to know if there was a child involved, though. But we'll cross that bridge when we come to it. Another hour searching and we'll call it a day. Tomorrow will be a long one, and if they're all involved in this, that will be the same for the foreseeable."

"It's not my day in tomorrow, Skipper, but do you mind if I come in anyway?"

"I thought you'd never ask."

• • • • • • • • • • •

Meredith waited until seven o'clock that evening until he gave in and called New Zealand.

"Meredith."

Meredith could hear the resignation in Steve's voice.

"Is she there?"

"No. Nor is she near the building. I can't get her for you. She was up with the lark and has gone to swimming training with Martha and the kids. They have to train before school."

"You gave her my message."

"I did, and I'd say she understood it. She was emotional."

Meredith closed his eyes. "Was that last night or this morning?"

"Last night. I take it she hasn't been in touch."

"No. You told her about the timescale."

"I did and she said good for him. I have no idea what she meant by that. What did it mean? I've been trying to work it out. I thought you might be jumping on a plane or something."

"Something far more dangerous than that. Tell her I called. Sorry to bother you. I'll try to stop."

"I will. Look, mate, that was a generous offer, I'm not sure I could have made it. If you meant it, who knows what the future might hold? It's clear you still love each other, and I can understand it from Patsy's viewpoint but not yours. You're a big man, Meredith. It's a comfort to know you'll be there for her if she ever needs you, even if this particular boat has sailed."

"Good. Glad I bring comfort to someone, and that wasn't sarcastic. Have a good day, Steve. Look after her for me. Call if you think there's anything I should know."

Meredith hung up and punched the wall. Rubbing his knuckles, he walked to the back door and lit a cigarette. She needed him now but just couldn't see it. Perhaps once the baby was born she'd feel differently.

He blew smoke towards the wilted tulips. Summer was around the corner. It would be winter in New Zealand soon, if it hadn't arrived already. Patsy had swapped one cold climate for another. A shower was needed. Emily would think his standards were dropping if he turned up in a state again tonight.

Chapter Twenty-Five

Brandon Farm

Mark shut the gun cabinet and walked into the kitchen. Everything seemed normal but it wasn't. It's like the house knew someone else was going to die. Perhaps it would be him but he knew for sure it wouldn't be Thomas. He turned and headed for Thomas's room.

Thomas looked up and smiled as he zipped up his bag.

"Thanks, Dad, I didn't think you were going to let me go."

"You've been a good boy. Lucky they still had room. Come on, you'll be late."

Thomas picked up his kitbag and put the strap over his shoulder. It made him list to one side. Mark took it from him.

"I'll carry it down the stairs. Hurry now."

"Can I say goodbye to Mum? I won't see her for a week."

"Better not, you don't want to be ill while you're away. Think what your mates would say if you gave it to them."

Thomas considered this for a moment and nodded. "Yes, okay. Everyone would be mad at me."

As they walked through the kitchen, Thomas looked around. "Where's Nan?"

"She had an errand to run. It's why I'm taking you." As Mark closed the door behind him, he wondered if Thomas could feel it, too.

A few hours later, Cissy walked across the yard, careful to avoid the spray as Mark hosed it down. "You let him go to camp?"

"Yep. He was lucky they hadn't filled the numbers." Mark turned off the hose.

"What changed your mind?" Cissy asked.

"I didn't want him to be here."

"You've decided then?" Cissy's head dropped to her chest.

"I'm going to sleep on it." Mark turned away, threading the hose into loops as he did so.

"One more night, aye?"

"Yes. One more night." Mark blinked away his tears.

That evening, when all the jobs had been done, and the farm was in as good a shape as it had ever been, he unlocked the door to the bedroom and smiled at Susan.

"Do you want a shower?"

"Yes, please." Susan knew better than to beg him to free her. That made him angry. While he was feeling happy, she had a chance at staying alive.

Mark looked at the tray as he untied her wrist. "You didn't finish your dinner."

"No. Think it's because I'm not working, my appetite isn't what it was."

"Not long, now." He stroked her face. "Come on."

Susan didn't think her legs would carry her as far as the bathroom. What did that mean, not long now? Did he want her to be clean when he killed her. Oh God, was he going to do it in the shower? That would be easier to clean up. Her step faltered, and she fell against him. He put his arm around her.

"Steady on. Do you need to go? Shall I wait outside?"

Susan whimpered and shook her head. It wouldn't be in the shower.

"I can come in and watch?" Mark smiled at her and followed her into the bathroom.

When Susan had finished, he wrapped her in a towel and walked her back to the bedroom and locked the door. Sitting her on the bed, he helped her dry herself. Then he stripped off until it was just the key hanging around his neck.

"I love you."

Afterwards, he pulled her into his arms. "Do you know my father listens to us? That's why Mum made us have this bedroom. To punish him."

Susan chose her words carefully. "I thought he might be able to. She really hates him, doesn't she? I didn't realise that at first."

"She does. Do you hate me?"

"No, Mark, you've been kind to me, apart from that first time, you know."

"I didn't mean to hurt you, it was just...I'm sorry."

"It doesn't matter. It was a long time ago. You've made up for it since." Susan wondered if now was the time to ask him again to free her. Now when he'd satisfied his need and was soft and gentle. But his next words told her that would be pointless.

"Whatever happens tomorrow, know I didn't want to do it, and I will always love you. Always."

"Why? Mark, what might happen tomorrow? What?" Susan pushed herself up onto her elbow and looked down at him.

"Let's worry about it then. I'm tired. We need to sleep." Neither of them managed much sleep, and dawn took an age to arrive.

Chapter Twenty-Six

Meredith watched Emily skip down the steps to the car. Wearing skinny jeans, a fitted shirt, and carrying some form of jacket, she tried to get control of her hair as a stiff breeze whipped it around her face. She grinned at him as she climbed into the car.

"Evening, Meredith. Lucky I didn't go to any trouble. I must look a sight. It wasn't quite dry." She leaned towards him and kissed him on the cheek. "Drive, James, I'm very hungry."

"Evening, and you look lovely. I like the wild look."

"Is that why you've taken to pushing me into hedges? Ulterior motive. You scrub up quite well yourself. You didn't look like that this morning. I can't believe you made it to the gym. And I have to ask, nipple clamps?"

"Too long a story. You had to be there." Meredith smiled. "It was very funny though. I go for the entertainment as much as any physical benefit."

"Well, although I don't want to inflate that ego, whoever is making you laugh needs a raise. The physical benefits are worth it. Over there. There's a space over there. Oh, you missed it."

"You are hungry. We can always run to the restaurant."

They ended up parking on the other side of the road, a few hundred yards down from the restaurant. The breeze was now a chilly wind, and Meredith placed his hand in the small of her back as they trotted across the road.

"Oh Louie, look. It's the skipper and his friend."

Louie Trump twisted in his chair, did a double take, and turned back to his wife. "Linda, did you know he was coming here? Don't lie to me, I will be cross."

"Yes, of course I did. I had a massive lunch, I've got enough leftovers for another two, and you don't come to an Italian and have a salad." Linda pointed at the bowl in front of her.

"You should have told me. I'm not impressed. It's embarrassing. Very embarrassing."

"Then you would have said no. Are you not enjoying your cannelloni?"

"Not anymore. Have you finished?" Louie usually humoured his wife and rarely showed anger or embarrassment at her antics. Tonight, though, he was not amused. "I think we should leave."

"Louie, no. That would be even more embarrassing. Giorgio will think we didn't like it. I'm sorry but he was being shifty."

"No. He told you where he was eating this evening. He chose not to share the private details. I'm sure he didn't expect you to become a stalker. Because that's what this is. It's not simply being nosey, it's stalking. Finish your salad, please. I'll get the bill."

Linda grabbed his hand. "I'm sorry. I'm sorry. You do realise this is our first ever row. Oh no, I'm so sorry. You're right. We should go. I've also finished. Shall I ask them to box that up?"

Louie caved in. "No. Lesson learned. We have enough boxes in the fridge already. I'll get the bill, and we shall slip away without even acknowledging his presence."

"Their presence."

Louie ignored her, looked around and, spotting a server facing their way, raised a hand. Meredith spotted the movement and paused as they followed the waiter leading them to their table.

"Smile," Meredith told Emily.

"I am. What are you talking about?"

"Good, keep it there. You'll find out." Taking her elbow, Meredith steered towards the Trumps' table. "Trump. What a surprise. Loopy, you look wonderful, as always. Oh sorry, you haven't met. Emily, this is Louie Trump, my right-hand man, and this is the lovely Linda, Patsy's best friend, and lock finder. Trump, Loopy, this is Emily, one of my oldest and best friends." He looked at Linda as Trump got to his feet and shook Emily's hand. "And not Ben. Did you think I'd lied to you?" He struggled to hold back the smile as Linda blushed.

"Nice to meet you, Emily. I'd invite you to join us, unfortunately we're just leaving." Louie flapped his hand towards the table.

"Oh, that's a shame." Emily looked at Linda and held out her hand. When Linda took it, she placed her free hand on the top. "Linda, it's lovely to meet you. I'm sorry you're leaving, I know you must be missing Patsy as much as Meredith. Unfortunately, I've never met Patsy, but feel like I know her because Meredith never stops talking about her. Perhaps another time."

"I do. We all do. Yes, it's a shame we have to leave, perhaps—"

"Perhaps another time. DCI Meredith will be starving by now. It must be at least two hours since food passed his lips. Ah, there's the waiter. Bill please." Trump made the obligatory air squiggle with his finger. "Thank you."

Emily laughed. "He's never been any different. Do you know when we used to catch the school bus he used to wander up and down the aisle asking everyone to check if they had food they didn't want in their lunch box, and he'd only just had his breakfast."

Meredith held up his hand. "Ignore her. It was once. Once when I'd overslept and needed to eat." He bumped his shoulder against Emily's. "You've just had road rage because I missed a parking space because you were hangry. Did you know that was an affliction?"

Trump smiled. "Linda, love of my life, shall we leave these old friends to catch up?"

"Yes, of course. I must just visit the loo. Emily, it's a shame we can't have a chat, but thank you for being there for the skipper. He needs a friend like you." Linda pulled Emily into a hug and blinked furiously. "Now I'm getting emotional. Excuse me." Linda hurried away.

Trump held out his hand. "I'm sorry, sir. I had no idea."

Meredith shook his hand. "No apology necessary. I'm sorry you didn't get to finish your meal, though. Loopy said the cannelloni is good."

"It certainly was until I realised why I was whisked out for a surprise meal. I would suggest going whilst the going is good. She might decide to join you after all. Apologies, Emily, enjoy your meal."

Meredith led Emily back to their table. He waited until they'd been given menus before he kicked Emily's foot.

"Thank you."

"For what?"

"What you said. It was kind."

"I was being genuine, Meredith. If Linda is Patsy's best friend and has also been cut off, she'll be feeling very sad." Emily shrugged. "What did you expect me to do?"

"Just say 'nice to meet you', I suppose. I should have known better. You are a remarkable woman."

"I am. But shut up and choose your food. As you correctly pointed out, I am hangry."

Food ordered, Meredith smiled at her. "Shall we do this thing?"

"Not yet. I want to eat first. I refuse to let good food go cold because we're talking again. That was my fault last night. I've learned my lesson."

"As you wish."

"Meredith, you're staring at me. Pack it in."

"You are very easy to look at, but I'm not just admiring the view, I'm admiring your poise, your natural gracefulness, and—"

"And shut up. I don't blush. Never did. The food is on its way, and I refuse to be distracted until I'm ready."

"Message received. But you do, you know, blush. I'll tell you later." Meredith smiled as their food was placed in front of them. "Thank you."

Meal over, Meredith leaned back in his chair. "Are we doing this here, or would you rather be somewhere more private?" He sighed as the waiter appeared with the dessert menu. "Would you like a pudding?"

"Of course. I can't believe you don't want one."

Meredith held his hand towards Emily. "Just the lady, thank you. May I borrow your pen?" He took the pen offered and wrote on his napkin, folding it before handing the pen back.

"What's that?" Emily looked at the napkin.

"I'll show you later. Here or somewhere else. Or have we got to wait until you've finished your meringue?"

"You're in a rush, Meredith, Can't we wait until the meal's over? I'm feeling shortchanged."

"Maybe. No pressure. You enjoy every mouthful, I will."

“I’m not sharing. You had your chance, buster.” Emily looked around. “How long can it take to put a meringue on a plate and add a dollop of raspberries?”

“Not long. It’s drizzling the chocolate sauce and sprinkling...” Meredith picked up the menu. “Crushed pistachios, that takes the time.” His eyes twinkled. “It’s an art form.”

Emily smiled. “You are being very amusing tonight, Meredith. And it’s here.”

Emily finished her third mouthful and pointed the spoon at him. “If you don’t stop staring, I promise I will do something you won’t like.”

“I doubt it. What would you like me to do?”

“Oh, what about talking? Tell me about your day, tell me about the nipple clamps, and I can pretend I was there.” A woman walking past the table faltered and took a quick glance at them before continuing her journey. “It’s him, not me. He’s the one into pain,” Emily told the woman’s departing back. Meredith laughed, and Emily pushed the plate across the table. “All yours.”

“Not an inch of room. But thank you. Coffee? Leave or stay?” He watched her chest rise as she sighed.

“Stay, I think. Might be easier, depending on the outcome. And I said you had to go first but I’m happy to. Is that okay?”

“You’re in charge. I know what you’re going to say.”

“I don’t think you do.”

“Emily, will you please put me out of my misery?” Meredith coughed. “Sometime this evening would be preferable.”

Emily took his hand in hers and searched his face. “You’re concerning me now, Meredith. Making me nervous, in fact. Every time I think I can read you, you throw me off kilter.”

“Apologies. Would it make it easier if I showed you what I wrote on the napkin?”

“Is that your choice?”

“No, it’s yours.”

“You have no idea what I’m going to say.”

“Yes, I do.”

“I’m not arguing with you. Give it to me.” Emily held out her hand.

Meredith handed her the napkin, which she read, refolded and placed on the table in front of her. "Based on what?"

"The lack of lipstick. The comments about Patsy. And, I hope, that you want to have a better life than the one I offered." Meredith looked away and cleared his throat. "You deserve better than me. You always did. If we ever do this again, with or without benefits, I'm not driving. I need a bloody drink."

Emily banged the flat of her hand on the table. "Lipstick? You based this on lipstick?" Screwing the napkin into a ball, she flung it at Meredith as she tutted.

Meredith caught it neatly. "You didn't wear lipstick because you didn't want me to look at your mouth. Your plan failed, but it was a plan none the less. And I also gave you several other reasons. Shall we cover those?"

"Not really. What I said about Patsy was true. Genuine. I wasn't sending subliminal messages. As to the deserving bit, I do, I really do deserve you. But all of you. I can't do second best. It wouldn't end well. I'd like me and you to end well. I deserve that, too."

Meredith flattened the napkin and reached across the table and caught the tear, before asking for the bill. "You do indeed. I'll take you home."

"I don't want to go home. I want you to talk to me. What do you think, can we be just friends? What were you going to say? I knew I should have let you go first. I demand to know. No lies, I demand the truth."

"Do you know your cleavage blushes when you're angry?"

"Fuck's sake, Meredith, stay on track, answer the bloody question, and stop making me swear. What were you going to say because you were very keen to get it out there?"

"No, I wasn't. I was very keen to let you escape."

"So you wanted me to escape?" Emily asked.

"That we will never know. My heart said no, my head said stop being a selfish bastard. I hadn't made a final decision until you came out with naked lips. Subliminal messages were all over the shop. Come on, let me take you home."

"On one condition."

"Being?"

"Tonight is the night we celebrate our friendship and get all the sexy stuff out of our system."

"Let me get this straight. There's sympathy sex, and sex to get over sex. Is there any other type of sex I don't know about?"

Emily tapped her lips and looked at the ceiling. "I can't remember. But I promise to let you know if it comes to me. Is that acceptable?"

"I can hardly blame you for being forgetful at your age."

"Exactly. I thought you were taking me home?"

"I am."

• • • • ● • ● • • • •

When Meredith arrived home in the early hours of the morning, the first thing he noticed as he entered the house was the flashing red light on the answer machine. He glanced at the machine as he walked to the kitchen. Two messages. He had been intending to get a glass of water but eyed the whiskey still sitting on the table. Knowing he'd need a drink to listen, he opted for a glass of wine, and he filled the glass and emptied it in several gulps before filling it back up and returning to the hall.

He hit the play button and sat on the stairs, his head resting against the spindles.

You have two messages. First message received at twenty-one forty-five.

Hello, Johnny, I'm not sure why I was on a timer. I could guess, but I won't. Whatever is happening in your life, I hope you're having some fun and it's not all work and alcohol. Although, Maxine told me she'd seen you at the gym a few times. The gym! Well done. But to the serious stuff. Your offer is humbling. I'm not sure I could have done the same, roles reversed, and I know you mean it with all good intent, and much as I'd like to accept, I can't do it. I can't do it to any of us. Oh, I'm sorry, I promised myself not to get upset. So, here we are. You must move on. I would ask you to forgive me and not to forget me, try to remember all the good stuff. I've said that before. Sorry. Look, I'm going to go now, but for the record, I know there would have been hurt, and pain, but there should never be guilt. You are you, DCI Johnny Meredith. Don't change any of what makes you, you. Oh, boy. So much I want to say but what's the point? It will just hurt both of us. Goodbye, Meredith.

Message two. Received at twenty-one fifty-seven.

I forgot to say the most important thing. I love you. I thank you. And, yes, I'm still sorry. Onwards and upwards, Johnny.

Meredith left his wine untouched on the stairs, walked to the answer machine and hit the delete button. He knew he's probably regret it but it felt appropriate. Pulling his own phone from his pocket, he dialled New Zealand. It was three in the afternoon there, but an answer machine picked up his call.

"Hodge, this leaving messages is not you. You have never been a coward. But if this is how you insist we communicate, so be it. You might want to let me have a private number, though. I'm not sure Steve and Martha, and certainly not their kids, will want to hear some of what I have to say. But for the time being, I will say this: I will always be here, and the offer will always be open. When you come back, you will see nothing but joy and gratitude. But, right now, I don't know you. You are certainly not my padlock." Meredith hoped Patsy would understand the reference to their time in Paris. "I bumped into Maxine and in the roundabout way she speaks, I understand you've stopped speaking to her. That's not good news. Whatever your final decision, because that's yet to be made, you need help. It's daft for you not to make yourself as fit and well as you can be. For the child. For our child because we've got a piece of paper that says what's yours is mine. If you won't speak to Maxine, find someone over there. Oh yes, but if you stay with Maxine, use Zoom. She thinks you're doing okay because she can't see your body language. There's a challenge for you. You like a challenge. Come home, Patsy."

Chapter Twenty-Seven

Brandon Farm

Susan watched Mark get dressed. When he was ready, he took her to the bathroom and waited for her outside. Back in the bedroom, instead of tying her to the bedstead, he took her face in his hands and kissed her.

"Get dressed. I'll be back. I'm not sure how long I'll be, though."

"Mark, what's happening? What are you going to do? Why do I need to be dressed? Are you going to let me go?"

"No. Just get dressed."

The door closed behind him, and she heard the key turn in the lock. Her instinct was to bang on the door and demand he explain. But who would hear her? Charlie and Cissy, they couldn't do anything to stop him from doing whatever he wanted.

If she was going to die, she'd die in her nightie. Why that made a difference she didn't know but sod him. She'd had enough of being frightened, enough of doing what was expected. In this small way, she'd leave this world dressed the way she wanted. A thought occurred to her, and she smiled. Walking to the wardrobe, she lifted out her party dress. She'd bought it just before she came here, and still hadn't had a reason to wear it. Laying it across the bed, she rummaged through her drawer. Best undies, too, she reckoned. She placed them on top of the dress and sat at the dressing table, unzipping the makeup bag that hadn't seen the light of day for a year or more.

Dressed and made up, she smiled at her reflection. Who knew, when he saw her he might change his mind. She doubted it, but she'd always been an optimist. Plumping up the pillows, she sat upright on the bed and awaited his return.

Chapter Twenty-Eight

Meredith hadn't slept, and was on his third cup of coffee by the time everyone had arrived.

"Morning all, get yourselves sorted. Ten minutes and we'll kick off. Loopy, I'll give you the honour of taking the briefing. You can highlight all the bits we missed, and then we'll plan our attack, and hopefully carry out an arrest or arrests."

Linda looked shocked and, shoving the cake tin she was carrying into Seaton's hands, she hurried to his desk.

"Skipper, are you sure? I mean I can. I've done a note sheet for you, but why me?"

"Because, yet again, you were the one that found the last piece of the puzzle."

"Not really. But if you want me to. But you are okay, yes? You're not ill or anything because you usually get irritated when someone else is doing the briefing. You try to hide it but we all know. I don't want to irritate you two days in a row. Which brings me to my apology. I'm sorry about last night. I'm glad you have Emily. She was lovely to me. She's very pretty, very kind, and very understanding."

"I know. Go and get ready. You're forgiven."

"Yes, Skipper. I'll try not to let you down."

As Linda walked away, Seaton stepped up to Meredith's desk. Meredith rolled his eyes.

"Morning, Seaton."

"Emily? Linda has met Emily," Seaton whispered.

"Yes, as has Trump. I think they liked her."

"They what?"

"You heard. Seaton, do you have something to say because we've got an important briefing coming up?"

"So I heard, why Linda? I don't believe what you just told her." Seaton glanced over his shoulder to make sure Linda wasn't listening. "She'll drive you mad."

"Because she has all the facts, she found most of them. And I didn't sleep last night, and have a thumping headache? Anything else?"

"You haven't slept knowing what today might bring?" Seaton rubbed his brow. "I thought we were past all this."

"Me too. Sit down, shut up, and let's crack on."

Although the team were silent, Linda walked to stand next to the screen and tapped her pen on a mug, until Meredith held up his hand.

"Now, Loopy."

"Skipper. I'm not going to waffle on, but I've prepared a timeline of the key dates. You all know that Jasmine Jones and Louise Marshall went missing, their bodies later found buried on farms in the Reading area. I'm going to talk you through our theory of what happened to them. Although not why."

A map appeared and Linda pointed out the two red dots representing the burial sites.

"We believe that until their deaths they had been living on Brandon Farm, here. Owned by Charles and Cissy Brandon, it is also home to son Mark and a woman claiming to be his wife. She's not but I'll come to that. The burial site for Louise was on farmland owned by the brother of Charles Brandon, one Gerry Brandon. Whether the extended family knows about any of this has yet to be discovered because the skipper forgot to ask or show them the photographs. But he's had a lot on his mind, so we'll skip that bit."

Meredith pinched the bridge of his nose as George snorted. Linda grinned and continued. As she read through her notes, bullet points appeared on the board behind her.

"Jasmine Jones disappeared in the summer of 2002. On the third of January 2003, she married Mark Brandon, becoming Mrs Jasmine Brandon.

Her body was discovered in 2023, and we think she probably died around 2009 and she'd been killed by a single blow to the head.

Having died in 2009, the original Jasmine was replaced by Louise Marshall. Louise disappeared in 2010, her body found in 2018. She had been killed in what appears a frenzied attack with a blunt weapon. It wasn't until Jasmine's body was unearthed in 2023 that the two cases were connected, and we got the job of solving it, and it's been a long hard slog, and to be honest we missed a trick or two. But not to worry it looks like we got there in the end."

"Loopy, can we get back Louise Marshall, please?"

"Skipper." Linda cupped a hand around her mouth and in a dramatic whisper told the team, "I'm irritating him. I knew I would."

Meredith pursed his lips and Linda grimaced.

"So, Louise goes to the farm in 2010. In 2014, as Jasmine Brandon the second, Louise Marshall was treated for a broken arm having been crushed by a cow between a gate and a stone wall, and in January 2016, as Jasmine B the second, gave birth to a son, Thomas. Father named as Mark Brandon. What she did to be killed when her—"

"I thought you couldn't find that?" Meredith interrupted.

"That's because you asked for maternity records. I got this from the General Register Office. Took hours. They need to sort that out," Linda replied.

"When?" Meredith looked confused.

"Last night when I got in after meeting Emily. Oh. Anyway, someone—"

"Who's Emily?" George asked. "You haven't mentioned any Emily before?"

Seaton's eyes darted to Meredith, and he covered his face as Linda replied.

"Oh, she's an old friend of the skipper, she's lovely. Really nice."

"He's got a lot of those. You'd better carry on." George said, and jerked his head towards Meredith who had tilted his head towards the ceiling and closed his eyes.

Linda cleared her throat. "As I was saying, before George took me off track, someone replaced Louise Marshall. A woman claiming to be Jasmine Brandon told Will she had never seen the two women before, and said she'd lived on the farm for twenty-plus years, and kissed Mark Brandon. So, here are the questions. One, how did they get Jasmine number two and three to go along with it? Because the whole family must be in on it. Two, does the current Jasmine know what happened to the others? Because that's where Will did a skipper and didn't tell her they were even dead. And he's not had a lot on his mind, I don't think. Have you?"

"Loopy, question three is on the screen. Stay focused." Meredith winked at Will Kent. "Don't look like that. You're in good company, and Loopy can't discipline you."

Linda glanced at the screen. "Focused. Yes. So question three, if she didn't know they were killed, what was she told to make her happy to say she'd never seen them, even though they are younger versions of herself? Question four, who actually killed the two girls? Mark, Cissy or Charles? Question five, as we've yet to speak to Charles, has he been bumped off too? No record of death, but then there wouldn't be because they'd have buried his body like they did with the girls. Then I ran out of questions." Linda looked at Meredith. "Shall I sit down now?"

"If you would." Meredith stood and took her place. "Thoughts? One at a time. George."

"Too many people know. How do you get a brand new wife? Let's stick with Louise taking over and passing her off as Jasmine the first? There was a gap between one and the other, granted, but they must have people come to the farm. Someone must have missed her in the gap. And when she did reappear, she'd changed. I know it's happened but for it to be a success, more than those living in that house must know. My money is on the brother and his wife being in on it. But what have they got to gain?"

"I thought about that," Louie Trump volunteered. "Linda filled me in last night, so I had the advantage over you chaps. These farms are remote by necessity, surrounded by fields. People come and go, deliveries, even farmhands, if they have them, but how many people would go into the house? The original Jasmine Brandon had no friends in the area. The only people she knew were the Brandons, and perhaps the odd shopkeeper, a word here and there with the postman. Would they have had an active social life? They're up at the crack of dawn, work hard all day, etcetera. It's feasible that when Louise arrived, she kept herself distant. She knew her role was to be Jasmine. She took her name, and it would appear her marital bed, and when there were visitors, a glimpse here and there until she was recognised as Jasmine. The issue for me arises with the child. Thomas."

"Agreed," Meredith said. "But the child would have been too young to know. One mummy goes, grandparents and father are around, and a while later, another mummy appears. Before he starts school. And one of the grandparents could have done the doctors and the school run, because they're farmers they're busy people. As for family, not all families are close. How often do you see them? One of my sisters I only see once every four years. If I replaced Patsy with a lookalike in between time, would she know? I'd like to think so but it's not beyond the realm of possibility. So accepting all that worked because it has, how do we approach it now?"

The team had fallen silent, and Meredith waved his finger.

"What, I can't mention her name? Patsy is personal. This is work. We are about to arrest someone for the brutal murder of two young women, and we are about to shatter a young boy's world. We don't have time to mope about because we've got personal stuff going on. Do you think Patsy would want that? Would do that? For the record, I'm not about to replace Patsy. You all know that's not possible, so stop being bloody dramatic and tell me how you think we should approach this. I know what we're going to do. I want to know what you think. Will, you can kick off because the others are still smarting."

"We arrest them all, surely? Then find out who and why. But all the adults in that house are involved, if not the wider family. We start by arresting them and bring the brother and his wife in for questioning."

"We'd need to have social services involved because of the child," Daisy said.

"And an armed response. Someone in that house is dangerous. They might all be. Have they got a firearms licence? Most farmers do. But even if they don't, as we know from experience, they still might have a shotgun or two in there." George smiled. "Meredith, wouldn't it be easier just to tell us what we're going to do?"

"Probably. These are our arrests. There are four adults who need questioning by us because I don't want to bugger about updating strangers. So four of us have to go down there, but we will need the help of the local chaps because as George rightly pointed out there might be trouble, and we'll need transport to bring them back to Bristol. I've spoken to Carrington and the chief super. They've cleared our path to go today and to bring them back here. Thames Valley have no problem with that." Meredith glanced at the clock: it was nine fifteen. "I want this done and dusted during school hours. That child is going to be traumatised enough without being there."

"I take it the girls will be babysitting me. Can I at least book them in when you get back?" George asked.

"You can. This is the way I'd like it to work. One of us, possibly two, will go and knock and ask for a word. We're going to catch them off guard, and hopefully can make a couple of arrests before they all get wind of it and try to do a runner. We'll find out who else is where and pick them up. I'm suggesting me and Kent go in first."

"Is there a reason for that, sir?" Trump looked a little put out.

"There is. A good one. I've got no one sitting at home waiting for me. Seaton has a wife and kids, Linda has had enough on her plate lately, and although Kent has a romantic involvement, he cocked up just like I did. That okay with you, Kent?"

"Yes, Guv."

Seeing the look on Linda's face, he added, "That's just a precaution because armed officers will be on standby, at all times, and Kent and I will wear body armour. We all will, and bodycams, all of us. That way, everyone knows what's going on. Everyone ready?"

"What now? Literally now. No phone calls to make?" Seaton got to his feet and pulled his jacket off the chair without waiting for the answer.

"Yep. We have transport waiting to leave at nine thirty. Traffic willing, we're meeting the Thames Valley mob at eleven." Meredith walked to his desk and snatched up his phone. "Final questions."

No one spoke, but the men leaving for Brandon Farm collected what they needed. Meredith watched as Louie kissed Linda.

"Are you okay, Loopy? I'd say you could join us but I need you to speak to this chap and sort out the cam footage and anything else you can think of. We'll be back by teatime." He tore a sheet from his pad and handed it to her.

Ten minutes later, he chose to sit in the back with his men. There wasn't a lot more they could say until they got there.

Meredith leaned back and crossed his feet at the ankles. "It's been a long time since I went on a shout like this. I have to say I'm looking forward to it. Go on, admit it, you all are."

They all agreed, and when they lapsed back into silence, Will said, quietly, "Am I allowed to admit I'm a bit nervous?"

"Yep, and the reality will be it'll all be boring, and we'll have some long days ahead of us stuck in a little room with lukewarm coffee, but the nerves, the adrenalin will be what keeps you safe if anything goes tits up. It's why we cocked up. We were bored. We thought we had the answers without asking the questions. In fact, I'm hoping one of the Thames Valley boys is a knob. That way, I'll be pissy before we knock on the door. Any other questions?"

"So, Louie, you met Emily. Did you like her? What's she like?" Seaton asked, and Meredith's eyes narrowed.

"She was lovely. Very attractive, very personable, very kind to Linda, who was being Linda. She told a very amusing story about DCI Mere...Am I missing something?"

"No, you're not, Trump. Ignore him. He's trying to make sure I'm pissy before I knock."

"I am not. I was genuinely interested. So, did you decide?"

Kent and Trump watched Meredith closely. Seaton knew more than they did.

"Didn't need to." Meredith closed his eyes. "I wish I'd sat in the front now."

"Ah come on. She's attractive and all that other stuff, and you didn't need to? I want to know the journey I'm going to be on for the next couple of months."

"Don't we all. Everything is fluid, Seaton. No point in putting your foot down. It's all on the move. Fluid."

"I've got no idea what you're talking about. I'll find out, you know that?" Seaton replied.

"That's good to hear. When you do, let me know. Are we done with the questions?"

"Almost." Seaton grinned, as Meredith opened an eye to look at him. "If you had everyone on standby, why did you let Linda take the briefing?"

"I was feeling reckless."

"Now, that answer I do believe. No offence, Louie."

"None taken."

Chapter Twenty-Nine

Brandon Farm

Everyone knew their job, everyone was in position, and Meredith looked at Kent as he started the engine. "Are you ready, Kent? Shall we go and arrest a few people?"

"I think we'd look stupid if we didn't." Will Kent buckled his seatbelt.

"Couldn't agree more. Good news about the boy being away. That will give them time to sort something out for him."

"Yes. Mind that pot...not to worry. It's not our car." Kent grimaced as the loaned car bounced through a pothole.

Meredith drove up the drive and parked to the left of the farmhouse, giving the police marksman a clear view of the front door should it be necessary.

"Follow my lead. Keep your mouth shut until it's necessary. If there's going to be another cockup, let it be mine."

"I won't argue with that."

Kent stood a little behind Meredith as he rapped the knocker and pulled out his ID. A tall, burly man opened the door and frowned at them.

"Mr Brandon, DCI Meredith and DC Kent. We're making enquiries in the area, and wondered if we might have a word?"

Mark Brandon smiled, and stepping back, opened the door wider. "Come in. Take a seat."

Meredith and Kent walked into the farmhouse. Kent looked back as Mark shut the door.

"Guv."

Meredith turned and looked at the shotgun now aimed at him

"Everything okay, Mr Brandon? What's the gun for? You having problems?"

"You could say that. Sit down."

Meredith nodded at Kent, and they took a seat at the table.

"Would you like to tell us about them? We might be able to help." Meredith watched as Mark looked out of the window without changing his aim. "Are you looking for someone?"

"My mother. She should be back by now."

"Where did she go?" Meredith hoped the team was getting all this. They could pick Cissy up without her coming anywhere near the house.

"I don't know. She should be here. I don't know what to do now."

"Is your wife with her?" Kent asked.

"No."

"Where's Jasmine?" Meredith asked and Brandon took a step closer. One hand holding the shotgun, his other pressed to his chest.

"Why?"

Meredith shrugged. "Just wanted to make sure everyone was safe. You're wandering around with a shotgun, not something I come across every day, and to be honest, it makes me nervous."

"And me." Mark said. "Jasmine's safe. I made sure of that." Brandon lifted the string to reveal the key. "Now you're here and I don't know what to do. I had it planned. You ruined it."

Meredith cursed silently, although he was glad they'd averted whatever Brandon had planned. "You've locked Jasmine up to keep her safe. Is that what you're telling me?"

"I just said, didn't I?" Mark twisted his neck to look out of the window.

"Where is she, in the house or in one of the outbuildings?" Meredith asked.

Mark's eyes wandered to the ceiling. "She's upstairs."

"Are you sure? It's very quiet up there." Meredith looked up at the ceiling.

"Because he can't start banging. I warned him, not today, not today." Brandon repositioned the gun.

"Warned who? Your father or your son?" Meredith asked.

"My father. Thomas is at camp, thank God."

"Yes, I heard that was a last-minute thing. Who arranged that? You or Jasmine?" Meredith hoped he wasn't revealing his hand too soon, but the more information he could get out of Brandon while he was talking, the better.

"Me. I didn't tell Jasmine." Brandon rested the barrel against his shoulder and scratched his head.

"Why's that? What's happening today? Why was it important for your dad to keep quiet, and for Thomas to be away from the house?"

"Shut up, shut the fuck up. I'm thinking." Brandon repositioned the shotgun and pointed it at Meredith. "Where is she? Where is she?"

Meredith held up his hands as Mark Brandon paced up and down, mumbling.

"I'll shut up again if you want me to, but I'm guessing you're talking about your mother, perhaps your dad or Jasmine will know where she is."

"Jasmine hasn't seen her for days, and he's seen no one."

Meredith closed his eyes, realising they might be talking about corpses. "Have you hurt them?"

"Not yet. Do you want to see her?" Brandon demanded.

"Yes, sure. If you don't mind. Up to you." Meredith leaned back in his chair. "You're in charge, Mark."

Brandon marched to the door at the bottom of the stairs and yanked it open, but realising he'd have to leave them alone, marched back and pointed the gun at Kent. "On your feet."

Kent hesitated and looked at Meredith.

Meredith leaned forward. "I thought you were going to show me?"

"Stay where you are. If he does anything stupid, I'll shoot you." Brandon pulled the string over his head and threw the key to Kent, who fumbled the catch. Brandon watched him scramble from the chair and pick it up. "Top of the stairs, through the door on your left. It's the locked one."

Kent nodded and, keen to be away from the gun he took the stairs two at a time. He opened the door to his left and found himself on a small landing with a tiny window at the far end. Closing the door behind him, he rested his back against it and pulled out his phone and dialled Trump.

"Can you see what's happening?" he asked as Trump answered.

"Yes. You're both doing well. Armed men are immediately outside of the property. Can't get a clear shot without showing themselves. They're being told what's happening. Another unit and paramedics on the way. Go and check the girl, Will, and then get back downstairs. DCI Meredith doesn't think he has much to lose at the moment. If you're there, he'll be more considered in his actions."

"Yes. You're right." Kent hung up and went to the nearest door. Pushing it open, he found an empty bathroom.

"Who's there? Is anyone coming to sort me out? You bastards." A gruff voice called from the door opposite.

Kent pulled out his ID and pushed the door open slowly. Quickly taking in the hospital bed, and the hoist, Kent held the ID towards the man he assumed was Charles Brandon. The room stank. He'd obviously soiled himself. "Police. I'm guessing you're Charles."

"Why the hell are you here? Where's Cissy? Where's Jasmine? I tried to warn her, but if you're here I'm guessing she's dead, too." Charlie Brandon held out his hands. "Who's going to sort me out?"

"I'm going to have to ask you to be patient, sir. Stay here and stay quiet. Your son is quite agitated and has a gun, and we've yet to locate your wife and Jasmine. We're trying to find them. Will you do that for me?"

Charlie rolled his eyes and let his head flop against the pillow. "Cissy said she'd let me die in my own shit."

"We'll be as quick as we can."

Kent went to the last door, and his hand shook a little as he put the key in the lock. He pushed the door open slowly, and Susan's eyes flared in recognition as he stepped into the room. She flew off the bed.

"Oh my God. Thank God, have you got him?" Throwing herself into his arms, she wept into his shoulder as he patted her back.

"Mark's downstairs. He has a gun and is holding my boss. He's agitated about his mother because he doesn't know where she is. Do you know?"

"I haven't seen her for days. He's had me tied to the bed. That door stayed locked. She never even bothered to come and talk to me. Mark took me to the bathroom and brought my food. Has he killed Charlie? I haven't heard him banging today."

"He's alive. In a bit of a mess but we'll sort that out later. You're not injured?" Kent gently pushed her away from him and looked her up and down, hoping his surprise at her choice of attire didn't register.

"Not injured, and I'm not mad. Although, I must be, I suppose. I thought he was going to kill me today. He told me to get dressed, and I thought if I'm going to die I'll go out with a bang." Susan's head shot towards the door as Mark Brandon shouted up the stairs. "What did he say?" she asked.

"I didn't catch it. I'll shut the door. Stay there." Kent hurried back to the door at the end of the landing and pulled it open. Susan followed him out. "Jasmine, would you like me to—"

"Susan. My name is Susan. If anyone else calls me Jasmine I might kill someone myself. I've had enough. I'm not being locked back in that bloody room waiting for him to finish me off. Let's get it over with." Susan pushed Kent to one side, and he grabbed her wrist. She turned to face him. "Let me go!"

"Jasmine, is that you? What's he doing to you?"

"Susan, he's got my boss down there. Don't piss him off," Kent pleaded.

"Jasmine, get down here now. I've got enough on my plate." Mark's voice was commanding, any hesitation gone.

Susan yanked her wrist from Kent's grasp and ran down the stairs, pushing Mark Brandon in the chest as she entered the kitchen.

"My name is Susan. Susan. Say it. If you're going to kill me, do it now. You and this bloody family have too many secrets. Do it in front of them. Go on, do it now. NOW!" She shoved him in the chest again, and he stepped back. "I was a good wife to you. A good mother to poor Thomas. What are you going to do to him when he gets in from school and finds you've killed another mother?"

She lifted her arms to push him again, but he caught her forearm and yanked her close to him. Kissing her forehead.

"I wasn't going to kill you, Jasmine. Couldn't do that. I love you. I was keeping you safe. That's why I locked you in. She couldn't get to you then."

Meredith watched the scene play out. His mind racing. Unless Mark really was delusional, he might be telling the truth. He was about to ask about Cissy when Susan exploded again. Meredith saw Kent step quietly into the room behind Brandon.

"SUSAN. Say it. I will not be Jasmine bloody Brandon for one more day. Say it."

"Susan." Mark smiled at her. "My Susan."

"Right. Good. Now why have you got that gun?"

Mark's eyes shot to Meredith, and he lowered his head and whispered in her ear. Susan looked up at him.

"Why?"

"Because she killed Thomas's mum. She hit her, and she hit her, and she was getting jumpy because of the stuff on the news, and I didn't want her to kill you." Mark's eyes never left Susan's.

"Cissy did it? She told me she ran away, baby blues. What about your wife? The first one."

"She said it was Dad. Said he was trying to force himself on Jasmine, and then he killed her when Mum found them. They were in the shed. He got away."

Susan put a hand on his chest. "Where's the hammer?"

"What hammer?" Mark looked confused.

"Cissy told me that you had to bury Jasmine because your prints were on the hammer and your dad hid it. He told Gerry where to find it if anything happened to him," Susan explained.

"I don't know anything about a hammer. Why would he tell Gerry that?"

Meredith cleared his throat. "May I speak?"

Mark turned to face him. "No."

Susan stroked his arm. "Mark, listen to him. He's a policeman, you have to listen to the police."

Meredith tapped the table. "Sit down, Mark. Sit down and tell Susan what happened."

Mark hesitated. "What if she comes back?"

"She's an old lady, Mark. You've got the gun. Come on, I'll sit next to you." Susan pushed Mark towards the table.

"To be on the safe side. Kent will stand in front of the door. I want no one coming in here until you've told Susan. Kent." Meredith jerked his thumb towards the front door. His message was for the officers outside not Mark.

Mark placed the gun on the table and sat opposite Meredith. Susan dragged a chair to sit next to him.

"Cissy told me you found your dad trying it on with Jasmine. Your dad killed her. You grabbed the hammer and dropped it when she moaned. Is that not what happened?" Susan asked gently.

"No. I wasn't there. I was in the top field with the feed. When I came down for lunch, she was in the barn bellowing for him to come out. I asked her what was wrong, and she took me to Jasmine. She was dead. She told me Dad had killed her after trying to have sex with her. When he saw Mum, he blamed Jasmine and hit her and killed her. Then he ran away. She was trying to find him. She asked me to help."

"And you found him?" Meredith asked.

"Yep. Up in the hayloft. I dragged him out and asked him why? He said it wasn't him, it was her. It was all her fault. I got so mad, I whacked him, then I picked him up and I threw him down. Then Mum came in. She kicked him hard. But he didn't speak. I thought he was dead, too."

"Why didn't you call the police?" Meredith asked.

"Mum said it was best not to. Said you'd put me away for killing my father, and then what would she do? She'd be all alone on the farm, and it wasn't my fault. It was his. Me being locked up wouldn't bring Jasmine back. I didn't want to go to prison. I wanted Jasmine. So I did what I was told."

"You buried Jasmine? That was kind of you."

"Yes. Planted some bulbs for her, too. But not that day because when I put Jasmine in the back of the car, Dad called to me. He wasn't dead. He was crying. Mum told me she'd go and speak to him. When she came back, she told me I wouldn't go to prison if I did what I was told."

"Mark, why did you listen to her? She's ruined your life, you great lummox. I think your mum killed Jasmine, not your dad. Don't you?" Susan looked at Meredith. "He's not lying, he doesn't know how to."

"It certainly sounds that way. Tell Susan what happened to Thomas's mum."

"She was nice, not like Susan but she was funny. Then she had Thomas." Mark grinned. "He was so tiny. I was happy again, then."

"Her name was Louise." Meredith told him. "Why did she agree to pretend to be Jasmine?"

"Mum said no one would ask questions if we got another one. Dad would keep his mouth shut if we looked after him. So Mum went to Bristol to find her. She paid her to help us because Jasmine had died. But she had to pretend to be my wife, or people would know. She took a long time to be my wife, but she did. I never made her. Then she had Thomas, and I loved her for that. Not like I loved Jasmine, not like I love you." Mark grabbed Susan's hand, and she inclined her head.

"Why did you hurt me? That first time? Do you remember?" Susan looked over at the sink.

"Because Mum was getting angry. Said she was paying you to be a proper wife, and she'd have to sort you out. I didn't want her to hurt you. Not like she hurt Jas...Louise. So I made you be a proper wife. I told you I was sorry but I was keeping you safe."

Susan smiled at him. "Thank you."

"What happened to Louise? She was being a proper wife. She'd even had a son for you. Why did she die?"

Thomas shrugged. "Because she was going to tell. Dad told her I'd killed Jasmine and buried her and thrown him out of the loft. Mum said we couldn't have that. I cried, and she said it would all work itself out, we'd find another Jasmine. And we did. We found you." Mark frowned and wagged his finger. "Is that the hammer you meant? That's what she did. She hit her and hit her. It was obvious she was dead but she wouldn't listen. She just kept hitting her."

Susan reached up and brushed his tear away. "It wasn't your fault, Mark." She looked at Meredith. "What happens now?"

"Now we speak to his father and find Cissy Brandon. Then we'll all have to go to the police station and sort this out."

Mark was nodding. "I knew that. That's why I sent Thomas to camp. I was going to kill Mum, and probably Dad. But I was going to let Susan take the car and escape first. So she wouldn't be in trouble, and she wouldn't go to prison. I love Susan."

"I can see that, Mark. But why would she go to prison? It seems to me like she had no idea about Jasmine and Louise?"

"When we saw that thing on the telly about them, Mum said we had to keep Susan away from the police. Keep her at the house because if the police knew they'd died here, they might think Susan knew about it, they might even think she'd done it. That wasn't fair."

Meredith stood up, and leaning across the table, put his hand on the shotgun. "I'm taking this, Mark. You haven't killed anyone and you're not starting today. Is that okay?"

"What will you do when Mum comes back?" Mark asked as Meredith slid the gun away from him.

"Hopefully lock her up for a very long time. She won't hurt anyone else, Mark. I promise. Kent's going to open the door now, and some officers will come in, and they will have to handcuff you. It won't be for long. Then you'll come down to Bristol and we can get this all written down, okay?"

Meredith nodded at Kent, who opened the door. Two armed officers ran in, and Meredith held up his hand. "Calm down. No need for any drama."

Mark grabbed hold of Susan. "I'm sorry. Will you visit me in prison? Will you look after Thomas for me?"

Susan looked at Meredith. "Can I go with him?"

"Yes. You need to come too. I'll see you soon." As Mark was handcuffed, Meredith turned to Kent. "We should go and speak to the father, and then we need to find Cissy Brandon."

Kent's nose wrinkled. "Send the paramedics up first. He needs cleaning up. He's going nowhere."

Meredith nodded and watched Susan and Mark being taken to a waiting car.

One of the officers hung back. He waited until they were in the car. "We found Cissy Brandon, five minutes after you came in. She was in the barn."

"Good job. Get some paramedics up to the old man. I'd like a word with Cissy."

"That ain't gonna happen. She hanged herself."

"Right. Well, that will save the taxpayers some money. Grates, though. Where are those paramedics?"

"I'll go and get them." The officer turned smartly and left Meredith and Kent in the kitchen. "You did well, Kent."

"I did nothing. Do you reckon he was telling the truth?" Kent asked. "I do."

"I hope so. Cissy Brandon obviously dominated him. But he knows right from wrong, although he believed everything she told him. Hope he gets a good brief. He might not do time. I think he's paid the price for being a member of this family."

"What about Susan? Seems like she cares for him. She believed him, and she thought he was going to kill her. Did you see the relief on her face when she found out it was Cissy, not him?"

"I did. Fingers crossed there's hope for them. Mind your back." Meredith pushed Kent to one side as the paramedics came in. "Top of the stairs to the left," he told them.

"You want them to have a happy ever after, don't you? Susan, Mark and Thomas."

"That's what I want for everyone. I'm going soft in my old age."

Chapter Thirty

When Meredith finally got home that night, he had three messages waiting for him. The first was from Emily.

"Hi, Meredith, do you ever answer your mobile? I'm not sure why you have one. It's half past six. I was thinking of going to the cinema. Front row, in full view of everyone, but it starts at eight. If I don't hear from you, I'll assume you think I want some sort of sex I've yet to find a name for. I don't. You just looked sad when you left. I want us to be happy friends. Oh, yes. On that point, why the hell doesn't Julia know about Patsy? Well, she does now. She wasn't happy. Sorry. Call me."

Meredith glanced at the clock. It was eight thirty and taking a seat on the stairs he listened to Julia's message.

"Meredith, I've just been speaking to Emily. How are you? Why didn't you tell me? How are you? Emily tells me she's resisted your charms so far, so put those charms away. Out of sight. She doesn't deserve you on the rebound, although I know it will be tempting for you. Oh shit. Who am I to tell you what to do? I love you, Meredith, I want you to be happy, and Emily is my oldest friend. I knew her before you did, so I'm asking you to think things through. All I want is for you both to be happy, so I'll have to trust the pair of you to make the right decisions. Why don't you take some time off? Come over and stay with us for a while. How are you? I'm jabbering now. Please call me."

Meredith sighed and listened to the message from Patsy.

"It's me. You've got to stop calling. I won't be embarrassed into taking your calls, and the kids are all under fifteen. They shouldn't hear what you might want to say, I'm guessing it would be censored under normal circumstances. Remember them? Normal circumstances? So, the reason for my call is to ask you to stop calling, but also to promise you I am going to speak to Maxine again. I've already left a message, but I've yet to hear back. 'Bye, Meredith. I'm going to make myself better for everyone. Your calls might hinder that."

Meredith's lips vibrated as he emptied the air from his lungs. That was a low blow. She knew he'd not know what to do. He went upstairs and pondered it while in the shower. Then going to the bedroom, picked up his phone and dialled New Zealand, and smiled when the answer machine picked up.

"Message for Patsy. Thank you. Remember, you need to have video calls. I love you and am looking forward to your next message. That's a thought, send me a video one, at least I'd be able to see you, if not touch you. I need to touch you. But not knowing who's listening, I'll tell you more next time."

He hit the call button and dialled out again.

"He lives and breathes. Too late, we'll have to go another time," Emily said as she picked up the call. "I'm in the supermarket, and nearly at the checkout. Why has everyone decided to shop in the middle of the night like me?"

"It's not ten o'clock yet. What have you bought?"

"That's why you're calling, for my shopping list?" Emily asked.

"Yes, I was calling because I'm starving and have got nothing in. I wondered if you wanted to join me for a late supper. I wouldn't have called, not given our new arrangement but you called me. But as you are now exactly where I should be, I wondered what was in your basket."

"I've eaten. Hours ago, so I shall have to refuse. I can grab you something and drop it round if you like. I got my car today, and the offer of a new job, which was unexpected as I've barely unpacked."

Meredith froze. Whatever happened from here on in, Emily couldn't come here. That would be even worse. He lay down on the bed and closed his eyes.

"That sounds interesting. Is it?" Meredith asked.

"Not sure. I don't want to make the wrong choice for the wrong reasons. So I told them I'd think about it. I'm next. Shout now or forever hold it. Do you want me to get you something?"

"No, I'll order something. I'm too knackered, and too lazy to go shopping or cook something. I'll catch you soon."

"Oh okay. Give me a call at the weekend if you're about. And speak to Julia, Meredith, she was actually at a loss for words. She's never at a loss for words."

"Will do. 'Bye, Em."

"'Bye."

Meredith pushed himself off the bed and went down to the kitchen. He picked up the pizza he'd grabbed from the corner shop on his way home, put the oven on and poured himself a glass of wine. Emily had sounded disappointed, but she shouldn't have offered to come to the house. Patsy's house.

• • • • • • • • • • •

The next morning, he went to the magistrate's court and was pleased to see Susan was there. He needed a word with her and walked across to sit with her for a while. He took a seat behind Mark's barrister, leaning forward to speak to him and settling back when the clerk got to his feet.

"All rise."

When they brought Mark in, he looked totally lost. Susan waved to him, and although he smiled, the confusion remained. The charges for concealment of a body and grievous bodily harm were put to him. He pleaded guilty as directed.

The magistrate looked at the barrister. "I believe you have an opinion on bail?"

The barrister explained Mark's mother had dominated and coerced Mark into all the illegal acts, and that he was no threat to the public, and would appear in court as required. Then, happy that the prosecution and the police had no objection, Mark was freed on bail pending a formal hearing.

Susan had told Meredith she would stay with Mark to look after Thomas until the outcome of his trial. She had nowhere else to go, and with Cissy and Charlie gone, it would be a doddle. Meredith hoped the pair of them would settle down to a quiet life. Depending on what Charlie had to say, Meredith doubted Mark would get a custodial sentence. Charlie was in hospital, and a place in a nursing home was awaiting his release. Meredith was going to see him the next day. There had been no rush to interview him. Cissy was dead, Mark in custody and Susan free and hanging around of her own free will.

There was still a lot of paperwork to do, and the chief super was threatening a visit. Meredith didn't relish that, so settling himself in a café, he called the office.

"George. Brandon got bail. Susan Beddow is taking him back to the farm. Me and Seaton have got an early start in the morning, and yesterday was a long day. I'm calling it a day. Send them all home. Tell Seaton to pick me up in the morning."

With that sorted, he texted Emily.

Just got out of court, and I'm done for the day. I'm going for a stroll along the waterfront. What time do you finish?

Ten minutes. Are you offering food?

Of course.

Where shall I meet you?

Over dinner, Meredith told Emily about the Brandons.

"So all in all a decent outcome. I hope she sticks around for him once it's done and dusted. He'll never cope on his own," Meredith concluded.

"You old softy. But then we knew that." Emily smiled at him.

"Put your lips away, Andrews. Tell me about this job you've been offered."

"It's a senior manager role, more money, company car, private medical and—"

"You're telling me you're some sort of whiz kid and I'm forking out for dinner?" Meredith laughed.

"I think you'll find I paid for the pizza. And what do you think I've been doing for the last thirty-odd years? Shit, Meredith, how did that happen? Who let us get old?"

"I think you'll find I'm in my prime. So, what's the catch?"

Emily pursed her lips and laughed when Meredith snapped. "No lips. Just words."

"There's no catch. It doesn't start for a while. They've not even got the premises yet, and I liked being back in Bristol. But..."

"But you need to move onwards and upwards, and you can't do that properly here." Meredith reached across the table and took her hand. "I'm sorry. I'm always fucking sorry, but I won't ruin your life. Not again. I think you should take it. You should put your brightest lipstick on and take those lips out into the world. Just make sure he's worth it."

"Don't you make me cry because I haven't cried yet." Emily looked away and blinked. "I don't want a man, Meredith. I wasn't lying about that, but you're right, maybe I should. What news on Patsy?"

"We're not talking about Patsy, we're talking about you. Where is this job?"

"Exeter. I like Exeter."

"Yes, been a few times. My brother lives there at the moment."

"Oh yes, the brother Ed. I've heard about him from Julia. She said he was very nice. Did you like him? You've had more to do with him than Julia. What's he like?"

"A nicer but stupider version of me, if I'm being honest. He's intelligent but just sort of bumbles along. Red can handle himself but will never take the lead. I like being settled, now I'm in my prime, he seems to like wandering aimlessly. He's good to his mother, other than causing her and Patsy to be abducted." Meredith shrugged. "He's just a bloke. Devilishly handsome, I'm told."

"For just a bloke, you've given him some serious consideration. That's good. I'm glad you like him. So he looks like you?"

"I just said, devilishly handsome."

"I'll be the judge of that. Have you got a photo?"

Meredith scrolled through his photographs. "That's him with Patsy the last time he was passing through."

Meredith smiled as he passed her the phone.

"No, it's not. That's you. Patsy looks lovely, and very young."

"Scroll to the next one."

Emily gasped as she looked at the half-brothers side by side, and made the photograph bigger, moving the image about as she inspected it.

"Oh my God. I only know it's you on the left because of the clothes. You'd never wear those shorts. Wow! So two Merediths were inflicted on the world."

Meredith smiled. "I forgot to mention he has no taste, absolutely no taste at all."

"How old is he?"

"Don't know, in his forties. Hang on, are you sizing him up as a replacement, and a toy boy one at that? Oh, no, do not go there." Meredith wagged his finger.

Emily laughed. "I'm sorry, I make my own rules. That sounded like you were telling me what to do, so I know you can't be serious. Or does that thought offend you? Is the cradle-snatcher offended? How old's Patsy?"

"Forty next birthday. She looks much younger."

Emily nodded and sighed deeply. "I think it's time to go home."

"Have you got your car?"

"No. Nor have you, I hope, after all that wine. I can walk from here."

"Then I shall escort you."

When they reached her building, Meredith stopped at the gate and pulled her into a hug.

"Thank you. I needed company tonight."

"Are you not coming in?" Emily asked.

"I don't think that would be wise. The ink on the agreement isn't even dry. I do have some self-control."

"Shame, because the goodbye sex was very good."

"It was, in your words, spectacular. Don't start downgrading it. But there was no agreement in place the last time."

Emily patted his back. "Good man. And you are, Meredith. You got there in the end. I hope she comes home."

"She will." Meredith tightened his hug. "Oh, Emily, I'm going to miss you. But I think this needs to stop. It's not doing either of us any good. You are temptation."

"I noticed. You need to go now. Right now because I can feel your temptation growing. Perhaps when Patsy comes home, we can go back to being normal friends. I'd like that."

"Me too." Meredith kissed her on the cheek, released her, and shoving his hands in his pockets, headed for the taxi rank.

When he got home, the light was flashing on the answer machine. He looked at it for a moment.

"Not tonight, Patsy," he said, and headed up the stairs.

Chapter Thirty-One

Meredith checked the time. Seaton would be here soon. He walked to the hall mirror and checked his tie. Allowing his hands to drop to the table, he ran his finger over buttons on the answer machine.

"Sod it." He pushed the play button.

"Hello, Meredith, it's Maxine, I wouldn't normally do this as you know, but I've just had a very long chat with Patsy, and I thought you should know..."

A little while later, Meredith ran down the stairs and pulled the door open. "Come on, Seaton, don't stand around." He slammed the door and hurried towards Seaton's car.

Throwing his bag and his jacket onto the back seat, he was buckling his seatbelt before Seaton had left the doorstep.

"What's the hurry? I'm early. I thought I'd get a coffee," Seaton complained, as he started the car.

"You're okay to see Charlie Brandon on your own, aren't you?"

"Yes, of course, but why? Have you got somewhere better you need to be?"

"Yep. Heathrow."

"The airport?"

"Seaton, don't ask stupid questions. Yes, the airport. And you have two hours to get me there. We should make it in good time but it's the M4, and it's Heathrow, so I am ordering you to floor the accelerator at every given opportunity."

Seaton turned and smiled at him. "Is Patsy coming home?"

"She is."

"What time does her flight land? I'm sure she'd rather you were late and in one piece."

"It doesn't. I'm going to get her."

"You're flying?"

"Another stupid question. Don't think I'd make it if I swam."

"But you don't fly. Do you know how long it takes to get to New Zealand?"

"I'm trying not to think about it but thanks for pointing it out."

"Ah, that is good news. When did you speak to her?"

"About four months ago."

"She knows you're going, doesn't she?" Seaton turned to look at Meredith.

"Nope. Eyes on the road, one piece, remember?" Meredith flicked his finger towards the road ahead.

"Guv, do you think that's wise?"

"Seaton, I'm about to get on a very big and very heavy plane for more hours than I care to think about. Take a guess."

"Point taken. Have you booked a flight?"

"We haven't even got onto the motorway yet. How many stupid questions do you think I can cope with before we get to the airport?"

"It'll take your mind off the flight. But I'll shut up now."

After thirty minutes, and cruising down the motorway in the fast lane, their stories ready should they get stopped. Meredith sighed.

"Big sigh, Guv. Getting nervous?" Seaton asked.

"Yes. But not about the flight."

"Tell me to mind my own business but why now?"

"Because I reminded her that we have a marriage certificate. It's a long story, Seaton. Patsy isn't pregnant. She never was. Her period stopped, either because of the shock of the attack, the lack of nourishment, or possibly the start of the menopause. But she thought she was pregnant and didn't know how to tell me because we'd agreed after she lost the baby that we wouldn't try for another. In a fit of boredom, she started sorting through some junk and found the letter confirming I was no longer able to produce, and the date told her that the baby couldn't be mine, so she assumed Deacon had raped her."

"But he wasn't capable of that."

"We know that, but having tried to block it all out, she wondered if she'd blocked that out too. A normal person would have got a pregnancy test, but she wasn't normal. Not then. She didn't know how to tell me and didn't want to get rid of it. So instead of getting better, she got worse. Finally deciding that she loved me too much to ask me to be father to a rapist's child."

"And yet you would have."

"It's never the children's fault. Ever. And I don't think I can live without her. I mean, I'd live. Might even enjoy myself now and again. But it would be survival, not living. She saved me the first time, and she's going to do it again. And if you ever tell anyone I said that, we'll fall out big time."

"Emily was surviving, was she?"

"No, Seaton. My lovely Emily was so much more than that. I've had some shit times, Seaton. Times I wouldn't wish on my worst enemy, but I've been lucky enough to have had some remarkable women in my life. Emily was one of them. I refused the final goodbye sex last night, and the sympathy sex, and the getting the cards on the table sex, or maybe it was no more sex sex was pretty special. But I refused it because the most remarkable woman of all is going to come home. Eventually. Now I'm going to make that happen."

"You're making me jealous again. How many types of sex are there? But before you answer that, you know Patsy might say no, don't you? To coming home. I mean, is she better now? Don't you go damaging her any more than she already is."

"If you weren't driving, I'd kiss you for wanting to protect her. Do you know that?"

"Glad I am then. How did Emily take the news you were jumping on a plane?"

"I didn't know at the time. Didn't hear the message until this morning. I decided not to listen to it last night. If I had, I'd already be in the air." Meredith shuddered. "Terminal three, take a left. I haven't told her yet. I'll call her once I've checked in."

Seaton drove into a forbidden lane and jumped out of the car. "I'm going to get a ticket for this, you can pay me when you get back." He held out his hand, and when Meredith took it, pulled him forward and slapped him on the back. "Good luck, Guv."

"I don't need luck. I'll have Patsy."

Meredith trotted away and into the airport, the fingers on both hands crossed.

About the Author

Thank you for reading Gone. I hope you enjoyed Meredith & Hodge's latest adventure as much as I did. If you did, I'd be grateful if you would be kind enough to leave a review on Amazon when you have a moment. Constructive reviews are invaluable to authors. If you would rather contact me personally, the details are below. If you want to read more of my work, you can grab a free ebook copy of The Making of Meredith, the prequel to the Meredith & Hodge series, if you sign up for my mailing list at https://www.mkturnerbooks.co.uk/about

ABOUT THE AUTHOR

I escaped the corporate treadmill in 2010. I began writing quite by chance when a friend commented, "They wouldn't believe it if you wrote it down!" So I did. I enjoyed the plotting and scheming, creating the characters, and watching them develop with the story. I kept on writing, and Meredith and Hodge arrived. Then, in 2017, the Bearing women took hold of my imagination, and the Bearing Witness series was created. In 2023, it was The Little Compton Mysteries and I am currently working on the JJ Jenson series. In between all the new ideas, I do, of course, keep going back to Meredith & Hodge.

I am married with two children, two grandchildren, and a German Shepherd. We live in Bristol, UK.

I would love to hear from you, and can be contacted here:

Website: https://www.mkturnerbooks.co.uk

Printed in Great Britain
by Amazon

53001565R00145